JAMAICAN ME GO CRAZY

KEISHA STARR

Jamaican Me Go Crazy. Copyright ©2018 by Keisha Starr.
All rights reserved.
Printed and bound in the United States of America

Published by
ExSTARdinary Publishing
Baltimore, MD 21215
Email: exstardinarypublishing@gmail.com

ISBN: 978-1-7322376-0-5

Library of Congress Control Number: 2018941136

Dedication

This book is dedicated to Kaydin and Kyrin Michael Hill; My joys, my boys! I love you both beyond the moon and stars in the sky. I thank God every day for blessing me with two loving, fun, cool, and energetic sons. You both have inspired me in more ways than you could possible imagine. If you don't remember one thing about your mommy, remember that she always followed her dreams, and want the both of you to do the same. Never allow anyone to tell you the sky is the limit when there are footprints on the moon!

Tyran Hill, my partner in life and Christ.... This book is also dedicated to you because you've supported me throughout the entire process and have devoted your time and talent to ensuring that we put out quality work. As I always say, thank you for being our very own John Q.

Last, I dedicate this book to my entire "crazy Jamaican" family who stands behind me in everything that I do. We've overcome obstacles that would have divided most families, yet rather than crumble, we climbed and persevered through it all. John, Barbara, and Rallin live on forever! #JBR4Life

CHAPTER 1

Behind Every Strong Man... There's a Stronger Woman!

I've always known I was cut from a different cloth. I mean, it was just so obvious in the way I walk, talk, shit even in the way I ate my food. My whole demeanor was unique, and I've always felt it down in my bones. I was different and I was at peace with that.

I'm a feisty 23-year-old hottie with golden caramel complexion. I have thick, long black hair that falls to the center of my back; and yes, it's "home grown not salon sewn". My nose looks like a little button, and people are always raving over my deep dimples, telling me how much they accentuate my smile.

My eyes are my secret weapon, however: light brown, slightly chinky, with long captivating lashes. I have some Korean features, inherited from my grandmother on my father's side. My breasts sit on my chest like two fresh California grapefruits, and my ass is as plump as a sweet Georgia peach. I don't have a single scar, bump, or any other shit females complain about. I'm neither tall nor short, roughly 5'6. Just straight flawless super model material. Now tell me why I shouldn't feel the way that I do?

You can blame my self-confidence on the way I was raised, but if you ask me, my hometown is responsible for my swagger. I'm from Baltimore, Murderland, home of the Wire. When you come to my city you either walk away with a warm smile or lay cold dead in them mean streets.

Before I go any further, allow me to introduce myself. My name is Jamaica Johnson but my friends call me JJ for short, and no I was not born in Jamaica, although my mother was. She migrated to America three years before I was born. I guess they could take the woman out of the island, but they couldn't take the island out of the woman, because when I was born the only name that came to mind was *Jamaica*.

As a young girl, I spent most of my time running up and down the street of Beehler Avenue, which is one of the best neighborhoods in the world. The entire Park Heights community was the shit, despite the crime, drugs, and poverty. For entertainment, all I had to do was step off my porch and Lucile Park was right there. Drug transactions, shootouts, gang wars, prostitution; you name it, and it was going down in the park, and I loved it all!

Growing up in the "hood" wasn't difficult. My parents provided us with the best, and we always had more than the rest. Our house stood out from everyone else's on the block. We had a closed-in front and back porch, a vegetable garden, and a huge swimming pool with a wooden deck. So yes, I lived up the Heights, but, my parents set trends most people couldn't keep up with, and for that reason, they were and still are, a well-respected power couple.

My parents couldn't take a decent shit without people gossiping about it, especially my daddy. Every nigga tried to be in his inner circle, every bitch tried to fuck him, and everyone's motives were the same. They were all looking for a come up.

To me, he's Delroy Johnson, to everyone else around the way, he's Lucky, the owner of five Mercedes Benz Dealerships in the DMV area. Delroy is extremely handsome, keeps his body in top-notch shape, and on top of being a dapper ass street nigga, he's also filthy rich. All the bitches, young, old, and in between, throw themselves at him, not giving two fucks about his wedding band. My dad's a high roller, and no, he's no longer in the streets, just in case you were speculating. Years ago, before we moved from the Park Heights community, my father was the neighborhood kingpin. He had the entire district on lock, from Park Circle straight back to Jew Town; however, he was careful about staying low key, and he used his best friend, Milk as the front man.

There were always packages coming in and out of our house. For years, I thought my father worked at a warehouse and was packaging goods for a tree company until I got old enough to know the difference between weed and tree leaves. They damn sure smelled different.

My mother tried to protect me from the game. She came up with clever excuses when I asked questions about why we couldn't have company in our basement or why she kept money in the wall instead of the bank. The more she tried to hide the truth, the more curious I became.

I learned a lot about the drug game, not so much from my father, but from my mother. It was instilled in me at a young age that money was everything, and obtaining illegal money was okay as long as you didn't get caught. My mother was a pro. She carried it like a true Jamaican Bella Mafia.

Mary was born and raised in a notorious neighborhood in Kingston, Jamaica called Jungle. Many things that couldn't take place in America were overlooked in Jamaica, and my mother wanted a better life. She realized very young that she was beautiful and her body could be used as an asset. At sixteen, my mother was already fucking older married men and taking their money. She wasn't out shopping and splurging on designer handbags and material bullshit like some of her friends. She used the money she received from her sugar daddies to pay bills, while putting cash aside so she could one day open a salon.

I guess you could say my mother was a responsible "hoe," getting by just fine until the condom popped and she ended up pregnant by someone's husband. That's when reality hit her ass hard. The baby daddy made no attempt to man up, which was obvious when he handed her some abortion money and told her to get lost. Mary didn't believe in abortions, but knew she would have problems getting by as a sixteen-year-old single mother.

So, against her will and belief, she laid on the abortion table, bawling as the doctors suctioned her fetus and dignity out of her body.

From that day forward, my mother was never the same. She knew she desperately needed to change her lifestyle, but felt that Jamaica was holding her back. So, she formulated a plan. After busting her ass in school, Mary received an academic scholarship to attend college in the United States under a student visa. She worked her way through college, where she met my father at a frat party.

Right from the start they attracted like magnets and fell deeply in love. After six months of dating, they married. She put it on his ass, I guess! One year later, my mother filed and was granted citizenship. Not much longer after that, I was born, followed by my sister, Rochelle.

When my parents met, my father was already doing a little hustling to make ends meet. My mother convinced him to go all the way out kingpin style. She masterminded a plan that outlined how long they were going to hustle, who they were going to do business with, and how they were going to clean up their dirty money. My father gets all the credit, but my mother was the brains behind all that shit. Mary dealt with all the out-of-state transactions, while my father regulated the local streets. She would take me on trips with her sometimes. I guess she thought I wasn't old enough to understand what was going on. What my mother didn't know was that she was creating a monster. I studied her moves, admiring how she shifted from my tender mother into a gangster bitch in 2.3 seconds. Mary would pack my suitcase and tell me we were going to visit my grandmother in Texas. I was a little confused because my father's mother was dead and my other grandmother lived in Jamaica. Shit, up until I was ten, I actually thought children could have more than two sets of grandparents.

"Remember baby, if anybody asks where are you going, you say to see my grandma and tell them how much you love and miss her, okay," my mother coached.

When we arrived, I never saw this infamous grandmother. We would check into a fancy hotel, and order tons of snacks. Later that night, my mother would take out my new doll and rip it open. That's when I realized money was stuffed inside the doll's stomach.

The next day after making the drug deal with some scary Mexican dudes, we would go to the movies or to an amusement park, then fly back home. These little trips were always fun and exciting.

My parents did their thing for years, but around the time I turned sixteen-years-old, things changed. One night while my sister, my mother and I were home, a knock came to the door. I answered it and saw my father's friend, Milk. Milk and my father had been best friends since middle school, so they were more like brothers. He was also my godfather and spoiled me with money and gifts when he came around.

"Who's at the door?" my mother screamed from upstairs.

"It's Uncle Milk," I answered, as I opened the door to let him in. It's hard to explain, but once I opened the door and saw the look on his face, a funny feeling came over me.

"Hey, baby girl. Who's home with you?" he asked as he looked around the house, with his hands tucked in his coat pocket.

"Rochelle is in the other room watching TV. Daddy's in Chicago and Mommy's upstairs cleaning up."

"So your father isn't here?" he asked, while looking in every direction.

"No." I walked back into the room with Rochelle. "But you can go upstairs to talk to Mommy."

I sat back on the couch and watched music videos. Less than five minutes later I heard my mother, along with some unfamiliar voices, carrying on a conversation in the living room. I paid it no attention until my mother walked into the room with a man pointing a gun behind her back.

"Ah weh di bloodclaat ah gwan?" my mother screamed.

"Where is the fucking money?" the man asked with the gun still pointed at her.

"I don't know what you're talking about," my mother cried out. "Please, my kids...I don't want them seeing this shit. Can you please just leave because I do NOT know where my husband keeps his money."

"Bitch, I know you're lying because Milk said you and Lucky had a shipment come in last night, so hand over the drugs or the cash," he demanded.

"How many times do I have to tell you I have no clue where Lucky puts the money or the product? I don't handle that shit. I'm here taking care of my kids. That's my job. Lucky handles everything else. I swear to you," my mother pleaded.

Before she could say another word, the man slapped her across the face. His hit was so powerful, it knocked her to the ground. That's when I lost it.

"Don't put your fucking hands on my mother," I screamed as I charged the guy and began punching away at his face.

He blocked all my hits until he pushed me down beside her. "You better sit down before I pop your little ass since you want to act grown." He then lustfully zoomed in on my young body with his perverted looking eyes. "I got something for you if you think you're grown with that phat ass of yours. I like them young, so don't fuck with me. If you over ten, I will stick it in." He busted out laughing and high-fived his friends.

Just as he approached me, Uncle Milk walked into the room carrying a bag filled with my parents' jewelry. "Leave the kids out of this and focus on the money. That's my fucking goddaughter so no one, and I mean absolutely no one, touch her." He walked over to my mother. "Mary, you know I love both you and Delroy, but I know you guys are hustling behind my back and cutting me out of major deals," he said, explaining his motives for running up in our house. "I didn't even know about the shipment coming in last night. I heard it through the grapevine, which in my eyes is disloyal. We supposed to be fucking family and you think you can cut me out? Just give me the shipment or hand over the money and I'll leave you alone."

Splat!

My mother spit directly in his face. "Fuck you, Milk. I can't believe you're doing this to us. We're family, for God's sake. You have men in ah mi bloodclaat house ah point guns pon mi pickney dem and threatening fi fuck my daughter. You better bloodclaat kill me right now because you gone too far with this, and mi would rada dead before mi give you ah bumbaclaat ting."

Milk wiped the spit from his face. "You know you just fucked up, right?"

"Mi nah know ah bloodclaat ting and neither do you." My mother showed no weakness.

The tension in that room soared from zero to one million and then, Milk and my mother began debating about who was shadier.

As they argued, another man walked in. He was ugly as sin, blacker than tar, and had a deep scar that stretched from his right earlobe to the tip of his lip. He looked like the devil himself.

All along I thought Milk was in charge, but it was apparent that he was working for this guy because he started calling all the shots.

"Look, I'm going to be late for my daughter's recital. If she doesn't give up the money, then pop her ass and let's go. I'm not leaving empty-handed so it's either the drugs, money or blood." He walked back through the door, continuing to give orders. "Hurry up, man. I need to record this recital for my wife. My daughter is playing the Virgin Mary and I want to be early so I can get a good seat. You know how them church folks be."

Here he was ordering his flunkies to hurry up and murder my mother so he could get a good seat in *church?* It was apparent he had no regard for human life, and I knew then that my mother was as dead as Elvis Presley if I didn't do something.

"This is your last warning, Mary. Give me the money or the work," Milk said.

"Fuck you, Milk. Like I said, you betta kill mi because I'm not giving you shit!"

Milk looked deeply into my mother's eyes to see if she was serious. She didn't flinch, didn't beg for her life. She just stood there giving him the *'it is what it is'* look.

This pushed Milk to his boiling point. "You know what, kill this bitch," he ordered.

The child molester who wanted to fuck me earlier, happily pointed the gun to my mother's temple, and cocked it. "You're a stubborn bitch. Too bad you're about to be a dead stubborn bitch. Kids say goodbye to your mother."

I almost had a heart attack. I knew where my parents kept a bulk of their money so I jumped up. "No, don't shoot. I'll take you to the money. Just please don't hurt my mother," I begged.

"Little girl, you have one minute to show us the cash or all y'all dead," the guy promised, with the gun still pointed at my mother's head.

"Follow me," I insisted. I began walking upstairs, with the men and my mother following closely behind. The sound of their tennis shoes behind me made my stomach nauseous.

"Jamaica, stay out of this," my mother demanded. "Don't show them anything."

I'd always respected my mother, but this was one time I ignored her. She repeatedly told me to be quiet and became furious that I disobeyed, but I didn't care. They were going to kill her and I had to do something to stop them.

I took the men into my parents' bedroom and opened the closet. "It's money behind there, but you have to break it open."

Milk knew the ins and outs of our house so he went to the garage to get my father's tools. He returned with hammers and power tools and handed them to the other guys. They banged and drilled until they ripped through the wall and just as I promised, the money was stashed right there.

"Alright, we got something here," one man announced, as he pulled out a bag.

They opened it up, saw stacks of Benjamins, and became excited. "Jackpot! Now this is what the fuck I'm talking about," he added as he removed bags of my parents' money.

That night, niggas left our house with over $700,000 in cash and $50,000 worth of jewelry, but most importantly, they didn't leave with our lives. That was all that mattered to me.

"Come on. We have to get the fuck out of here right now," my mother yelled once the men left. "Don't stop for anything." She grabbed Rochelle and me and damn near yanked us out the door with no shoes or jacket.

We jumped into the car and drove directly to my mother's friend, Penny's house. We rushed through the door and she immediately called my father. My mother was crying hysterically, but what I remember most was she wasn't crying because some niggas were just about to murk our asses. She was boohooing because all her money and jewelry were gone.

"All our fucking savings down the drain. They would have never found that fucking money had Jamaica not showed them. I understand she was trying to help, but I kept telling her to sit down and shut up. Them weak-ass niggas was all bark and no bite. They weren't going to do shit, especially Milk's punk ass."

I didn't know what my father was saying on the other end, but there was a period of silence where my mother kept shaking her legs and banging the table.

I couldn't believe what I was hearing. I thought I was the hero, but I guess I was the fuck-up who ruined everything.

My father sat on the phone with my mother for hours giving her specific instructions. I couldn't hear everything they said, but I remember overhearing my mother say, "We definitely have to move because I don't feel safe in that house anymore."

That was when my spirit dropped. I was not moving from the Heights, robbery and all. That was my home and I wasn't about to make some niggas run me away from my friends.

My father stayed away from Baltimore and we laid low at Penny's house for a couple of months. Life changed drastically.

My mother didn't have access to thousands of dollars anymore, so we had to make due with whatever my father sent. The very tight budget drove her insane. She was miserable all the time, and didn't hide the fact that I wasn't her favorite person in the world.

One night as I was getting ready for bed, I overheard my mother on the phone talking to my father. "So Milk is taken care of, right? Good, I hope his soul rots in hell. We put that nigga on and he thought he was entitled to half of everything like he was the one taking trips and risks. He didn't even know how to bag up when we brought him under our wings, but this nigga hollering about we're doing business behind his back and he wants his share. Well, he got his share. I hope he enjoyed his last days with it."

My heart sank a little because I knew what that meant, and even though Milk did us dirty, it still felt weird to hear that he was dead.

My parents continued their conversation and as time passed, my mother's tone and overall attitude became happier than it had been in a month.

After she hung up, she danced around the room, shouting, "Halleluiah! Glory... Glory!"

"What's going on?" I asked as I walked into the room to see my mother with the biggest Ronald McDonald smile. You would have thought she won the damn lottery or better yet, that her money was still behind the wall in her closet.

"Your father just called. We're moving to Harford County. We're going to be a family again. Yesssss God," she belted.

Harford County? *Where the fuck is Harford County?* I was in disbelief and I was pretty sure it was written all over my face. "Harford County? We're not going back to Park Height? What about my school? What about my friends? What about Myesha? I can't leave my best friend."

"Trust me, sweetheart, this move is for the better. The school system is better and the neighborhoods are safer. This will be an excellent place to raise our family. Besides, Myesha can come to visit anytime."

We were moving away from Park Heights! That meant I had to start my life completely over. That meant I had to leave my best friend. I didn't want to move, but understood why we had to.

My mother wasted no time packing. And just like that, the next morning we shipped out to Harford County to meet up with my father. I was extremely happy to see him. I couldn't remember a time in my life when my father was absent, so for him to lay low for months felt weird. I ran into his arms like I hadn't seen him in a million years.

We stayed in an extravagant hotel for a couple of months until the day of settlement on our new house. We moved into a spacious six-bedroom house that resembled a mini mansion. We had a built-in movie theater and an indoor swimming pool. We had our own cook and even a lady who came to clean and wash our clothes every week. We were living it up, but my spirit was down. I loved our new home and yes, it had everything built to our desire, but my heart belonged to Park Heights.

My parents weren't idiots. Although I only knew about the money stashed in the wall, they had money hidden elsewhere. Once we moved up in the world, my mother decided it was time to wash their dirty money, so my father opened a small used car dealership: Lucky's Cars. After two years, his business did so well, he moved up to selling used Mercedes Benzes, and then from there his business grew so fast.

He got various banks to loan him money, as *if he needed it,* to open his first Benz dealership. He became so successful that along with his dealership, he purchased my mother her own beauty salon: Unique Hair and Feet.

From that point, my father became a business mogul. He used his street smarts and hustling mentality to gain respect from business elites all over.

So, there I was stuck in Harford County, living a life that most kids my age dreamed of, yet I was miserable. I missed the neighborhood gossip, fights, and excitement I experienced down in Park Heights. Most importantly, I missed Myesha. Something had to give and it had to give quickly. I needed out of Harford County AKA Whitesville, so I had to come up with a master plan.

CHAPTER 2

*A Closed Mouth Can't Get Fed and Closed Legs
Can't Get Head*

Six months passed and I was still stuck in Harford County. Unlike Park Heights, where I was the most popular kid on the block, I was damn near invisible here. I didn't have any friends and to be honest, I wasn't looking for any. Yes, I had my sister Rochelle, but we were on two different planets. She was a tomboy, I was a diva, and our personalities clashed frequently.

After months of seeing me mope around, my parents finally had mercy on me and allowed Myesha to start coming over on the weekends. When the summer rolled around, she practically lived with us. This worked out perfectly for Myesha because she was going through her own problems at home.

Myesha was very pretty; just like me. Her complexion was a little lighter than mine. She had a round face, bright hazel eyes, and the fullest lips you'd ever find on a girl. I would say Myesha was about 5'2 and had an eye-catching figure. Although, I was shaped a little better, she had lots of curves with a phat ass donkey booty.

Myesha's family wasn't rich but they weren't poor. Everything I had, she had, too. Her mother was a nursing assistant at a prestigious nursing home in the richer area of Baltimore and her father was the manager for a large construction company.

Myesha's mother had just found out she was pregnant two nights before their lives made a turn for the worst. A drunk driver hit Myesha's father's car off the road while he was driving home, killing him instantly. I didn't think Myesha ever recovered and neither did her mother, Mrs. Kendra because a couple of months after her sister was born, Myesha's mother fell into deep depression when reality kicked in that her husband was truly gone. She began drinking hard liquor daily and when that stopped working, she started on stronger substances, like cocaine and heroin. For a while she was stealing pain medication from her job. By the time her supervisors realized she was stealing their Percocet and Morphine, she was already addicted to heroin. She lost her job and became very ill, leaving her unable to perform her motherly duties.

When Myesha received an eviction notice taped to her front door, she had to grow up faster than she anticipated. Her mother and baby sister became her responsibility, too stressful for a teenager.

Myesha and I had our own issues. I wanted to get back to the city and she wanted to escape the madness that was taking place at home. The irony was I longed for the madness she was running from. We knew we needed to make some moves, but just didn't know what moves to make. We were both sixteen years old. Most girls our age would have tried to get permits to work for scraps all summer long. That wasn't me. We needed to come up with a better plan.

One night, while Myesha stayed over my house, we made a vow we would be successful no matter what. "Myesha, we have to get some money together so I can move back to the city. When I get my place, you can come live with me. We can take your little sister with us and put your mother in rehab." I laid down with my legs crossed, staring at the ceiling. "We need some real money, not chump change," I advised her.

"Jamaica, how are we going to make this work? No one is going to rent us an apartment. We're too young. Plus, we have to pay rent, gas and electric, water bill, and what about food? It sounds easy but it's real out there." She continued, "We can get summer jobs or maybe start our own business."

She sounded stupid as hell to me. I gave her my pissed off face because that was exactly what she was doing. I knew she didn't think I was going door-to-door selling fucking Girl Scout cookies or some shit like that. Instead of blowing her off like I normally did, I tried to reason with her.

"Do you know what it takes to open up a business? What are we going to sell? It takes money, Myesha; money we do not have. I'm telling you, my mother had two jobs but she still did some hard hustling to get where she is today. Only rich people can afford to work and live comfortably."

If there was one thing I learned growing up, it was you had to walk a little crooked to get straight and you had to do a little wrong to get right!

I sat and broke the game down to Myesha because she was naïve to these streets. She kept talking about opening a business and I looked at her like, *What the hell are we going to sell?* The only thing I was sure everyone wanted was me. The girls at my school wanted to be me and boys wanted to be with me. With that last thought, suddenly it hit me.

I looked at Myesha and then back at myself. Myesha was gorgeous and I was a dime times two. We were young, but we certainly didn't look our age. "I got it, girl! We could market two products that's sure to sell; Myesha and Jamaica."

Myesha looked at me like I was crazy. "JJ, what the hell is you talking about? Do you mean sell pussy? Girl, you know I got a man, so please don't go there. Not to mention, I got too much pride and..."

I laughed in Myesha's face. I had to interject before her blood pressure went sky high. "Look, I got a lethal weapon concealed in my draws. The day I let this off, Baltimore is going to shut down. I'm not talking about selling my body like a cheap whore. I'm talking about going out, finding a cow, and milking him for all he's got. We need a baller with riches and rank on the streets. All we need to do is trap one stupid motherfucker. That's what my mother did, now look how she's living. I'm not saying my father is stupid, but come on; he married my mother six months after meeting her. She had to throw some serious pussy on him."

"The only man I'm throwing serious pussy on is Marcus. I'm pretty sure there's other ways to get money besides being a gold-digger."

"You're throwing serious pussy on Marcus, but is he throwing serious cash back at you?" I snapped. Before she could answer, I answered for her. "No, he's not! He don't do shit for you. Basketball is the only thing that Marcus got going for him, and even that's not promising because making it to the NBA is not guaranteed. First of all, his grades are fucked up and he's always getting kicked off the basketball team, so that nigga probably only get into a community college when he graduates. I'm the one always hitting you off to pay your neighbor to watch you sister, when your aunt can't. I'm the one that gives you money to get your nails and hair done. I'm the only one you can turn to when you need help, but you hollering out the only man you're throwing pussy on is Marcus. Girl, you may as well start throwing pussy on me because I'm doing all the boyfriend duties."

As usual Little Miss Sunshine ignored my rant and kept talking about opening some damn business. After a long, dragged-out conversation, I realized I wasn't getting anywhere.

"Look, Myesha, I'm not trying to be smart, but you handle your situation your way and I'll handle mine. I need real money, not chump change and your solutions aren't lined up with my needs. Let's just agree to disagree and take care of our own situations. Goodnight!" I turned off the TV, dimmed the lights, and closed my eyes. I was on a mission!

The next morning, my mother dropped us off at Towson Town Center to go shopping for summer clothes. Knowing good and well that Myesha's mother was somewhere smoking up her social security check, she hit Myesha off with a few hundred as well.

Although Myesha thought we were there to shop, I was there looking for a new friend. I lied to my mother and told her that my classmate, Paula was meeting us at the mall and that her mother was picking us up. I even told her we were going to the movies just to buy some time. My mother didn't suspect a thing!

"You two be safe and don't talk to strangers. There's some real crazy people out here. And be home by ten o'clock," she ordered.

I reassured her I would be there by nine. I almost convinced myself.

As soon my mother pulled off, Myesha and I headed into the lady's room to put on the clothes I'd packed for us that morning, while everyone was still asleep.

"Here, change into this and put on some make-up," I ordered as I handed Myesha her outfit for the day.

We went into the bathroom stalls and tousled to get our clothes on. After we dressed, we walked out and looked at each other. We both looked extraordinary. I was sporting an ass hugging mini skirt with a light blue tank top. Myesha changed into a pair skinny jeans and an off the shoulder belly-skin top. Little Miss Sunshine didn't even question why we changed our outfits; she just liked the way we looked. It wasn't uncommon for me to steal my mother's clothes and change in the school bathroom. Myesha knew all my tricks, so she paid me no mind and asked no questions about my motives today.

When we stepped out of that bathroom, we transformed from teenagers to women. Everywhere we turned, boys as well as grown men were trying to holler. Typically, I ignored them, but today I stopped and took numbers, although I didn't see anyone worth my time. From noon to four, we walked through the entire mall and I didn't see a fool with money in sight. Everyone I met was either my age, which meant they were living off of their parents, or they looked old and broke as hell.

I was frustrated and Myesha was getting tired of walking. Mind you, at this time she was still clueless to my plan.

"Jamaica, we've looked in every store at least twice. My feet starting to hurt. Where's your friend who's supposed to meet us? And what time does the movie start?"

What a koo-koo brain.

"Look, Myesha, there's no friend coming. I only said that so my mother wouldn't come back. I was hoping we could find a couple ballers here, but it's dry as shit today."

"A baller?" Myesha questioned. "What are you talking about?"

"Remember I told you we needed to find some niggas with money so that we could lock them down and make them take care of us? That's what this whole trip to the mall was about. There's no friend coming. What fucking friend do I have besides you? Come on, girl, use that brain God gave you."

"So you tricked me? Why would you do that? I told you that I'm with Marcus, and I'm not looking for another boyfriend." Myesha started to flip out, damn near causing a scene in the middle of the mall.

"Please shut up, Myesha. You're bugging the hell out of me. You know what? Since you're so in love with Marcus, why don't you call him and tell him to come pick us up? Oops, I just remembered his broke ass don't own a bike much less a car."

"At least I got a man. If you had somebody, you wouldn't be out here looking thirsty at the mall."

"Bitch, please! You've been with Marcus for over a year and you don't even have a friendship ring to show for it. Like I said, tell him to swing by on his skates and pick you up so you won't have to worry about getting home."

Myesha's entire body tensed up, as we argued back and forth. After speaking my mind, I walked off to the front entrance to call my mother. Myesha continued to argue and I continued to ignore her. Just as I prepared to make that call, my attention was drawn to a truck heading my way. I glanced inside and saw my future baby daddy pushing a black on black Porsche truck. The dude inside was fine as hell and I was instantly love-struck.

He was bumping Jay-Z's *American Gangsta* CD and at that moment I knew I'd found my own American Gangsta. I had to get his attention. Myesha was still standing behind me ranting, but all I heard was blah, blah, blah. She was in her feelings and I was feeling a little something-something for Mr. Porsche.

"Myesha, forget all that shit," I interrupted. "Do you see that fine ass boy? I know that nigga got some loot."

Myesha spun around about three times trying to figure out who I was talking about. Finally, when she locked eyes on the target, she shook her head, and I knew she was going to have reservations about the situation, as usual. "I see the truck, but that's no boy sitting inside, that's a grown-ass man. He's not checking for you. A man like that wants a woman. He'll probably be more interested in your mother."

Myesha busted out laughing, which fueled the fire in me to prove her wrong. Nobody doubted Jamaica Johnson's man pulling skills, especially this lame dame. "Boy, man, they're all the same. They all think with the same brain between their legs."

"Well, go for what you know." Myesha shook her head, still laughing at me. "Go ahead and get your love connection on, baby." She could barely get her words out without laughing.

I pulled my hair from the ballerina bun it was in and made it fall to the middle of my back. I refreshed my lipstick and topped it off with MAC gloss to draw attention to my plump, sexy soup coolers. Nothing turns a man on more than seeing a sexy chic with seductive shiny lips. It made them think about getting their dick sucked, and I didn't have a problem with being the main attraction of many fantasies.

Although I was still a virgin, my little coochie had been jumping for about a year now. I'd heard sex stories from my classmates and Myesha, so I'd been eager to try it out.

Myesha reluctantly waited on the curb, as I sashayed across the walkway. Oh, I was giving Mr. Porsche my America's Next Top Model walk, too. When he looked up and saw this ass jiggling, he damn near crashed into the car in front of him. He beeped his horn to get my attention, but I kept walking. Turning around on the first round made a girl look pressed. Finally, after his second attempt, I turned.

He put his window down and motioned for me to come his way. "Let me talk to you for a second," he said.

I wanted to run and jump into his arms like the white folks did on TV, yet I found the strength to keep my cool.

"If you think I'm worth the walk, come to me," I challenged. I was young but not a fool. You had to lay shit down from day one so these niggas would know. If you walked to a man once, he'd always expect you to walk to him.

He smiled, showing off his pearly-white teeth. When he finally stepped out, I felt like I had gotten myself in a tight situation. His body was ripped. I mean Vin Diesel kind of ripped. This was no boy all right, this was a real man.

"I can't believe you were just going to walk by with that beautiful smile," he said. "You have to give me the honor of at least knowing your name."

I caught a glimpse of my reflection in the mirror of his truck; my face was painted red. The boy had me blushing and that was not an easy task.

"It looks like you were about to leave. Can I walk you to your car or do you need a ride somewhere?" he asked. His baritone voice stimulated my curiosity and intrigued me to get to know him better. Something told me he was going to change my life. Whether it was for the better or worse, I didn't know.

"I don't see a problem with you giving me a ride. Can I at least get your name before I jump into your truck? Right now you're a stranger and my mother told me to never ride with strangers," I said.

He smiled, thinking it was a flirtatious joke. Little did he know, my mother just told me that shit a couple hours ago. I laughed to myself because the irony of it was thrilling to me.

"My name is Deshawn, but you can call me Shawn for short," he said.

"That's a nice name," I said. "My name is Jamaica, but my friends call me JJ."

With us formally introduced, it was time to roll. Deshawn opened the door for me like a gentleman. "Well hop in, pretty lady. Now that we're acquainted, I can give you that ride and maybe get to know you a little better."

«I'd like that," I said as I pulled my hair back behind my ears to accentuate my innocence.

The boy couldn't stop looking at me. I knew he was captivated, but little did he know, I was captivated by him, too.

I sat beside him blushing up a storm, and I almost forgot about Myesha. I looked up and saw her waving her hands like a bird taking flight. Leaving her dumb ass would surely teach her a lesson: *Never underestimate Jamaica Johnson!*

As foolish as she was acting earlier, she was still my best friend, so I couldn't leave her stranded. Besides if I did, her dumb ass would probably call my mother and blow up the spot.

"Oh, wait a second. I got so caught up in our conversation I almost forgot about my sister. Do you mind if she rides with us?" I asked.

"Your sister?" Deshawn asked, looking around at all the girls walking in and out of the mall entrance.

"She's right there across the street; the one standing next to the guy in the blue shirt." I was tempted to say 'she's the asshole with the stupid look on her face'.

"Sure, tell her to come on," Deshawn said.

I gestured for Myesha and when she came over, let me tell you, sweat was dripping down this bitch's forehead. The timid little girl looked like she was about to pee in her pants and blow my motherfucking cover.

"Hello," Deshawn said as Myesha sat down in the truck.

"Awww… Awww hello," she replied sounding nervous as hell. I swear I wanted to hop over in the backseat and slap her timid ass.

"So where do you live, sweetheart?" Oh shit, where did I live? Damn, I almost forgot I was someone's sixteen-year-old child. I couldn't pull up to my house in Vin Diesel's truck. I had to think quick before he became suspicious.

"Park Heights," I said, hoping Myesha didn't make a sound. I gave him Myesha's address and sat back quietly, thinking, *Jamaica, how are you going to get out of this one?* My parents were serious about me staying away from our old neighborhood and here I was on my way back there. I just hoped that I didn't run into any old problems. You know, the problems that made us move from that area in the first place.

We pulled up about twenty minutes later and my heart pounded like steel drums in a go-go band. Myesha exited the truck, not even saying thank you for the ride. After she left, Deshawn and I sat inside, talking, getting to know each other.

"So, are you free tonight? I would love to take you out if you are," he asked.

"I just finished writing a huge research paper, so lucky for you, I am free," I said.

"Research paper," Deshawn replied. "Are you in college? I love a cute girl with her head on her shoulders."

"I am. I'm sophomore at Morgan State University," I said, lying my ass off.

"That's good shit. I'm shocked you don't have a date tonight. A pretty, educated woman like you is usually tied down already. You know what they say, the good ones are already taken."

"I could say the same thing about you," I said. "Are you single, or do you have a girlfriend stashed somewhere?"

Deshawn smiled. "I don't have a girlfriend, but maybe you can change that after tonight." I didn't have to see my reflection to know that I was blushing. My entire body felt warm and tingly. "How old are you?" he asked.

Oh shit, why was he asking me this? Did I do or say something to blow my cover? What the fuck!

"It's rude to ask a lady her age, especially when she doesn't know yours," I said, trying to buy myself some time.

"I'm not trying to be rude, sweetheart. You mentioned that you were in college. I'm just asking questions to get to know you so that I could plan our date. I don't mind telling you my age. I'm twenty-six-years old. I'm an old head." Deshawn laughed as he put his hand over mine.

"Twenty-six isn't old. You're not even thirty yet. I'm nineteen so does that make me a young head?"

"No, it makes you legal enough to have fun with me," Deshawn said.

Wow, this man is ten years older than I am! Who would have thought that he would actually believe I was nineteen-years-old?

I swear when pussy is in front of a man, they became dumb, deaf, and blind. I was playing a dangerous game, but as the saying goes, "Scared money don't make no money." I needed to make moves and this guy could be the key. I could tell he had limitless potential, and could be exactly what I needed to take that journey into adulthood.

CHAPTER 3

Oh What a Tangled Web We Weave

After Deshawn pulled off, I went into Myesha's house, trying to come up with a plan. I needed to stay out tonight with a grown man without getting caught. That was my mission. Now, all I had to do was come up with a workable plan.

Myesha stood by the front door shaking her head. "You're way in over your head, Jamaica. There's no way this is going to end on a good note."

"Well, it has to work because he's coming back here to pick me up for our dinner date," I explained.

"What? Are you crazy," Myesha screamed. Her eyes almost popped out of her head. "Your parents are going to kill you when they find out, and on top of that, you made a date with a man who looks grown enough to be your father. Just like all your other schemes, this shit is going to flop."

"Stop saying that. It could work out. I just have to think of something believable and I'm going to need your help." I grabbed her hand. "Please cover for me. I swear, this can be what we both need."

The more I tried to convince Myesha, the more she shot my idea down. "I'm telling you, Jamaica, you don't even know this man, but you're making plans to go out with him."

I was in creep-mode so I honestly couldn't hear a single word Myesha said. The truth was I tuned her out a long time ago. Shit, her thoughts and opinions had been on mute since last night.

"Chill out and let me handle this situation," I said. "You being nervous is starting to make me nervous. I just need you to have my back and cover for me."

"Sure thing. Just don't say that I didn't warn you," were Myesha's last words about the situation.

From thereon, I went into gangster mode just as my mother use to do when she was making drug deals. I had to think like her so I could get away with my plans.

I sat for a long time, putting my story together, making sure that I was prepared to answer any questions. After much deliberation, I came up with something convincible.

I took a deep breath and called my mother. She picked up laughing at a joke my father was telling in the background. I was relieved they were both in a good mood. As soon as she answered, I gave her no time to ask questions.

"Mommy, Myesha really needs me to stay with her tonight. I promise I'll stay inside the house the entire time," I pleaded.

"Wait a minute. Why is Myesha's home number coming up on my Caller ID? It seems you're already at Myesha's house," she sternly replied. She was pissed off already.

"Well, Paula's mother is still outside. She said it would be easier for her to drop Myesha home first since she had something to pick up on this side of town. I came in to say hi to Mrs. Kendra and she's very sick. Myesha is depressed and crying, so I didn't want to leave her alone. I would tell her to ride back with me, but she has to babysit her little sister." There was a period of silence. I didn't know how this was going to play out, because silence could be deadly with a Jamaican woman. "I swear I wouldn't be asking if Myesha wasn't hurting so badly," I added.

"Myesha's crying?" my mother asked. "I guess it is stressful for a young girl to see her mother suffer like that." She paused for another second. "Okay, you can spend the night, but make sure you sleep with your pocketbook glued to your hands. Sleep with it under your pillow because Kendra will clean you out. Take your diamonds out of your ears, wrap them up in tissue and stuff it in your bra."

"I will, Mommy," I answered. "I love you. Bye!"

"Okay and Jamaica, we will talk about this later. You should have called me before going to Park Heights. This conversation isn't over by a long shot, okay?"

"Yes, Mommy, I understand and I know that I was wrong. I apologize."

"Okay, good night. I love you. Call me if you need me."

The second my mother hung up, my ass was in Myesha's closet trying to put together a nice outfit. I'd bought clothes from the mall earlier, so it was just a matter of finding the right accessories and handbag to bring my look together.

I'd purchased a black knee length pencil-fitted dress with leather sleeves that hugged my body tightly. There was almost no room for me to breathe. I borrowed a black and gold clutch, black pumps, and some gold accessories that matched my dress perfectly. The hook-up was sexy as hell.

I spiral curled my hair and Myesha beat my face to the Gods. My nails and toes were already polished with a French white tip, so it took no time for me to transform into supermodel mode.

Deshawn arrived at eight and was driving a money green BMW. I almost didn't recognize him when he pulled up. The nigga was a baller without a basketball and I couldn't wait to trap his ass. He looked dapper in a pair of True Religion jeans, white t-shirt, and grey Burberry cardigan. His look was clean-cut and neat, which was totally different from the oversized clothes the boys at my school wore.

Deshawn opened the door for me like a true gentleman. As I switched my phat ass past him and stepped into the vehicle, I caught a glimpse of him eyeing me down like I was a tender piece of prime porterhouse steak.

"You look amazing," Deshawn said.

"Thank you." I smiled, revealing my beautiful dimples.

Deshawn kept looking over at me and showering me with compliments the entire ride, and I kept blushing and accepting them.

"I really mean it, baby. You look stunning."

"You're looking fine yourself. I love what you're wearing and your cologne smells *delicious*." I had to throw in a compliment too because if there was one thing I knew, it was that men loved to feel just as important as women. "So, is this your car, too?" I asked.

"Yeah this is my ride, baby. I don't drive other people's shit. If I don't own it, it's not for me," he answered.

We cruised down Interstate 83 South, toward downtown Baltimore, where the majority of the main attractions were located.

"Sit back and relax, Ma. We're going to have an amazing night."

I loved a man who took control and Deshawn was doing just that. It felt good to be an adult for one night. I had no rules. All I had to do was sit back and relax as Deshawn ordered.

The rest of the night was like magic. Deshawn took me to a restaurant in Little Italy called, Moe's. As soon as we walked in the hostess greeted us and asked Deshawn did he wanted to be seated in his special section. He told her yes, and she took us upstairs to a secluded section of the restaurant. He ordered a bottle of champagne as we sat by candlelight getting to know each other. The waiter didn't even bother to ask me for ID, and it was obvious that Deshawn had pull up in here.

"Do you have kids?" Deshawn asked as he took a sip of his champagne.

"Kids? I'm only nineteen. What I look like having kids," I replied, rolling my eyes at the thought of being somebody's mother. Hell, I'm still a kid myself.

"You act like that's a weird question. It's girls that's barely in their teens with two or three kids."

"Well, I'm not one of them. I'm focused on my education," I said.

"What are you studying in college?"

"I'm majoring in business management. I hope to open a chain of successful boutiques one day."

"I can see you doing that. I may even invest in your boutiques if your proposal makes sense," he said as he chuckled.

"Oh, I have to come up with a presentation and proposal to get you to invest in me," I asked.

"You damn right," he replied as we both burst into laughter.

"So, you asked me did I have any kids, but you never told me if you had any," I said.

"Nah, I don't have any kids, but I wouldn't mind having a few little soldiers running around the house later down the road."

"Well, I want a little diva to follow in her mother's footsteps and take over my businesses when I retire," I said.

"A little diva is going to need a few soldiers around to protect her. I'm just saying," Deshawn said, as he smiled and shrugged his shoulders.

I smiled back, thinking how cute it was that he was joking about having a future with me.

Our meal was finger-licking good and our conversation was stimulating, even for a young teenager like myself.

I tried my best not to act my age, especially when the buzz from the champagne kicked in. God knew I'd never had a drink in my life so my tolerance level was low. However, even though I was a little tipsy, I was able to keep my composure. For us to be ten years apart, I was able to carry on an adult conversation with him. I was always mature for my age and tonight it paid off.

I'd heard of fairytales with such scenarios, but never in a million years did I think I would be sitting here wining and dining with a real man. Last night, I was constructing this plan in my head and tonight, I was already living it out.

After dinner, Deshawn and I drove around, not going anywhere in particular. We just cruised the town and continued to get to know each other.

"Why are you single?" I asked, catching him totally off guard.

"Why am I single," he repeated. "That's an interesting question. I'm probably single for the same reasons that you are."

"And what might that be?" I said.

"People not meeting up to my expectations. I have high standards, so I expect the woman that's going to be with me to set her bars high, too. Baltimore females either fucked too many niggas or they want to be niggas."

"And what about the men here?" I said, jumping in defense mode. "Most are pill popping wanna-be hustlers, and the decent ones are on the down low." I snapped my fingers three times like the queens did.

Deshawn busted out laughing. "Well, there you have it. Like I said before, we're both single for the same reasons." I started to laugh, too. "Besides, most females can't handle my lifestyle. It takes a special kind of woman to deal with me and keep me intrigued."

"Oh yeah, so how am I doing so far?" I asked. "Am I keeping you intrigued?"

"You wouldn't be here with me if you wasn't," he said, as he bit his sexy ass bottom lip and looked deep into my eyes.

I didn't know if this man was running game or if he was serious. All I knew was I wanted him, and I wasn't ending this date without him wanting me.

Living in Deshawn's world for the night was fun. He took me to parts of Baltimore I never knew existed. My parents would have died if they found out I went to half the places. Every stop we made, Deshawn got out the car, came back with knots of money, and asked me to count it for him. I didn't have to ask what he did for a living because it was obvious. Hell, I've seen this scenario played out before by my parents, so I knew what was up. I was drawn to his world, as if I belonged there all my life.

I licked my fingertips, and flipped the dollar bills back as I counted out the stacks. I was too pumped because my man was in charge, well at least he was going to be my man very soon.

Around midnight, we began to wind down and mellow out.

"Are you getting tired?" Deshawn asked.

I guessed he sensed that I was exhausted as hell after I started yawning. "Yeah," I told him.

"Okay! Let me get you home."

As Deshawn jumped onto I-83 North toward the beltway, I knew we were not heading for Myesha's house. In fact, we were heading toward I-95 New York.

"Umm excuse me, where are we going?" Did he think I wouldn't notice his little detour?

"We are going home; *my home*. You're not afraid to spend the night with me, are you?"

My mind told me no, but my body, particularly the lower parts, was telling me it was only one night, what was the harm? Deshawn put his hand firmly on my leg and massaged my inner thigh, looking back and forth from the road to my eyes.

My pussy began to clinch. A part of me was scared as hell, but as far as I was concerned, there was no turning back.

"Oh it's not a problem," I assured him. "I just wasn't aware we were going back to your place. You should have told me about your plans. I didn't pack anything to sleep in." That was what I said, but inside I was thinking: *Oh my goodness I didn't expect this to be happening so soon.*

"You don't have to worry about that. You can put on one of my T-shirts when we get in the house," he suggested with a smile.

"How nice of you to share your T-shirt with me," I joked, as I sat back, closed my eyes, and daydreamed about what the night had in store.

We drove so long I couldn't tell what exit Deshawn took. I had fallen asleep and he shook my legs softly, before walking to my side of the car and opening the door.

I stepped out of the car and was taken back. His house was just as big as my parents'. Not only did I see the Porsche truck he was driving earlier, but there was a chromed silver Maserati parked beside it.

I walked into the house and was even more impressed. Deshawn's house was eloquently decorated and lavish. The living room was spacious, with large, tall ceilings and an enormous gold crystal chandelier centered in the middle of the room. The cherry wood and gold classic Italian-style leather sofas accentuated the long silk gold curtains that hung from the king-size triple paned windows. I immediately took my shoes off, because God knows I would die if I scuffed his beautiful chocolate colored hardwood floor that looked like it was never walked on before.

Deshawn gave me a quick tour of the house and showed me where everything was located. I felt overwhelmed by just being there with him. As Myesha pointed out, Deshawn was no boy.

Speaking of Myesha, I had to call her to check in and make sure everything was going smoothly on her end. I knew she would be expecting me to come home and I didn't want her calling my parents when she woke up in the morning and I wasn't there.

I called, and told her I wasn't coming home and Little Miss Sunshine went off.

"Jamaica, you just met this man."

"Look, I'll be there in the morning, okay? I can't talk long because he's in the next room. I'll text you every hour if that makes you feel better."

"I sure hope you know what you're doing. You're always acting on impulse and one day it's going to catch up with you," Myesha warned.

"I know but I can assure you that I'm safe. I'll be fine. Just hold me down if my parents call your house for any reason tonight."

Before hanging up, Myesha gave me the "be careful" speech and explained that Deshawn could be a rapist, serial killer, and a bunch of other crap. I understood her concerns, but they weren't sufficient enough to make me change my mind. The danger excited the hell out of me.

Finally, after Myesha said her piece, she hung up and I went back to grind mode.

Deshawn came back into the bedroom, walked into the master bathroom and turned on the shower. I should have had sex a long time ago because every little thing he did sent shivers up my spine. The sound of the pouring water turned me on like crazy. With every drop that fell from the shower, I had my own little drops falling into the center of my panty, as I laid in his bed contemplating about what the night had in store.

He walked back into the room, picked up a remote control, pressed one button, and a TV came scrolling from the ceiling.

I tried to act like it was normal for a TV to pop out like that because I didn't want to seem pressed, but I mean the nigga had a fucking TV dropping from his ceiling.

Deshawn handed me the remote. "I'm going to take a shower. Make yourself at home."

"Thank you. When you're done I would like to take one myself," I replied.

Deshawn walked over to one of his drawers in his dresser, and took out a wife beater and a pair of boxers. He then walked into the hallway, to his linen closet, grabbed a wash cloth and bath towel, before heading back into the room and handing them to me.

"There's another bathroom down the hall. Go ahead and help yourself."

I thanked him, walked into the bathroom, and set up the shower. My little head was on cloud nine. I felt like a woman and there was no way in hell I was going back to being treated like a child. If he allowed me to, I would run away from home and live with him forever. I would cook, clean, and do all my womanly duties just to live here and not have to follow my parents' rules ever again.

I stepped into the shower and the warm water hit my body, causing a shivering sensation to run through me. Now this was bizarre because I took many showers in my life, but this one seemed unbelievable. Thunderbolts flooded my love button and drove my hormones into overdrive. I looked down at my tender breasts and saw that my nipples were hard. The more I squeezed them, the more aroused they became. I explored every part of me, and every part yearned for Deshawn.

I couldn't stand it anymore. With fire in my eyes and sex on my mind, I stepped out of the shower, naked as the day I was born, and walked back into Deshawn's bedroom. I was going to fuck the shit out of him. I'd never even French kissed, yet I knew I was going to suck his dick until I got to the center of his Tootsie Pop.

Deshawn was still in the shower when I opened the bathroom door and walked inside. The image of his bare body standing behind the glass shower made my natural juices seep out of me like a hand squeezed Florida orange. It was like I turned into some kind of animal that had to have him, and no one was going to stop me.

I opened the shower door and stepped inside. Deshawn looked at me with a stunned expression. I didn't say a word. I walked underneath the steaming water and began rubbing soap all over. I closed my eyes as I caressed myself from head to toe. Deshawn's big cock arose before my eyes. It was long and thick like a sugarcane, and damn it, I had a sweet tooth.

I got down on my knees and without hesitation, I opened my wet mouth and thrust my tongue around Deshawn's flesh, nearly swallowing him whole. The way he moaned and slowly grinded his body into my face, while using the tiled walls and shower handle to stabilize himself, only made me propel his cock further down my throat. I wanted to suck the life out of him.

I wrapped my hands around his thick dick and jerked his flesh back and forth, while moving my lips in every direction possible. The whole thing couldn't fit in my mouth, nevertheless, I sucked and sucked until tears rolled down my cheeks.

"Ohh shit…shit…suck this dick." His cries of ecstasy were pleasuring me, so much that I lifted his manhood and sucked his tender love balls. I slurped from his balls to his dick, and deep throated him like crazy. He grabbed a handful of my hair, threw my head against the tiled wall.

"You want me to fuck your mouth, don't you?"

I softly whispered, "Yes, Daddy," as I stared into his eyes and nodded to assure him that my answer was YES!

"You want this nut to squirt all over that pretty ass face of yours? Alright, well here it goes. Umm Ummm …Shiiii Shiiiii Shiiiit." Deshawn tightly closed his eyes and let out a loud moan. The nigga was damn near on his tippy toes with his dick standing over my face.

I closed my eyes, opened my mouth, and the next thing I felt was my mouth being filled with Deshawn's cream. It was warm and tasty.

When he was done, I licked my lips. "Hmmmm, that was delicious." I was so proud of myself. My first time giving head and I made the volcano erupt.

I thought Deshawn would have been worn-out, at least that was what I was told. Myesha told me after Marcus bust a good one, he was barely able to walk straight. To my surprise, she was dead wrong. Deshawn picked me up, carried me into his bedroom, and laid me on his bed. I seductively opened my legs as wide as I could and welcomed him to lay down between my threshold.

Deshawn climbed on top of me, pulled my body down toward him. "You want to play rough, huh? I got something for your pretty ass." He began kissing all over my body. He licked from my earlobes to my cheeks, to my lips. He licked from my lips to my chin, to my neck. His tongue traveled from my neck to my breasts. He sucked on my right nipple and swirled his tongue across my chest to the left nipple. He pushed my plumped breasts together and sucked them at the same time, then licked straight down to my navel. Nothing on earth ever felt this fucking good to me. When I felt his long, thick, wet tongue travel from my navel to the peak of my juicy pussy, I almost lost my fucking mind.

Deshawn swirled his tongue down the center of my phat pussy and began caressing my clitoris with his tongue. From that point, I could not refrain from screaming. I swear I nearly broke this nigga's neck off when he inserted his tongue in and out of my opening. I was new to this, nevertheless, I rode his face like I was in a Derby. I grabbed his head and push his tongue deeper inside of me, crying, screaming, and begging for more.

"Baby, don't stop. I'm about to cum," I shouted in ecstasy.

Just when I felt an explosion of juices rushing through my tunnel of love, Deshawn lifted his head, plunged his big dick inside my tight pussy, and began knocking down every inch of my innocence. I was in pain, yet I didn't want him to stop. I cringed every time he moved. My pussy was too inexperience for this kind of work. I had to come clean and tell him that he was my first or he would kill me.

"Deshawn, wait I have to tell you something. This is my… my…this is my first time. I've never been with anybody before, so please take your time."

It was like talking to a brick wall. Deshawn banged and plunged his dick inside my pussy.

Finally, after repeating myself two or three more times, he stopped and said, "Look Shorty, you don't have to lie to me. I won't think any less of you. We're two grown adults doing grown things. I know this pussy is tight and all, but virgins don't do the shit you just did to me in the bathroom."

There was no convincing him. If I wanted to be in this adult world, I had to adapt to adult things. So, I took the "D" like a "G" until Deshawn climaxed for the second time. He collapsed on top of me.

After laying for roughly a minute, Deshawn got up and began rolling a blunt. I walked over and wrapped my arms around him. He smiled at me and kissed my stomach. You would have thought we'd been together for years and were madly in love.

"What's up, baby? Are you hungry?" he asked.

"No, I'm not, but I have something to talk to you about," I nervously stated. The truth was I didn't know how he was going to handle the news about me being sixteen, but he needed to know. I wanted him to be my man, but I couldn't start this relationship with lies.

"What's up?"

"Look, when we met earlier, I was really feeling you and I wanted to get to know you better, so I bent the truth a little."

Deshawn laughed. "What, are you a man or something? If you are, please keep that shit to yourself because if you tell me that, I'll have to kill you." He continued to laugh as he sparked the blunt and took a draw.

"Please be serious for a minute. Like I said before, I like you and I know if you knew I was only sixteen, you would have…"

Deshawn's attention quickly shifted from his blunt to me. "What? You're how old?" he asked with rage in his eyes. He snapped before I could respond. "Look bitch, I just met you so don't play these types of games with me. I'm a serious man and I don't play around like that." The look in his eyes told me I was in trouble. I wished I could have disappeared and went home.

I began crying hysterically, and at that point, my true age came shining through. "I'm sorry. I tried to tell you that I was a virgin, but you didn't believe me."

"You didn't try to tell me shit. You told me you were nineteen. You came in here sucked and fucked me like a motherfucking woman, then you lay this shit on me," Deshawn screamed.

His deep rigid voice scared the hell out of me. All I could do was cry. He jumped up and pulled a suitcase from under his bed. I thought he was getting a gun.

I screamed, "No," repeatedly, but he kept ignoring me. I backed up toward the door so that I could run out, however, when he opened the suitcase I saw that it was only filled with money. Deshawn counted out a bundle and handed me five grand.

"Here, take this and keep it moving, Shorty. I don't ever want to see you again. Don't call my phone, as a matter of fact, I'm changing my number. Just put your shit on and let me get you home."

As I dressed, I was thinking five thousand dollars was a lot of money, especially if you were as young as I was. It was like winning a million dollars. Any other chick would have jumped at the opportunity for a quick come up, but not me. Maybe it was because he treated me so good or because he was my first. I didn't know, but I was weak for Deshawn.

"I don't want your money, just please take me home. You don't have to worry about me. I won't tell anyone about tonight. I would never bring drama your way."

"Yo, take this money and keep it moving Jamaica, or is that even your fucking name?" Deshawn asked, while looking at me sideways.

"I'm sure it's a gas station somewhere around here. You don't even have to take me home. I'll find the nearest one and call a cab," I replied as I shamefully made my way out of the room where we'd just made steamy love. I bent down on the way out and pretended to fix my shoes. When Deshawn wasn't looking, I threw the money to the side of the sofa. I wasn't about to take some hush money from a nigga who just fucked me. If he wanted me gone, I was gone. All that other extra shit was irrelevant.

I left Deshawn's house feeling like a damn fool. I played myself big time. I should have kept my mouth closed and fucked him until he caught major feelings for me. That way, by the time he found out the truth about my age, he would have been too pussy-whipped to leave.

After walking fifteen minutes, I found a Crown's Gas Station about three blocks up. I went inside, grabbed a bottle of water, and called a cab. They said my driver would arrive in ten minutes, however, thirty minutes later, I was still waiting. It was a long night for me, and was exhausted.

I sat on the curb outside of the gas station and rested my head against the wall for about a minute before I floated into dreamland. Just when Mr. Sandman decided to send me a dream, I was startled by a male voice.

"Damn, you're just full of surprises, huh?"

I awakened to see Deshawn sitting in his car staring at me. "First, I find out you're sixteen and now I find you sleeping outside."

I quickly sat up and fixed my hair. "Well, I had a long night. Unfortunately for me, it ended before I could get any sleep so here I am," I sarcastically replied.

Deshawn reached under the driver's seat, pulled out the money he'd given me. "Why didn't you take the money?"

"Because it's not about the money," I replied, barely able to look at him.

"Then what is it about, Jamaica?" he asked.

"You tell me. You told me to stay away from you. You said to never call you again, but here you are with me. Why did you come for me?"

Deshawn wasn't prepared to answer that question. He just sat in silence, so I answered for him.

"You're here because you like me. I know we could make this work, but I won't force you."

"Do you think it's that easy? A nigga could face jail time fucking around with you. Yo, you lied and that could come back to haunt me one day."

"I won't allow that to happen," I promised.

"This is too much. I'm not looking for a girlfriend right now. I was just looking to have a little fun and kick it with a cool ass chick, that's it."

"We could make this work if you're open-minded about the situation," I assured him. "Just give me a chance."

Deshawn let out a loud sigh and stared as I got in his car.

We sat and had a real serious ass conversation until the sun came up.

"You can never, and I mean never tell anyone about this relationship. I'm going to jail if anyone finds out about this. Do you understand me? I'm getting slapped with rape charges and I have too much going on to have to deal with that type of heat," Deshawn firmly stated, as he stared me down. "This is not a fucking game, so from here on, all the games that you play have to stop. You can lie to everyone else, but me."

"I will not keep any secrets from you from this point on," I assured him. "All I'm asking is for a chance, that's all."

"I'm going to give you that chance, but you have to follow my lead. There's going to be times when you want to be with me, but can't. You have to be mature enough to handle that. There's going to be times when you're tempted to tell people about us. You have to fight that temptation. If you're ever confronted by your parents or the police and they ask about me, exercise your right to remain silent. You have to put your big girl panties on now, Jamaica. Do you think you can handle this situation?"

"I don't think so, I know so," I said, as I reached over and turned his face toward mine. "We can make this work and I promise, you will never regret this. I don't want to hurt you. I'm trying to get to know you, and hopefully fall in love with you, so that we can make them little soldiers and diva that we talked about earlier." We both laughed and stared into each other's eyes for a short while, processing our inner thoughts.

"I'm serious, Jamaica. Don't let me regret this, especially since I was initially lied to and involuntarily put into this situation."

"I promise you have nothing to worry about. I will never bring trouble to your front door," I said.

Finally, at the end of our conversation, Deshawn decided to give me a chance. He laid down a laundry list of rules and I agreed to follow them. It wasn't easy but I got my man, just as planned.

From that night, our relationship blossomed into something special and now, we were madly in love. Deshawn kept me in place, and to be honest, my parents should thank him. He made sure that I stayed in school and got good grades. Even when I wanted to ditch to be with him, he declined and told me if I failed even one class, our relationship would be put on hold until I got back on track. I got straight A's after that warning.

Life couldn't have gotten any better for me. I had my man and I was ready to take on the world. As the song said, I'm a movement by myself, but I'm a force when we're together. Yes, I was good all by myself, but damn it, Deshawn had made me better!

CHAPTER 4

Be careful what you wish for

A heavy burden lifted off my shoulders when my 18th birthday rolled around. I didn't have to hide my relationship any longer. I felt legal, regal and ready to take on the world. Deshawn was happier than I was to let the skeletons out of the closet. It was the best year of our lives.

I was already fly as hell, but I became the shit after graduating from high school. Not only did my parents purchase the royal blue S500 Mercedes Benz I'd been asking for, but they also set up a $30,000 trust fund for me to start any business of my choice after I graduated from college. I guess that was their way of making sure I graduated from Morgan State University.

I was majoring in business management, while Myesha took a different route and enrolled into a fashion design school. We made a vow to one day put our degrees together to open a fashion boutique. The chips were falling in the right places. So when I decided the time was right, I brought Deshawn home to meet my parents. *What a BIG mistake!*

Turned out my father knew Deshawn from back in his hustling days. Deshawn was a young hothead working for my father's rivals. All hell broke loose in my house when Deshawn walked through the door. `

"What the fuck is this nigga doing in my house?" my father asked as Deshawn and I walked into the living room to greet him and my mother.

"Wait, Lucky is your father? You never told me that Lucky is your father," Deshawn said as he pointed to my father with a confused look on his face.

"I wasn't aware that I had to," I replied. "I didn't know you two knew each other. What's the problem?"

"The problem is you're not going out with this fucking nigga. This little punk never liked me, especially after I ran him and his clown ass friends off my block."

"What?" I asked. "Why would he do that? Deshawn what is he talking about?"

"Your father and I have history, but I had no clue you were his daughter. He's been out of the game for years, so how would I have known that? Not to mention, he never ran me off no block, I moved to a block that was more profitable. Nobody ever made me do shit that I didn't want to do." Deshawn was talking to me, but he kept smirking and looking at my father like, *nigga what, what's up?*

My mother pulled me aside. "Jamaica, where did you meet this guy?" she asked. "I just don't see how y'all paths crossed."

"It doesn't matter where I met him. I love him and he loves me, and I'm not leaving him." I walked off from her and stood beside my man. "Daddy, whatever happened in the past is in the past, let it stay there. He's been very good to me and he loves me."

"He loves you," my father replied. "You think this nigga loves you? Look, I'm going to say this one last time, get this nigga out of my house before he gets carried out." I looked into my father's eyes and saw that he was serious. Although he was not in the streets anymore, he still had connections and he was still Lucky.

Deshawn wasn't the least bit moved by my father's threats. He had an unbothered expression on his face, and it was apparent that both of these stubborn men weren't going to be mature about the situation.

"Let's go," I said to Deshawn. "This was a big mistake."

"You fucking right it was a big mistake bringing this nigga up in my house. Jamaica, you're not a child anymore. As your father I'm telling you that this man is dangerous and conniving as fuck. He stole a lot of money from people, including me and did some other foul shit. If you continue to see this nigga after I specifically told you not to, you better ask him to pay all your bills and take care of you from hereon."

"You're not being fair," I replied. "You didn't even give him a chance to apologize for whatever her did in the past. He may have been a different person back then, but he's changed. He's been nothing but good to me and we're in love."

I professed my love for Deshawn, but it was like talking to a brick wall. My father had his mind made up and he wasn't going to change it for me, or anyone else.

"You heard what I said, right? If you continue to see him, you better be prepared for the consequences. Most importantly, don't ever bring this nigga back around my motherfucking family again."

I assured my father that Deshawn wouldn't step foot back inside his house, however we would continue seeing each other.

My father didn't like that one bit, so he told me that I was cut off financially from this moment on; as if I needed his money anymore.

Deshawn took care of me in every aspect, and I called him Big Daddy anyway! I was a grown ass woman and I wasn't going to let my father dictate my life.

After seven months of fighting the cause, my father gave up, but he said, "When that relationship turns upside down, don't expect me to rescue you."

That was fine because my relationship was solid. I loved my father, but this was my life. Now that my parents agreed to stay out of my relationship, everything was flawless until Deshawn fucked up and asked me some stupid shit that made my stomach turn.

We were lying in bed one night, watching television, when Deshawn got up, walked into the hallway, and came back holding a box of Jean Paul Gaultier perfume; one of my favorites.

"This is for you, beautiful," he said as he handed it to me. "I brought it for you this afternoon when I was at the mall."

"Thank you, baby," I said, as I took the bottle from him and placed it on the nightstand. "You're so sweet." As I said before, Deshawn took good care of me and was always showering me with gifts.

"It's not a problem. You deserve the best." He replied, as he leaned over and kissed me. "Why don't you open the box?"

"There's a bottle that almost full still sitting on the dresser. I don't need to open this one just yet. I'll put it in the cabinet until the other one is finished."

"Nah, open it and make sure it didn't break because I dropped it earlier and it hit the ground hard," he said.

"Okay," I replied. "You better not had smashed my damn perfume," I jokingly said as I opened the box. I pulled out the bottle of perfume and looked it over; everything was fine. "It's not broken, baby."

"Are you sure?" Deshawn asked. "I think you need to look at the bottle real good."

I looked at the bottle again, and saw a sparkling object sitting on the spray area that I didn't notice before. I took the top off and removed the object. It was a three carat marquise cut diamond ring with diamond clutters embedded on a double band. The ring was stunningly beautiful. It literally had me speechless for a couple of seconds.

"Deshawn, what's this?"

"Jamaica Johnson, will you marry me?" He was on his knees and everything like we were in a romantic novel, standing in front of a fucking white horse with wings. What? Marriage? Where did my bad boy go?

I looked into his eyes to see if he was joking. I was eighteen-years-old, having fun in college, and wasn't prepared to be trapped into a marriage. I loved him, but damn, let a sister live a little. Why was he changing up the game now?

I didn't know what to say because I didn't want to lose him. So, to spare his feelings, I accepted his proposal, and before I knew it, my mother and Myesha were planning my wedding.

As months passed by and my wedding day came closer, my love for Deshawn began to deteriorate. I was making a name for myself up at Morgan State, just as I did as a youngster around Park Heights. I joined a few organizations, like the Caribbean Students Association and the National Society of Leadership and Success. I was invited to pledge different sororities, and every time I turned around, people were giving me party invites with free tickets. I was even voted Miss Morgan State University during my first year of college. People began to hear about the hot girl, with the rich family, who pushed the Benz. Everyone wanted to hang with me.

Then, I didn't know if it was because of my mother's yams, bananas, and dumplings, but my ass got rounder, my breasts stood up like implants, and my body became curvaceously stunning. I became sexier than I even imagined.

Deshawn couldn't handle all the attention that I was getting, so he became overly obsessive. It was pathetic how he followed me around like a "pussy watchman," as the Jamaicans would say. I couldn't shit comfortably without him accusing me of letting another nigga wipe my ass. He totally jumped out of character.

Deshawn even started to verbally abuse me; calling me sneaky bitches and hoes for every little thing. He damn-near smothered me, and at times, I wondered if he was marrying me because he loved me or because he wanted to have more control over me.

I was fed up with his insecurities. Bad enough he was cramping my style with this marriage bullshit, but I was missing the fun of being young. All my friends were dating and having a ball. I realized I wanted to enjoy the freedom of being free. Finally, my parents couldn't dictate my life but now this *man* was trying to. Oh, hell no!

One night while Deshawn was at the club collecting his money, I gave him a call. I was being a coward, but I was too afraid to hurt him face to face. Deep down, I still truly loved Deshawn, but just didn't want to be stifled by his love anymore. Leaving a break up message on his voicemail seemed like the right thing to do. So, when his voicemail picked up, I spoke directly from my heart.

"Deshawn, I know you may not be able to understand what I'm about to say, but lately, I've been unhappy and I've tried to cope with it, but I can't any longer. I feel like I'm living a lie and I want to do what's best for the both of us. You've been so good to me and I don't want to hurt you, however, I need my space so I can grow. You're stifling me and your love is literally taking my breath away, and I mean that in an unhealthy way. I need time to live my life without limitations so I can truly understand who I am. I want you to know you hold a special place in my heart and I still love you very much. Call me as soon as you get this message so we can talk. I love you baby. Bye!»

I was a real bitch to leave such a sensitive message, but it is what it is. Seasons changed and people changed and our relationship was no different.

Right after I hung up, and I mean, the very second I hung up, I called Myesha and scheduled a, "Welcome back, Jamaica," girls night out. My bestie and I linked up and went to a predominately white club in Fells Point, Maryland. We partied like we never had before.

I danced with every man in the room. Hell, I think I even danced with a couple females, too.

"I'm sad about your breakup, but bitch, I'm soooooooo happy," Myesha confessed. "I feel like I got my sister back."

"Shut up, girl. I didn't go anywhere." After five shots of Patron, I was done. My words were slurred and I could barely stand up but, my best bitch and I were reunited and I couldn't wait to hit the streets as a free agent.

"I can't understand a single word you're saying. Let's get back out on this dance floor and show these people how we get down," Myesha said as she got up from her seat.

Of course, I joined her and we partied the night away like two teenagers with no cares in the world. I honestly couldn't recall a time when I had this much fun. It felt like I was locked up for twenty-five years and just got paroled.

When I arrived home that night, the first thing I did was check my call log, but there were no missed calls from Deshawn. I called him, but he kept sending me to voicemail. I realized he was in his feelings. I was a little sad because I didn't want our relationship to end this way, but this was his decision.

Two months passed by and I still hadn't heard from Deshawn. It was like our relationship never existed. I tried to call him on numerous occasions, but he wouldn't answer. One day, I called his cell and house phone and they were both disconnected. I took that as a sign that he'd moved on.

I was walking out of school after attending my last class one evening. I was stressed out and exhausted from a dreadful two-hour dr calculus exam and just wanted to get home and crawl into bed. It was cold, dark, and gloomy outside.

The majority of the students were already on their way home. I had stayed back to speak with my professor.

The walk to my car was long and exhausting. The trees were naked with only frozen branches hanging off. The air was brisk and dry, causing smoke clouds to form with every breath I took.

I hit the alarm on my car, opened the doors, and literally dropped into the driver's seat. As I put my key into the ignition, a huge knife was plunged into my neck. Afraid to turn around, I threw my pocketbook to the backseat.

"Please take it all. I have four hundred dollars in cash and my bank code is five-five…"

"Shut the fuck up, bitch. I don't want your money." The voice, it was too familiar. It was a voice I'd been hearing for years, but tonight, it wasn't pleasant at all.

"Deshawn, what are you doing?" I asked. I smelled the aroma of Bvlgar's Men's cologne, his signature scent.

"Shut the car off and you better not make a fucking sound." He plunged the knife deeper into my throat, pinching my skin.

I was scared shitless. I knew he would hurt me, so I did exactly as I was told. From the corner of my eye I looked around to see if there was anyone around to help me. Where the hell were the fucking campus police who always came around writing tickets and harassing the students?

Deshawn grabbed my hair and forcefully turned me around to face him and when I did, I saw a familiar face in an unfamiliar way. His eyes were bloodshot red and his face was cold and heartless. I screamed because I was staring at the devil himself.

"Somebody help me, please! Oh my God, please help me!" I yelled like I had never yelled before.

Deshawn began hitting me in my face and calling me all types of bitches and whores. I couldn't fight him off even though I tried.

"Don't hurt me. I'm sorry. Deshawn, please don't kill me," I pleaded.

"Don't kill you? Bitch, when I'm through with your ass, you're going to grab this knife and stab your own fucking self," he threatened. From the callous look of his piercing eyes to the menacing tone of his voice, I knew he meant every word. Deshawn's next demand was to start my car and drive to the back of the empty campus. I stalled for as long as I could, but once again, I did as I was told.

After parking, Deshawn dragged me out of the car by my hair and beat me like a fucking man. The blows to my head and chest nearly knocked me unconscious.

"After all the fuck I've done for you, you think you can just leave me? I could have gone to jail for fucking with your lying, conniving ass." *Swoooop*! Deshawn inflicted another blow to the side of my face. The impact nearly disconnected my head from my neck.

I screamed out in agony, but that only made matters worse.

"A nigga treated you like a queen and wifed you and you took that shit for granted. Let's see how you act when I treat you like the whore-bag that you are." *Swoooop, Swooooop, Booooom*! Deshawn's blows poured down on my body like a waterfall. He wasn't having mercy on me whatsoever.

I had to think because time was running out. He could kill me and I needed to get to his heart and try to use the love he once had for me to control the situation. There had to be a drop of love and compassion left in his heart for me and I had to find it quickly.

"Deshawn, baby, I never stop loving you. That's why I kept calling after the break up. I wanted to speak to you to let you know I was experiencing last minute jitters, but they quickly went away. You wouldn't pick up for me and eventually changed your numbers, so I assumed you didn't want to be with me anymore." I hoped and prayed my reverse psychology worked because if it didn't, I was dead.

I spent the next five minutes pouring my heart out to Deshawn, and after a while, the beating slowed before stopping. He looked deeply into my crying eyes, as if he was trying to read my mind. I was hoping he would see the pain he'd caused and let me go. If he just allowed me to walk away, I would have kept my mouth shut and not told a single person.

"You mean you didn't want to call off our wedding?" Deshawn asked softly.

"No I wanted to be with you. I still want to be with you," I answered while staring hopelessly into his eyes.

He'd always told me my eyes were the most beautiful thing on God's earth, so I hoped my gaze would do some damage control.

Deshawn went from being deranged to warm and compassionate. "So why did you leave that message on my voicemail?"

"I was having cold-feet. My mother says everyone goes through that stage when they're getting married for the first time."

"So you still want to get married?" Deshawn asked.

"Yes, baby that's exactly what I'm saying," I quickly answered.

A relived expression washed over Deshawn's face. He gently caressed the back of my neck. "I'm so sorry, baby."

Words couldn't explain how happy I was to hear that come out of his mouth. He was remorseful. He called me baby. His touches were gentle, and I felt a sense of relief knowing the nightmare was finally over. Although my entire body was sore from the beating, I just wanted to get in my car and get the hell away from this sick bastard. I wasn't thinking about contacting the police or letting anyone know what occurred. I just wanted to get away.

Deshawn continued to massage my neck as he kissed my lips and whispered into my ear, "Jamaica, I am truly sorry."

I replied, "It's okay. I'm sorry, too."

"No baby, I don't think you understand. I am really, really, really sorry... I'm sorry for falling for a lying ass slut like you." *Swaaaaaap*! Deshawn slapped any thought I had of escaping out of my mind. "Bitch, you must think I'm some kind of fool. You needed space, right? You needed space so you could fuck other niggas! You wanted to be a thirsty ass bitch. Well since you love dick so much, let me give you some right now."

He began ripping my clothes off with his knife. The blade cut my skin. Once I was completely naked outside in the cold, it dawned on me I was about to get raped.

Deshawn unbuttoned his jeans, pull his already erect dick out of his boxers, and jerked it to make it even more erect. The entire time he called me all types of sluts and warned me he was going to fuck me senseless.

I screamed out for help but it was pointless, so I closed my eyes and laid on the cold concrete as my first love raped and repeatedly beat me. He beat me so much, I blacked out for a couple minutes, and as I regained consciousness, he was still on top of me pounding his husky body between my legs, choking me, and biting my neck until he broke my flesh. The whole time he kept yelling, "You'll never love another man again. I'm going to make sure of that!"

Fifteen minutes later, which felt like eternity, Deshawn lifted up from my weakened body and as I laid helplessly on the ground, he ejaculated on my face. All I could do was close my mouth and shut my eyes.

After pulling his pants up, Deshawn walked over to me and graciously helped me off the ground (yes, I said *graciously helped me*).

"Baby, let me help you get up off this cold ground." He'd changed back into the charming Deshawn I'd met at the mall as he brushed the dirt from my hair and ripped clothes.

"Deshawn, why'd you do this to me?" I asked feeling both horrified and confused.

"What did I do?" he asked calmly.

I didn't have an answer because it was obvious what he'd done. I stood there for a good minute, looking at him to see if he was serious. I guess he became annoyed by my silence because he screamed, "Bitch," and then composed himself. "I mean, baby, what am I doing to you?"

I knew then that I was dealing with a mad man.

"You didn't do anything. I'm sorry, I didn't mean to say that. It came out wrong," I corrected.

Deshawn walked me to my car and opened the door so that I could sit down. He then leaned inside, softly kissed my lips, and asked, "So do you want to see a movie tonight?"

I couldn't believe my ears. "Sure, that sounds fine," I replied. This was the type of crazy shit you only saw on the news.

"Okay, so let's catch a late movie and grab dinner afterwards. I know how much you love sushi, so we can hit one of those sushi bars you're always nagging me to take you to," he suggested, as I sat before him with a busted lip and blood still dripping from my nose.

"That sounds good," I said again with a fake smile. I didn't want to say the wrong thing, so I kept my responses brief.

"You have dirt all over you and your hair is all over the place. Go home, get pretty, and meet me later with your bag packed."

"My bags? What bags?"

"Your bags, silly. I think it's time for us to take this relationship to the next level. I want you to move in with me."

"Live with you," I repeated, as I wrapped my hand around my finger to stop the bleeding. "Oh yeah, I agree, we need to take this step so that we're never apart," I replied, as a sickening feeling ran through my body and made me nauseous.

After making plans with me, Deshawn strapped the seatbelt around me. "Drive safe, baby. There's some crazy motherfuckers out here riding around drunk and reckless. I don't need any of them hurting you."

"Sure thing. I'll drive carefully," I promised.

"Don't forget what I said. I'm not playing any games with you, Jamaica. If you tell anyone about tonight I'm going to hit you where it hurts. I'll kill your entire family in front of you and then keep you alive to torture you until I'm bored. After that, I'm going to kill you, too." Deshawn never made idle threats, and I knew for sure he would do exactly what he said. The severe migraine I had from his massive blows to my head reminded me just how real shit could get with him, so I wasn't taking his threats lightly.

"I promise I won't tell a soul. I'm going home to freshen up and I'll be right back out to meet up with you."

"Okay, sweetheart. See you soon." Deshawn closed my car door and walked off.

I pulled off and wasted no time getting the hell away from there the very second he turned the corner. I must have driven about 120 miles per hour on the highway. My legs were trembling and my entire body felt like it was hit by a dump truck multiple times. To be honest, I didn't recall the entire ride home. All I knew was I saw my front door and wasted no time getting my black ass behind it. I ran inside, slammed the door, and bolted the locks shut. Once inside, I fell to my knees crying. I didn't even notice my parents in the living room until my father went off.

"What the fuck? What happened to you, Jamaica?" my father screamed. He jumped up from the sofa and covered my half naked body with his jacket. "Who did this?"

I just knelt there, weeping.

"Oh my God, Lucky. Look at her face. Jamaica, talk to us. What happened to you? Who did this?" my mother asked.

I wanted to tell them everything, but I remembered Deshawn's warning. I was dealing with a psycho, so I lied to my parents to protect them.

"I was driving home and this girl cut me off, so I cut her back off. We got into an argument at the light. Then we both got out of our cars and started fighting. Her friends jumped in and banked me. They drove off before I could get the license plate number."

"Exactly where did this happen? What street? What intersection? What was the make and model of the car? How many girls were in the car?"

Question after question were thrown my way. I tried my best to answer them but the truth was, I was too exhausted and physically drained to keep up with my lies. I just needed to take a hot shower and pop one or two Percocets that my father kept in the bathroom for his back spasms.

Lucky and Mary were too smart for that shit, though, especially my mother. She took one look at me. "Your story sound bloodclot bogus. No girls beat you up. I bet you any amount of money Deshawn did this to you," she screamed in her Jamaican dialect.

Deshawn! The sound of his name sent chills through my body and I burst into tears. "Look, I said some girls jumped me, now leave this alone. I just need some rest, okay? Please back off," I pleaded.

I tried to walk up the steps, but my mother pulled me back down and continued to question me. My father, on the other hand, didn't ask any more questions. He grabbed his coat from the closet and walked out the door.

I knew where he was going. I tried to stop him, but I could barely walk. My mother tried to stop him, but she had no luck either. The last thing I heard before my father pulled off was him talking on his phone: "I need you to call Blacks and have him meet me at the spot right now. We have something to take care of tonight."

After he drove off, my mother turned and said, "You need to be seen. Put some clothes on and let's go."

"I'm okay. I just want to take a shower, go to bed, and forget about tonight," I tearfully begged.

"Maybe you think this is up for discussion so let me rephrase myself. Go upstairs, get dressed, and let's go or I will call nine-one-one and have them escort you out of here." My mother's eyes popped out of her head like she was possessed.

Everyone in our household knew when them eyeballs come out and start moving side to side, she meant business. Realizing that I had no choice, I got dressed and headed to Harford County General Hospital.

Before I knew it, my mother and I were sitting in an examination room. The nurse, social worker, and doctors all questioned me about what went down and I stuck to my guns. I told them the same story I'd told my parents.

"I was jumped by some girls during a road rage dispute."

My mother kept interrupting, telling everyone she suspected I was lying, however, I was not a minor. I was a grown ass woman, giving these medical professionals my statement. And although I suspected that everyone in the room knew I wasn't telling the truth, there was nothing they could do. They had to go with my story.

After the examination, I thought I was going to be discharged, however, three police officers walked into my room. They told me my story wasn't adding up and explained that my medical examination and test results revealed that I was severely beaten and raped. My mother almost passed out when she heard that one, because up until now, she only suspected that Deshawn beat me up. Nevertheless, I told the police officers the same story.

This only infuriated my mother even more. She went off in front of everyone. "Are you going to let Deshawn get away with this? Why are you protecting him? Tell the police what they need to know so they can go and arrest him."

"I just want to go home. I don't care what the test shows, I was jumped by some girls. It's a simple case of road rage." I jumped off the examination table, grabbed my belongings, and stormed out the door.

One of the police officers followed me. "Excuse me, ma'am. Would your mother happen to be talking about Deshawn Burris?"

How did he know Deshawn's last name? My mother didn't know his last name and I sure didn't mention it. "What if it is? What does it mean to you?" I asked.

"Oh it means nothing to me, but if it's Mr. Toe-Tag Deshawn, as we so like to call him down at the precinct, it means a whole lot to you. That man is not to be taken lightly and if for any reason he's after you, you have a serious problem."

I stood in disbelief. I broke down and cried on that cop's shoulder like he was my fucking father. It was like I couldn't control my tear ducts. I felt helpless and trapped.

"He said he would kill me and my family if I betrayed him, and I don't want to upset him more than I've already done. That man is crazy. He has multiple sides to him and I saw them all tonight."

The officer shook his head. "Deshawn Burris always finishes what he starts, and if you believe he's just going to let you go, he's hit you one too many times. You need to give us a statement so that we can get this punk off our streets."

It was evident that the officers wanted Deshawn badly. They spoke with such passion and anger toward him. They shared several chilling stories about murders that Deshawn either committed himself or paid to have done. They said they could never arrest him because people were too afraid to testify against him, and the ones who were brave enough, always came up missing or dead. I couldn't believe it. I knew he was in the streets, but I had no clue this monster side of him existed until tonight. How oblivious could I have been?

After an hour of interrogation, I told the officers everything. In other words, I snitched. I told them how Deshawn and I met and explained what he did to me tonight. Even worse, I revealed his drug connections, nationally and locally, and prayed it was enough for them to get the conviction they were looking for to lock him away for a long time.

The officers made me call Deshawn to confirm our date. He told me to meet him at the normal spot, which was the club where he collected his money. The entire time I was setting him up, I kept thinking this wasn't going to end right. I felt it deep in my bones.

With the police's protection, I pulled up to the club at 10:00 pm and called Deshawn to let him know I was outside.

"Okay, hold tight for about fifteen minutes while I count up this money."

That fifteen minutes felt more like fifteen hours. It was torture sitting outside, wondering if Deshawn knew what was going on. Were these police officers really concerned about my well-being or was I just another bait to capture their suspect? And the most alarming question of all, if this doesn't work out, would Mr. Toe-Tag kill me and my family?

Deshawn walked out of the club fifteen minutes later and made his way over to my car. I couldn't tell you why he was smiling, but I could say he looked like he was up to something, or should I say he looked like he knew that I was up to something. Nonetheless, I tried to keep my composure.

As he opened the door and sat inside the car, I felt a rush of anxiety. The feeling was so overwhelming that I almost opened my door and ran out. However, my fears went away when Deshawn leaned over and gave me a kiss. "You know that I love you, right?"

I nodded and said, "Yes," although after what he did to me, I seriously doubted that he did. The beating, the rape, and the ejaculation on my face all confirmed that Deshawn had no love for my ass.

Deshawn asked, "You know that I know you more than you know yourself, right?"

"Yes," I nervously answered again, wondering where he was going with this conversation.

"Then you should know that the Jamaica I know wouldn't show up for a date with me after I whipped her ass the way I did. The Jamaica I know wouldn't even stand for that shit." I looked down but Deshawn turned my face back toward his. "Do you remember the last thing I said to you?" I didn't answer because my mind was wandering all over the place. Again, Deshawn repeated, "Jamaica, do you remember my warning?"

Before I could answer, about fifteen police cars rushed down on us and surrounded my car. One officer ran over to my car with his gun drawn and pulled me out. I looked back at Deshawn as I was being escorted away and he sat there, still smiling. He didn't say a word or try to run, he just kept smiling.

It was complete mayhem after that. After the police officer took me away and placed me in my parents' car, multiple officers with guns drawn, rushed down on Deshawn, and started yelling, "Get out of the car and get down on the ground."

Deshawn peacefully opened the door with both hands up in the air, before kneeling and clasping his fingers together behind his head.

I watched from afar and what I remembered most was the incessant smile on his face. It was unsettling because the Deshawn I knew wouldn't go down without a fight, even with police officers involved.

Deshawn was arrested and charged with a first degree assault, first degree rape, statutory rape, and criminal harassment.

I was a nervous wreck during the months leading up to his trial. I didn't know what to do or who to trust during this time.

Deshawn's silence made me nervous. He was basically letting me know that he was going to follow through with his threats. I hoped the judge sent his ass away for good. That was my only guarantee to walk away victorious. Although Deshawn could very well put money on my head while in prison, he had more influence on the outside than inside.

After countless months of looking over my shoulder and living in fear, Deshawn's trial finally began. With my life in the prosecutor's hands, I went on the stand and testified against a man the police coined "Toe-Tagger of the DMV."

I identified Deshawn as the man who raped and brutally beat me and gave background information on all the criminal activities that I witnessed him engaging in over the span of our relationship. They asked how we met and I gave a complete statement, including the fact that I was only sixteen and he was twenty-six when we first hooked up.

The next day, the defense attorney presented his case on Deshawn's behalf. He portrayed me as a lying, conniving, gold-digger who used him for his money. He said that I lied to him and told him that I was nineteen-years old, which was true, but he said that it wasn't until six months later that Deshawn found out my real age when he stumbled on a letter from the Department of Motor Vehicle laying in my car. His lawyer also had a copy of the initial police report, stating that I told the officers my injuries came from a road rage incident and argued that I didn't identify Deshawn as my attacker until I was influenced by the police department, who already had a personal issue with him. He even stated that Deshawn was racially profiled by the police and gave accounts of six criminal cases against him that were dropped due to lack of evidence. If that wasn't bad enough, Deshawn's lawyer called two bartenders and the owner of the club where he was arrested, to say that he was inside partying during the time when I was attacked. When that motherfucker got through presenting his case, I looked like the monster and Deshawn looked like the victim.

After four days of the prosecution and the defense presenting their cases, I was sitting back in the courtroom nervous as hell as the judge read his verdict. Deshawn was found guilty of all charges: first degree assault, first degree rape, statutory rape, and criminal harassment.

I'd gone back on my word and broke my promises to him. The night I lost my virginity, I swore to him this day would never come.

After reading all the charges and the maximum sentences and fines they carried, the judge started to say a bunch of legal terms I didn't understand. The one statement that stood out the most was, "You are therefore sentenced to the term of five years, with the possibility of parole within three."

When I heard that shit I literally felt my heart hit the floor. *Five years, what the hell!* That was all he was getting was five measly years that he could probably do standing on one hand? Where the hell was the justice system that was supposed to prevail? It seemed more like the justice system derailed if you asked me.

I looked at the police officers and state's attorney, who all held their heads down to avoid making eye contact with me, and knew I was dead. Man, Bob Marley stood a greater chance of being alive than I did.

Deshawn reclined back in his chair like he was chilling in his living room watching a Baltimore Raven's football game. He hired some big shot lawyer, who somehow convinced the judge to be merciful with his sentencing. He got the best of us and he knew it. The smirk on his face said it all.

I had to leave before I burst into tears. As I picked up my purse and exited the courtroom with my parents, Deshawn began to mock me.

"He raaaaaaped me when I was sixteen years old," he blurted out, imitating me in a southern belle kind of voice. "Oh my God, he took my innocence away."

People started to chuckle. Even the judge looked like he was cracking up on the inside. I felt mortified.

Suddenly, Deshawn's second personality surfaced and that was when shit got real. "Bitch, you were a whore who lied about your age until you sucked my dick and let me bust in your mouth. Then you told me you were sixteen." Deshawn shifted his attention from me to the judge and blurted, "Y'all niggas really going to convict me of rape? I didn't rape this bitch. The only thing I'm guilty of is trying to turn this hoe into a wife." He shifted his attention back to me, but this time when he looked into my eyes, something clicked and this nigga went ham. He jumped from his seat, sprung toward me in attack mode, but the guards restrained him. It took damn near three of them to hold him back.

The judge looked stunned, and it was evident that he didn't have control of his courtroom anymore.

"You slut bitch. When I come home, I swear it could be fifty fucking years from now, you're going to pay for this shit, Jamaica."

For him to make treats and act in such of an aggressive manner with guards, police officers, and a judge in the same damn room, I knew I was playing on the wrong team. No one could protect me from him; not even my parents and all their money.

After Deshawn's trial, I withdrew from college for an entire semester and fell into deep depression. I fell off for a hot minute, but as I said on the day I broke off the engagement with Deshawn, "Seasons changed and people changed." With the help of my parents and some much-needed counseling, I bounced back like a basketball.

Today, I'm 23 years old with new goals in life. I'm a little older and a little wiser. If Deshawn didn't teach me anything, he taught me that I have to protect my own. I have to protect my heart, my life, and my dreams. I have to create my own lane and cruise in it. Now, I live by one rule and that's "Do what makes Jamaica Johnson happy!" Everything and everyone else is secondary.

CHAPTER 5

Winter Rose

Although I overcame the Deshawn era, he did accomplish one thing. He destroyed my ability to love. I dated here and there, but I never allowed myself to fall for anyone. Now I understood what he meant when he said I would never love again.

I questioned every guy I went out with, wondering when was he going to show me "that" side of him. The side that was crazy. For this reason, I kept everyone at a distance and never got into anything too heavy, which made my *situation-ship* with Terrell perfect.

Terrell was a guy I enjoyed seeing a little more than others. Most people called him Rock. He didn't inherit that nickname because he was a geologist. They called him Rock because that's what he sold. He was the newest big shot on the block, making a lot of cash and if it seemed like I was heading down a familiar path, you're right. Hey, what could I say? I loved them D-boys and if I was going to fuck with a dude, he had to be the nigga in charge.

Indeed, Rock was in charge. He had a gang of niggas working for him, and most people knew not to cross him, and the ones who didn't, learned the hard way.

Rock and I had the perfect arrangement. We both weren't looking for anything serious. I didn't require a lot of his time and sure didn't need his money. All I needed was some good loving from time to time and vice versa. Our little thing was fun and uncomplicated and if I had anything to do with it, it was going to stay that way.

My life was back in order and finally on the up-and-up. My parents were still doing their thing in the corporate world and making power moves that were productive for business, however, unproductive for their marriage. With successful Benz dealerships and a new trendy beauty salon, Lucky and Mary rarely had time for themselves.

My father started to mix and mingle with the elite crowd. He was always attending some out-of-town convention or meeting with business moguls to discuss investments. This also meant he spent a lot of time away from my mother because she couldn't just up and close her salon to travel with him. Well, actually she could if she wanted to, but as I explained, Mary was all about her paper, so she wasn't about to lose money just to be with her husband. Remember, this was the lady who was willing to take a bullet to the head before giving up her stash.

My mother thought it made sense, and was more profitable, for them to work separately and get together whenever time permitted. The little things they used to do, like taking elaborate vacations out of the country, were out of the question, considering they had separate schedules. Communication, respect, and time were just some of the essential elements of their marriage that became compromised, and my mother couldn't care less about all that, as long as the money rolled in.

Every time my father's schedule freed up, here came Mary convincing him to invest in something new. Just as she persuaded him to go big time in the drug world, she was now demanding that he expand his dealerships. So within no time, my father went from having one successful Benz dealership to five. With his success, my father was then able to upgrade and relocate my mother's beauty salon from a small storefront building to a three-tiered structure in one of the richest areas of Harford County. She hired ten other stylists, who worked on level three of her building. She hired three masseuses, three nail technicians, and a skin care specialist on level two. Finally, on level one, was my Aunt Pamela's Jamaican restaurant.

Aunt Pam was my mother's youngest sister, who migrated from Jamaica to America a couple of years ago. She lived with us for a while until my parents helped her purchase a house of her own, not too far from ours. My mother loved her baby sister, so she roped her into the family business. That way, she could make some real money, too.

With the stress of running multiple businesses, the love between my parents began to slowly fade away. Feeling like he needed an outlet, my father began to find happiness in other women, many, many women.

Lucky became a straight hoe, that was the best way I could put it. He was a handsome, successful, man, so of course, all the thirsty hoes appreciated the time, attention, and money they received from him. The messy part was that my mother was fully aware of what was going on, but stayed with him to maintain her lifestyle.

I, in no way, wanted to be that type of woman. I had dreams of having my own shit, but wasn't expecting handouts from anyone.

However, after graduating from college, I was hit with reality. I had my degree but didn't know what to do. Technically, I wasn't broke because my parents were rich and I had my after-college fund, but I had no clue about who I was as an individual. While I soul searched, I did a lot of partying, which infuriated my parents.

One morning while I was half-sleep enjoying the cool morning breeze ticking my body, I was rudely awakened by my parents hovering over my bed.

"Jamaica, get up right now. We need to talk!"

I knew what was coming next because it was our standard argument; especially after I had partied the night before.

"You need to get out of this bed and go find a job." My father was going off, but I kept my eyes closed and tried to tune him out. "You can lay there and pretend like you're sleeping, but I know you hear every single word I'm saying." The sound of his voice mixed with the six shots of Patron I had last night was a recipe for disaster.

"Okay, Daddy, I'll go look for a job as soon as I wake up," I assured him.

"No get your lazy ass out of this bed right now. I'm tired of watching you sleep throughout the week and party all weekend, while your mother and I are up at the crack of dawn busting our ass to support your lavish lifestyle. No one spends more money in this house than you, and you're the one who's unemployed."

I couldn't drown his ass out to save my life, so I finally opened my eyes. "Look," I replied, annoyed. "I said I'm going to look for a job today. Just get off my back a little," I snapped.

My father was always annoying, but he was being overly obsessive about me find a job today.

Of course my mother had to co-sign with him. Mind you, they didn't get along any other time, but when it came to tag-teaming me, they had each other's backs.

"It can be full-time, part-time, split shift, flex-hours; I don't give a damn what shift as long as your ass is working by the end of the month. You can't go through life thinking that your looks and your parents' money will always save you. Jamaica; you're a grown woman."

"A grown fucking woman," my father added. "Now get up and go put in a couple job applications somewhere. I don't want to see you laying around this house today."

After hovering over my head for what seemed like eternity, the wardens finally left my cell. Why were they picking on me? I didn't see them pressuring Rochelle and she was old enough to work. Just because she was still in school shouldn't exempt her from getting a job.

Not to mention that I wasn't broke. My $30,000 trust fund kicked in the day after my graduation, so I had a nice chunk of money. They should have been happy that I hadn't blown that already. Even after they left, my father kept opening my room door and demanding for me to get up so, I finally showered, got dressed, and called Myesha to see if she wanted to hit the mall before heading to work. I didn't have a job but Myesha did, a very interesting one at that.

Her mother, Mrs. Kendra was still getting high and Myesha's job at McDonalds wasn't paying the bills. To survive, it was either find a better job or live on the streets with her addict mother and baby sister. So Little Miss Sunshine found herself another job at a club called "The Den" and she went by the name of My'Nasty. Her alias was a combination of her real name and the word Dynasty — she said that meant "Myesha's quest to acquire an empire."

Typical Myesha, trying to make her bougie ass sound important. My'Nasty was the perfect name for a damn stripper, which is what she was. A lot had changed since we were little girls. Little Miss Sunshine was now shaking her ass for cash, which was ironic considering everyone expected me to be the one sliding down the stripper pole.

Anyhow, Myesha agreed to chill with me before going to work. I arrived at her house, honked the horn, and she came flying out the door with Mrs. Kendra running behind her arguing, stumbling, and slurring her words like a true west side junkie.

"You won't even loan me one dollar? What type of daughter are you? You're a selfish ass bitch."

Myesha kept power walking to the car, attempting to ignore the ghetto ass commotion her mother was causing.

"Go back in the house, Ma," Myesha yelled as she rolled her eyes and sat down in the car.

"Esha... Esha... Eshaaaaaaaaaa... Just loan me one measly dollar," Mrs. Kendra hollered as the neighbors snickered from their porch.

I saw one girl aiming her cell phone toward us and I knew what was up.

"Yo, people are recording this shit. They're going to upload this; tell your mother to chill out." I pointed to the girl so Myesha could see who I was talking about.

"Oh my God, please drive off. I don't have the time or strength to deal with this today," Myesha pleaded.

She didn't have to say it twice. I put my car in drive and zoomed off just in time to escape a lotion bottle Mrs. Kendra threw at my car as she screamed, "Well, fuck you, then," to Myesha.

"Wow, what's up with your mother?" I asked.

"I don't even feel like talking about her ass right now," Myesha replied with sadness on her face. "She's getting worse, Jamaica. I need to put her in rehab quick or she's going to die. I think she's selling our food."

"What? What do you mean she's selling y'all's food? You mean she's selling food stamps?"

"No, I mean she's selling food from our refrigerator. The other day we had a whole chicken, couple steaks, and some other things in the deep freezer. The next day I went to cook dinner, and the deep freezer was completely empty. I asked her what happened and she said what food? I swear, if it's not bolted down, my mother is going to sell it for crack."

"Is your aunt still keeping your little sister until you get things situated?" I asked.

"Yeah, that's the only good thing that I was able to do. I can't escape this madness, but I'd be damn if I sit back and let my sister go through this bullshit. As much as it hurt to send her away, I know it's for the best."

I didn't know what say. When I saw Myesha getting teary-eyed, I changed the subject.

"Girl, look at my outfit. Don't I look casket sharp?" I joked.

Myesha burst into laughter. "You sure do. What's up with this church outfit anyway? I thought we were going to hang out and shop today."

"I'm looking for a job," I answered with a straight face, trying my best not to laugh.

With one eyebrow up, Myesha looked at me. "Bitch, the only job you have is driving me to mine, so stop lying and tell me why you have on those khaki pants and a button-down blouse. Did you have to go to court today?" she clowned.

"No, but it sure felt like I was standing before a judge and jury." I told her about my parents nagging me. "I threw on this outfit and told them I was going to come back with a job."

"And they believed you?" Myesha questioned.

"Of course they did. I'm going to hang out for a little bit, maybe chill with Rock, and then head back home this evening and tell them about all the businesses where I submitted my resume."

"I hear that shit. Well, let's hit some malls now," Myesha replied, as she turned up the radio, reclined back, and enjoyed being chauffeured.

We drove around gossiping, sightseeing, and shopping. As we were making our way to the second mall for the day, I thought about my parents and it didn't sit right with me. They were starting to get on my last nerves and something had to give.

"Girl, I think it's definitely time for me to move out and get my own place."

"Move out? Jamaica, you don't have a job. You need to get something steady first or you'll have to ask your parents for money every month. Right now you don't have to ask them for anything, however, if you move out without finding a job, it can get pretty ugly."

"I can handle it."

She shook her head like she didn't believe me. "I remember the day I applied for work at The Den. I was staring at three turn-off notices and an eviction slip. My check from McDonald's was three-hundred-twenty-five dollars and forty-two cents, but I had over twenty-five hundred dollars worth of bills piled up in front of me. I swear I never had a panic attack in my life, but I had one that day. I swallowed my pride, took my ass down to the club and twerked until my back almost broke. Of course, it's not what I wanted, but it's what I was given. I didn't have a choice; however, you do."

Myesha was raining on my parade, but for the first time, I agreed with her. If I planned on moving out, I needed a job. However, a standard nine to five was not my cup of tea.. "I'm going to work something out because I can't stay there any longer."

"Look, just don't make any rash decisions," Myesha warned. "Think this out completely before making a move."

"I hear you. I'll think things over a little more and let you know what's up," I assured her.

We had just left the second mall and were sitting in the parking lot about to pull off when we ran into an old friend.

Nina Simmons, a whack ass chic from around my old neighborhood, pulled up and parked about three spots up from us in an all-white Audi R8. My eyes nearly popped out. I couldn't believe how good she looked and I knew for sure that couldn't be her car because she was always shabby and poor as hell.

Nina stepped out of that car looking like one of those rich white bitches shopping on Rodeo Drive in Beverly Hills. She looked fly as hell, and here I was, sporting some fucking khaki pants. I didn't want her to see me looking like this, especially after the way we used to clown her in high school.

Back in the day, Nina was skinny and homey looking. The boys used to bring soap to school and throw it at her because she had a funky body odor. Her hair was always long and curly, but was never done. She had bumps all over her light-skinned freckled face. She was underdeveloped, unpopular, and unwelcomed in our clique. She always attempted to sit at our table and talk, but no one ever talked back. To see her looking so stunning today was totally shocking.

As Nina walked around her car, her ass bounced behind her like two basketballs. Where did she get those from? This bitch used to be shaped like a number two pencil. Her hair was still long and curly, but full of body and life. And I knew for sure that her breasts came with a price tag because they were the size of Pamela Anderson's and she didn't have them a couple of years ago. Even the freckles on her face looked cute.

Nina hit the alarm on her car, tossed her hair in the wind, and proceeded to strut toward the mall like she was on a fucking catwalk.

"Turn your head away," I ordered. "Don't make eye-contact with that bitch."

Myesha and I both looked in every direction, but Nina's. I wasn't giving this hoe the satisfaction of shitting on me today, however, she spotted us anyway.

I was fiddling with the radio when I heard, "Hey, Jamaica. Hey, Myesha. What you girls been up to?"

The bitch didn't waste no time flashing her "bling-bling" diamond ring in the air, acting like she wasn't doing it on purpose.

I acted totally surprised and happy to see her. "Ohhhhhhh, hey Nina. I almost didn't recognize you," I said, throwing her a little shade in the mix. "How have you been, girl? Looks like life is treating you extra good."

"Well you know, I do what I do," she said as she stepped back and twirled like a damn ballerina.

"It's always a pleasure seeing someone from the school doing good. I guess we all doing big things," I said.

"Yes we are. I ran into a couple of old classmates and they said you were doing your thing, too, so congrats. Do you have any kids?" Nina asked me.

"Nope. How about you?" I asked.

"Hell no, girl. I'm too busy chasing that money to be chasing babies," Nina replied, with a sly chuckle.

I could see she was attempting to take this conversation to another level. She wanted to brag about her accomplishments and I wasn't going to open that door for her, however, Little Miss Sunshine had to go pump her head up by jumping into the mix.

"Chasing money? It looks more like you caught it, girl. That car had to cost you a pretty penny. That shit is fierce," Myesha complimented, sounding like a pressed ass groupie.

If looks could kill, I would have murdered my best friend by accident. I rolled my eyes at her so hard, they nearly rolled off my face.

"Girl, this old thing. This is a little birthday present from this dude I've been seeing. My baby spoils the shit out of me," Nina replied.

Wait? What! Nina had niggas buying her cars? What the fuck was I doing wrong? Now the bitch had my attention.

"That's nice of your boyfriend to buy you such a lavish ride. I'm guessing you two are in love. So, are there wedding bells in the near future?" I asked, plotting to get the drop on this dude who was so graciously giving bitches luxurious gifts. Shit, if Nina could get a car out of him, I knew my fine ass could get an apartment and some more shit. Nina was no friend of mine, so I didn't have a problem with locating her dude and running up on him.

"Girl, he's not my man, he's my baby, there's a big difference. You see, my baby has a wife so he couldn't possibly be my man. I take care of him and he takes care of me; it's a win-win situation for the both of us," Nina explained.

Bingo! Well there it was. Nina was selling pussy!

As Nina started bragging about her "baby," I took a good look at her from head to toe. She had a nice shape and an alright face. She couldn't compare to me though. Still, she had the power to get money from niggas. She was pulling off the plan I came up with years ago.

I was intrigued by her lifestyle. I had to hear more.

"So Nina, how did you meet your baby and how did you get close enough to his heart to make him so generous, without you falling in too deep?" I needed this information because I wanted to drive around, shop all day, and make mad money without breaking a sweat or chipping a nail. I wanted to pull up in my elaborate ride and have bitches jealous of me. My envy had turned into admiration.

"Simple as one, two, three," Nina assured me. "Trust and believe you can make money without even trying, Jamaica. All you have to do is go to every hot spot where the ballers are. Go to all the major parties, high class lounges, cigar bars, cars and bike shows, sorority step shows, golf courses, whatever it is, you just be there in the mix of it all. Make sure you're the hottest thing up in there and don't look obvious; just mix and mingle. Men are like prey wanting to be caught."

"I hear that, girl," I cheered as I gave her a high five. "I've been telling Myesha the same thing for years. These dudes nowadays ain't shit, which is why I use them before they use me."

Nina laughed, and stomped up and down as if she caught the Holy Ghost. "Preach that gospel, Jamaica."

Myesha rolled her eyes at the both of us, but she knew we were speaking the truth. "Well some people have to learn on their own, and I've truly learned my lesson to the point where I could obtain my Ph.D. in heartbreak," Myesha sadly replied.

"Yeah, I heard Marcus up and married some bitch from out of state. You know his brother still talks to my cousin, so I hear a lot about him. He's making money now, legal money at that, and showering her with everything. He just brought her a truck a couple of months ago. When I heard about that, I said that's messed up because Myesha held him down since high school and stayed loyal, and he goes away to college and marry some random bitty." Nina shook her head in disgust and so did I.

Tears filled Myesha's eyes but she did a good job at holding them back. She'd never gotten over the hurt Marcus caused.

Marcus began taking school more seriously when he realized that his basketball career was on the line, and by senior year, he had a lot of colleges pursuing him. He made so many promises to Myesha. He told her that once he got financially straight, he was going to marry her and change her life for the better. Well, that never happened. Marcus got a full basketball scholarship to Ohio State University, and got drafted to the Cleveland Cavaliers during his first year. As he began moving up, his relationship with

Myesha began falling down, until he eventually came out and told her that her and her crack-addict mother didn't fit into his new lifestyle — and he'd found some other chic who did. While he was at Ohio State, Marcus met a white girl studying pre-law, who came from a wealthy family. He proposed to her after three months of dating, and now, they were married and expecting their first child.

Myesha had never opened her heart to another man. She danced at the club, took their money, and kept it moving. She didn't even go out on dates, and when I tried to play matchmaker, it always ended horrible. I think Myesha was probably more broken on the inside than I was.

"He's the one who's losing out, Myesha. Get what you can get out of these niggas and don't get caught up," Nina suggested.

"That's motherfucking right," I cosigned.

We sat outside of the mall and talked for a long time, catching up on the latest gossip and hearing stories about Nina's life experiences. Time flew by and before we knew it, it was late as hell. Myesha had to call the club to let them know she was running late. Before leaving, we exchanged phone numbers and made plans to hang out.

Nina's words remained deep-rooted in my brain long after she left. Fuck niggas, get money, was already my motto, but now I planned on taking it to another level.

Nina was doing her thing, but to me she was going about it all wrong. There had to be a system for me to get these niggas money without compromising my body. I, in no way, was prepared to turn my body into a male playground, with men jumping up and down in my pussy like it was a trampoline.

After dropping Myesha off at work, I decided to grab a bite to eat. I was in the process of ordering my food when my cell phone rang. I looked down and sighed heavily.

"Hel-loooooo," I answered, dragging the word out so that my annoying-ass father knew I was annoyed.

"Hey, I'm just calling to check on you and see how the job hunt is going. I hope you're applying yourself, Jamaica."

"Daddy, I'm out here filling out applications and leaving my resume with everyone. I'm doing exactly what I said I was going to do," I lied.

"I don't care if you have an attitude, just as long as you find a job real soon. What time are you coming home?"

"I'll be home around nine. I have many job agencies to hit and some other businesses to visit, so I'll be home pretty late." It was only 4:00 pm so that little lie brought me a lot of time to waste. My mother usually came home from the salon at 10:00 pm and my father always strolled in after midnight. Plus, my sister was gone for the weekend, so I was about to chill and have the house to myself for the rest of the evening.

"I hope you're taking this seriously because your mother and I surely are. You have opportunities girls your age don't have…" Blah blah blah….

I tuned him out so I couldn't tell you what he said next. As soon as he said the last word, I quickly said good bye and hung up feeling relieved.

I was looking for a job alright, but not what he was expecting. I had to get a piece of Nina's fortune. I failed with my plans with Deshawn, but this time around I was "Triple M," *Much More Mature!* My parents didn't have to worry about me sitting doing nothing. I was about to make some serious changes in my life.

My new motto was, "Get rich or kill somebody trying, because I refuse to be the one dying."

CHAPTER 6

Daddy's Little Nightmare

I made my way back home to get some much needed rest. I was feeling a bit tired, especially after the employment sermon my father had preached. I walked into the living room and sat down to watch TV. Just as I picked up the remote, I heard a loud banging from upstairs.

Startled, I jumped from the couch and looked around. "Boom-Boom!" the noise sounded off again.

Who the hell is home and what the hell are they doing upstairs? It sounded like someone was banging on the wall or hitting something with a hammer.

Then I remembered Mr. Kipper, the nosey neighborhood watch captain, telling my parents about some recent break-ins. With my luck, I could have walked into a home invasion.

I grabbed keys from the coffee table and ran to the front door. As I opened it and made my way to the porch, I heard the banging again.

But once I was on the porch, I realized what was going on. It wasn't the sound of a burglar. It was the sound of someone getting it on.

Stepping back in the house, I heard faint sound of moans and groans, combined with a bedpost hitting the wall. Someone was upstairs having sex, good rough sex.

I slowly closed the front door. My parents were still at work and my sister, Rochelle was supposed to be at her friend's house.

But could it be Rochelle? Was my little sister getting her cherry popped in the house while everyone was away? Wouldn't that be ironic? My parents were coming down on me for partying hard and not setting a good example for my "innocent" little sister.

Determined to catch her little sneaky ass, I tiptoed up the steps.

"Oh right there, yes, yessssss." The sound was echoing from my parents' bedroom.

How nasty was that? She was fucking in our parents' room. "Fuck me……..fuck me hard, baby!"

The closer I moved toward the door, the more I realized the voice wasn't Rochelle's. I took my time and slowly opened the door, making sure it didn't make a sound.

As soon as it opened, I regretted it. Now, I'd seen and experienced some foul shit in my life, but this had to be the worst. I wished I had the guts to gouge my eyeballs out of my fucking head.

I stood in that doorway for thirty seconds, which felt more like thirty hours, and I knew my life would never be the same.

There was my father on his knees, fucking some slut from behind. He had a handful of her hair in his hands, as he pounded her into the bedpost. The two of them were going at it so loud they didn't even notice me.

I couldn't take the sight of my father's bare ass, so I cleared my throat to make my presence known. My father turned around; the stunned expression on his face was priceless.

Before he could say a word, I screamed, "Daddy, what the fuck are you doing? Please tell me that you're not cheating on my mother in her own home; in her own fucking bed!"

My father jumped out of bed, exposing his naked body. I felt disgusted for the both of us.

"Give me a second to get dressed and let me explain, baby. Just give me a second," my father begged.

"Let you explain? What could you possibly explain? I see what's going on. You're cheating on Mommy with this bitch. There's no explanation needed."

As my father attempted to put his boxers on, the slut jumped out of bed and started to retrieve her clothes.

As soon as she turned around, I literally felt my heart drop. Shit just kept getting worse. I walked closer, blinking to see if I was imagining things.

I almost couldn't get the words out. "Aunt... Aunt Pam is... is...is that you?"

She shamefully held her head down.

"Oh my God. Aunt Pam, you're fucking Daddy?"

The bitch burst into tears. I grabbed her fucking face and forced her to look at me.

"No, don't cry now, bitch. You're fucking your sister's husband? Your sister who takes care of you? Your sister who's helped you repeatedly? Your sister who went to war for you when this piece of shit didn't want to help you get your house and restaurant?"

Rather than answering my questions, the bitch played the victim and continued crying. I wasn't falling for this shit. I needed answers, so I decided to help her get the words out.

Swooooop... Swooooop! I slapped the bitch into another time zone. She tried to cover her face, but I slapped the bitch until she broke down and begged like a homeless person. "Please, please, I'm so sorry, Jamaica. I made a mistake."

"A mistake," I repeated. "How the fuck is this a mistake? A few minutes ago, you were begging him to keep fucking you, so tell me how is this a mistake?"

Aunt Pam couldn't answer that question. She stood in front of me, looking stupid as hell, flinching like a child every time I raised my hand.

My father had the nerve to try to stop me from attacking her. This infuriated me even more. I pushed his filthy hands off of me and gave him a look that made him know not to play with me.

"Oh, so this is why you were so eager for me to leave the house this morning, huh? Get up and get dressed right now, Jamaica. Apply yourself, Jamaica. Don't bring your ass back home until you fill out an application for every single job that's hiring, Jamaica." I repeated all the bullshit he'd said to me. "So this is why you called me earlier inquiring about what time I planned on coming home?"

"Jamaica, please listen to me; we didn't plan for this to happen. We're both sorry. It just ..."

"It just what, Daddy?" I screamed, cutting him off before he got a chance to tell me another boldface lie. "What could have possibly just happened except your dick got hard, Aunt Pam's pussy got wet, and the both of you decided to fuck, in my mother's bed?"

I was furious. The more my father talked, the angrier I got. To make matters worse, every time I looked at my aunt, I wanted her blood. At that point I totally lost it.

I grabbed a handful of my aunt's hair, pulled her to the ground, and stomped her ass. My father tried to restrain me, but I was in beast mode. It took him nearly five minutes to wrap his arms around my body so that I couldn't swing on the both of them, and even then, I kept kicking and spitting. I fought them until I didn't have any strength left.

"Jamaica, please don't tell your mother. This will break her heart. Your father and I made a huge mistake and we will have to live with this shame for the rest of our lives. Just don't make Mary suffer for this," Aunt Pam pleaded.

Was she really trying to convince me to keep this from my mother? I needed the bitch to get the hell away from me before I caught a murder charge. "Get the fuck out of my house and don't say another word to me, Pamela."

Knowing that I meant business, she shut her mouth and hurried to get dressed. "Just know that I will deal with you later," I warned.

Aunt Pam walked down the steps and I followed closely behind. She opened the front door and shamefully made her way out, but before fully exiting, she tried to reason with me one last time. "Jamaica, I'm so sorry. This will never happen again, I swear. Please don't tell your mother."

SWAP! I smacked her dead in the face once again, this time harder than before. When I pulled back, I swore I could still see my fingerprints across her cheek. "Didn't I tell you not to say another word to me?" I screamed out in rage.

The bitch couldn't talk. I literally slapped the words out of her mouth. As Aunt Pam held her face in agony, I slammed the door because our conversation was over. At least for now.

I took a deep breath and turned around to deal with my father, who was fully dressed and sitting at the bottom of the steps looking like a helpless child.

"Honey, can we talk?" he asked.

"Oh, now you want to talk. This morning you were acting holier than thou, standing in my room making me feel like shit. All along you were plotting and scheming to have the house to yourself so you could get some pussy from your wife's sister."

"No, Jamaica, you have this all wrong. I was not lying to you. I meant everything I said. I care about your future and want to see you be a better person than I am."

"Well, there you go. You have your wish because I'm already a better person than you are. "

My father let out a loud sigh out of frustration. I knew him well, so the fact that he couldn't control this situation was eating him up. "Honey, can you just allow me to explain what happened tonight?" my father pleaded.

"No, there's nothing to talk about. I've said all I have to say."

He continued as if he didn't hear my words, "Despite the circumstances, I've been a great husband, father, and provider to this family. I've always broken my back to ensure you all were good. So for you to just treat me like shit, without giving me a chance to at least explain myself, is unfair."

"Are you serious?" I asked. "You were just having sex with Aunt Pam; Aunt Pam, Daddy! You could have cheated with anyone in the world, but you chose to fuck your sister-in-law. And now you want to justify that by claiming you've always provided for your family? So I guess if I had your money and power and was able to provide for my family, I could walk around here like a God and do whatever the hell I please."

"No, no, no. You're twisting my words, Jamaica. What I'm saying is despite my flaws, I still take care of this family and bust my ass for you all."

"Let me ask you something. Do I look happy right now? Do you think when Mommy hears about this she's going to be happy?"

"It's like you don't want to hear my side. You already have your mind made up."

We were talking in circles. What my father was basically saying was, yes, I am a cheater, but I'm rich and can provide for my family so I should get a pass. He kept rambling for about twenty minutes, but, I wasn't listening to a single word. I was too busy thinking about how I could let this little situation work to my advantage. If he thought I was going to keep my mouth shut without getting something in return, he guessed wrong.

On the other hand, I didn't want to hurt my mother, and telling her would shatter her heart into a million pieces. Besides, my mother knew that my father cheated on her from left to right, but she never left him. My mother loved my father; however, she loved the life that he provided for her even more. It would take a miracle for me to convince her to leave him, and even then, I would have to have a lot of money to make her feel secure enough to walk away from her comfort zone.

As that last thought ran across my mind, it hit me. I knew a great way to make my father and aunt pay, like literally pay for what they did.

I walked over to our living room bar, poured out a big ass shot of Patron, and took it straight to the head, just as my father did when he had a long stressful day. I threw the shot back and looked at him with a devilish grin. He looked at me in astonishment. I'd never drank so much as a wine cooler in front of my parents, so to see me in this manner was shocking to my father. I laid down my ultimatum.

"Okay, you want me to keep my mouth shut about you and Pam? I can do that, but it's going to cost you. I want fifty-thousand dollars wired into my bank account no later than tomorrow afternoon. If the money is not there when I check my balance at noon tomorrow, all hell is going to break loose and I'm telling Mommy everything."

My father's eyes became filled with tears. I could see his hurt and pain, but I didn't give two fucks. "Fifty thousand dollars? Are you serious, Jamaica? You want me to give you fifty thousand dollars or you're telling your mother about what happened today?"

"That sounds about right," I assured him. "It's not like I didn't give you an option. You can choose not to pay the money. However, I'm pretty sure when Mommy finds out, she and her lawyers are going to chew you up into a million pieces and take way more than that from you."

"Wow. After all I've done for you, this is how you're going to repay me? This is how you're going to treat the man who gave you life?" My father was fishing for sympathy, but I didn't feel anything in my heart for him except hatred.

I didn't answer any of his questions for the remainder of our conversation because I didn't owe him shit. Instead, I wrote down my bank account information and handed it to him. "Here's my account number. You lose it, you blew it," I warned.

Knowing that I couldn't live under the same roof with my father and pretend like this incident never occurred, I decided to make a move. I walked upstairs to my bedroom, packed a few things, and left the house without saying another word to him.

After leaving my parents' house, my next stop was to visit my dear sweet aunt. She wasn't getting off that easy. If my father had to pay, she did too.

I banged on her door like I was the police for about three minutes. I heard her standing behind the door, but she wouldn't speak.

"Bitch, open the door. I know you're there. I can smell your pussy through the door. My father just got finished fucking you and I can still smell him on your whoring ass body." I was screaming loud enough for all her neighbors to hear. She quickly opened the door to avoid further embarrassment.

"Jamaica, I feel bad enough. There's no need to come here to rub it in my face."

"Oh I'm not here to do that; I came here for compensation."

She had the same confused look on her face as my father had. Aunt Pam wasn't filthy rich like my parents, but she was bringing in a rack of money from her business.. I knew for a fact that she had a hefty savings account and I wanted a piece of it.

"Compensation?" she repeated. "I don't have any money here for you, Jamaica."

"Oh yes you do, honey. Tomorrow you're going to get up bright and early, go to your bank, withdraw twenty thousand dollars, and then deposit it into my bank. Here's my account number."

Aunt Pam looked at me as if she didn't understand English. "Wait. What?" she asked. "Come on, Jamaica; please don't do this to me. I don't have that kind of money to just give away."

"And how does that affect me?" I asked.

"Are you seriously going to use this situation to take money from me? You're taking hard earned money that I worked my ass off for." Crying and pleading, Aunt Pam begged me to reconsider, but I wasn't trying to hear the bullshit. She didn't have any compassion for my mother when she was riding my father's dick, so why should I have any for her?

"Look, I give zero fucks about what I'm taking from you. My only regret is that you're not worth more so that I could tax that ass even harder."

Aunt Pam held her head down and cried. My heart was frozen and the sight of her was beginning to make me sick. I had to get the hell out of there before I start beating her ass again.

"You have until noon tomorrow to have that money deposited into my account. You and your boo can ride together because he's making a deposit, too."

I grabbed my purse, walked to the front door, and warned Aunt Pam one last time. "If you deposit that money at twelve-oh-one you'll be a minute too late and I'm going to fuck you harder than my father did." I walked out the door, leaving her standing there looking horrified.

I had one last stop to make, and it was the hardest. As much as I dreaded making this trip, I knew that I had to face my mother. Besides, she would become suspicious if I just up and moved out of the blue with no explanation. After stalling as long as I could, I finally found the courage to go see her around 6:00 pm. I walked into the salon and greeted everyone before heading upstairs to her office. As I approached her door, a sickening feeling came over me. I had to stop to get myself together.

I opened the door and visions of my father and Aunt Pam rolling around naked on my mother's bed replayed in my head. I knew then this wasn't going to be easy.

My mother was sitting behind her desk going over the books. She looked up and her warm smile melted my heart and made me feel like shit at the same time because of the tainted secret I was keeping from her.

"Hi, Mommy." I gave her a big hug. "What are you up to?"

"Hello, honey," she happily replied back. "I'm just going over the numbers for this month and balancing the checkbook. Is everything okay?"

"Yes," I answered. "Why do you ask?"

"Well, because you've never come to the salon to just hang out and it's pretty late."

I smiled, but the more I looked into my mother's beautiful brown eyes, the heavier my heart became. My eyes were weary and exhausted from fighting back tears. I didn't have the strength to pretend any longer, so I just started the conversation that I'd been dreading all evening.

"Okay, Mommy, you're right. I have something to tell you, and I hope you'll be able to understand where I'm coming from. I already know that you're not going to be happy with my decision, but please know I'm doing it to better myself."

A disturbed expression casted across my mother's face. It was like she already knew something bad was about to happen. Being the control freak that she was, she cut me off. "What's going on with you, Jamaica? I know something is wrong so just spit it out," she demanded.

"Ma, I'm not in trouble. I just came here to let you know that I'm moving out," I explained casually, hoping it would go over her head. Of course it didn't.

"You're doing what? When did you make this snap decision?" she questioned, looking confused.

"I've been thinking about doing this for a while. I weighed all my options and this is best for me."

"Is that right?" my mother asked. "So how soon are you planning to move?"

Without making any eye contact, I replied, "Actually I've already packed my things. I'm moving out tonight."

My mother's eyebrows nearly touched her hairline when I uttered those words. She looked at me like I was cuckoo for Cocoa Puffs. I was so nervous that I just kept on talking, hoping I was making sense. "I'm taking your advice and finally taking my life seriously. I need a job and more responsibilities. If I stay home, I will never get the drive to look for a job, but if I'm in the real world, then I will have no other choice."

"I never said you had to move out, Jamaica. All I asked was for you to find a job and stop partying so much. You don't ever have to move out." I heard the pain in my mother's voice. Just this morning I was snuggled under my blanket in my cozy bed, and now hours later, I was in here telling her that I'd packed my things and was moving out tonight. It was all happening so fast and I knew my mother had many questions, but I couldn't answer any of them. God knew I wished I could, but I just couldn't.

"I'm going to be fine. Please don't worry. It's not like I'm moving across the country. I'm still going to be right here in Baltimore."

"Why are you leaving so soon? Just this morning you were quite content with living at home. Are you leaving something out of this conversation? my mother asked. Oh, I was leaving a whole lot out. I was leaving the steak off of the plate and feeding her the sides. Still, I remained calm and tried my best not to break under pressure.

"Everything's fine," I reassured her. "I thought about the conversation we had this morning. It's time for me to get myself together and be the woman you raised me to be."

I tried to deflect our conversation back to the one she had with me this morning. I wanted her to believe this was her idea. Of course my mother knew me better than I knew myself, so she kept questioning my real motives.

I sat in her salon for damn near an hour explaining. After realizing she wasn't going to change my mind, she finally gave up.

"Look, you're a grown woman and as much as I would like to protect you from making stupid mistakes, I can't. It seems you have your mind made up, so it doesn't make any sense for me to waste any more time trying to convince you. Just do me a favor and break the news to your father because he's going to have a fit when he finds out about this."

My stomach cringed from hearing the word father. I wanted to scream that bitch was not my father, and he shouldn't be your husband. I quickly wrapped up the short visit with my mother.

"Okay, I'll call Daddy and tell him what's going on. I'm going to stay in a hotel until my apartment comes through. As soon as it does, I'll let you know where it's located. I'm not big on saying goodbye so please tell Rochelle what's going on for me." I gave my mother the longest hug known to mankind. I didn't want to let go; I wanted to just hug and protect her forever. Unable to fight back the tears any longer, we both cried in each other's arms for literally a half an hour.

When I finally left my mother's salon, I walked out feeling lost and overwhelmed with emotions. Inside my car, it hit me; I was officially on my own. For years I'd plotted and schemed for my freedom and now it was official. I was free from my parents. I was free from Deshawn.. Despite the tragic circumstances that led to this day, I was finally free from everyone's rules and was looking forward to creating my own.

It was late when I checked into the Marriott Hotel Waterfront. I ran a hot bubble bath and soaked my tired body in the steamy water until the temperature dropped about three times. If I said that I had a wink of sleep that night, I would be a liar. I stayed up the entire night crying, devouring a whole bottle of Pinot Grigio, and searching the Internet for apartments and condos. Although my mind was flustered, I was able to find a few places that met my high expectations.

I fell asleep snuggling my laptop on top of my stomach like it was an infant. As soon as I was able to close my weary eyes, the alarm on my cellphone buzzed off. After fighting the urge to hit the snooze button about a million times, I finally jumped into the shower, got dressed, and grabbed a large cup of coffee.

I spent the entire morning filling out apartment applications, praying something would fall into my lap very soon. At the same time, I checked my bank account, waiting for my deposits to hit. Finally, at 12:15pm I logged into my account and *boom*, it was there. My checking account had $3,500 and my savings account sprouted from $30,000, which was my after-college fund, to $100,000, including my father's $50,000 and my aunt's $20,000.

I almost had a mental orgasm. I had turned my lemons into lemonade and came out victorious, as always. This was just the beginning. My life had officially started. I had my freedom, my money, and a billion-dollar mindset that was going to take me places far beyond my imagination. It was officially my time to shine. Bling... Bling... Bling... Bitches!

CHAPTER 7

Las Chicas

Although I felt more accomplished than I've ever felt in my life, I was still homeless. I visited a million and one leasing offices, but it was hard to convince the rental agents that although I didn't have any pay stubs because I had never worked a day in my life and I didn't have rental history because I'd been living with my parents, I did have the means to pay my rent on time each month.

What should have been a day's worth of work, turned into weeks. I was almost ready to give up when I stumbled onto a beautiful spacious two-bedroom townhouse in Owings Mills that had my name written all over it. It was perfect because it was close to Interstate 695, which took me practically anywhere in Baltimore.

I called their rental office to see if they had anything available, and they did. This time when they asked about employment, I gave my mother's salon and told them I was the receptionist. My mother even created pay stubs for me. After turning over all the necessary documents to the rental office, I went back to my hotel. The next morning the lady from the rental office called to let me know that I was approved. She asked me to come in and sign the lease and pick up my keys. I was so excited, I had to scoop up my bestie so that she could see my first place and share this special moment with me.

We pulled into the apartment complex and Myesha's jaw dropped. She nearly lost her mind when the gateman buzzed us in. To me this was nothing, however, to Myesha, this was some real lavish shit going on. She was already gawking at the building, but when she stepped into my apartment and saw how spacious it was, she went crazy.

"Jamaica, where the hell did you get the money to move into this expensive ass place? How much is your rent? I know it's higher than a giraffe's pussy."

I laughed so damn hard I nearly choked. Myesha wasn't even trying to be funny, which made it even more comical.

"Twenty-five-hundred a month," I answered, while still laughing at her giraffe's pussy reference.

"What the fuck? You can't afford this shit. You've really lost your damn mind," Myesha replied.

Her concern for me was heartfelt. I knew she would spend the rest of the evening worrying about me, so I guessed it was time to fill her in on my dysfunctional family.

"I know you may not understand what I'm about to tell you, but there have been a lot of changes in my life. So much has gone down, girl, you wouldn't believe me even if you were there to witness the shit. I need you to have a seat, honey. Let me pour us both a glass of wine because you're going to need a buzz to take this in."

Myesha sat down on the carpet waiting for the scoop.

"Some foul shit went down between me and my father. Do you remember the day we ran into Nina?" I asked.

"Of course. We had a pretty intense conversation."

"Well, let's just say that day got even more intense for me after I dropped you off. When I went home, I sort of walked in on my father and my aunt."

Myesha looked at me like she was waiting for me to finish my statement. When I didn't say anything else, she said, "You walked in on your father and your aunt doing what?"

"Maybe I need to spell it out for you because it seems that it's not registering. I walked in on my father and my aunt fucking. Lucky was having sex with my Aunt Pam in my mother's bed."

"What! Wait a minute. What," Myesha screamed. "Please tell me you're joking."

"I wish I could, girl," I said, with my head held down. The thought of it all made me sick to my stomach.

I sat in my empty apartment with Myesha and told her everything that went down. I told her how I blackmailed them and logged into my account so she could see my balance.

"Oh my God. I can't believe your father and aunt did that to your mother. She loves them both so much," Myesha stated with disgust highlighted on her face.

"This shit isn't over by a long shot. I got something for their asses. Just wait and see," I assured my best friend, who knew me well enough to know that I meant business.

The next two months of my life flew by like a MiG-25 aircraft. Living on my own was a lot different from living home with family, but I made the best of it. Myesha stayed over almost every other night so that helped me. Still, the overall realism that I was finally on my own, felt both liberating and lonesome, depending on the mood I woke up in.

I was bored with nothing to do one night, so I decided to invite Rock over. As I mentioned, Rock and I were on the same page regarding the stipulations of our "situation-ship" so we had a fun, easygoing thing going on. I wanted some good dick and that boy surely knew how to sling it.

I wasted no time with small talk when he answered. I heard his sexy ass voice, and my pussy clinched. That was how sexually connected we were.

"Rock, I need to see you tonight. I'm feeling real hungry, and I need you to feed me." He loved when I talked dirty to him. That shit made him crazy.

"Oh yeah, you want me to slide through," he asked, knowing good and well that I did.

"Yes, come slide through and then slide on in," I added as I laid in my bed rubbing my pussy, thinking about how good he felt when he was up inside of me.

"Bet! I'll see you in a few."

I waited for my boo to arrive and in no time, he was knocking at my door. I opened the door and the smell of his cologne captivated my soul. He leaned over to hug me as I stood on my tippy toes and planted the juiciest, wettest kiss on him. I was wearing a sheer peach bathrobe that revealed my soft smooth bare skin. I let my long hair flow down to my back, which was still damp from my shower. My nipples were perky, my ass was shaking, and I made sure all my assets were visible to the eye. Every time my baby came over, I made sure I was flawless in every way, so he left wanting more.

"Thanks for coming on such short notice, baby. I was really missing you." I held his hand and guided him into the living room. Sitting down, I opened my legs just wide enough for him to get a view of my freshly semi-shaved pussy that sat up like a cuddly kitten. I guessed he loved what he saw because he opened my legs wider to get a better view.

"Damn that pussy looks goooooooood," he complimented, as a huge bough formed in the front of his jeans. That dick print sat on his jeans like his pants had been manufactured like that.

I kneeled in front of him, removed his erect sausage, and thrust it into my mouth. I worked his long pole with my mouth and just when I saw the "climax" expression on his face, I stopped, hopped up on top, and began riding him like a mechanical bull. Front, back, side, side, twirls, spins, and everything. I rode that motherfucker until all my natural juices ran down on his pole.

I was not a selfish chick. I got mine so I had to help my baby get his. "I'm not through with you yet. I have more where that came from," I seductively announced, as I climbed down, went to the edge of the couch, and bent my phat ass over. "Come fuck me until you bust in this pussy!"

"Yeah, that's exactly how I like it," Rock assured me, as he kneeled behind, then pushed my head down to the arm of the sofa, and propped my ass up in the air.

By now my pussy was drenching wet. He put his stiff dick inside me once more and began breaking my back out. I felt pleasurable pain with each thrust, causing me to beg for more and mercy at the same damn time. We were going round for round for roughly thirty minutes when I noticed Rock's strokes slowing down. I knew he was about to cum, so I talked a little dirtier. "Give it to me, baby. Bust inside this tight ass wet pussy," I demanded.

"Uhhhhhhh... Ohhhhhh Shiiiiiiiit.... Fuuuuuuck," is all I heard after that. Rock's warm molten lava exploded from his dick like an erupting volcano, and sent me into overdrive, causing me to scream in ecstasy as I reached my peak for the second time.

"Ohhhh, yeah...don't stop. Keep fucking me. Keep fucking me. Give me that warm nut while you fuck these walls, baby." I pinned Rock down to the bed and damn near rode the skin off his body as I climaxed. I deeply exhaled and collapsed on top of my baby.

I climbed down and fell flat on my stomach. Rock softly kissed my lips and fell out next to me. We snuggled for the next hour or so, watching reruns of Martin until we fell asleep in each other's arms. I was sleeping peacefully when Rock sat up in bed, causing me to wake up.

"What's wrong," I asked. "I was so comfortable, baby." I laid back down and pulled the pillow under my head.

"That's the problem, Jamaica; you're too comfortable," Rock replied, sounding a bit bothered.

I sat back up and looked at him because I had no clue what he was talking about.

"Now don't get me wrong, I don't mind coming over here and spending time with you like this, but at some point, you have to sit down and let a nigga know where he stands in your life. It seems as though you want to play house and I'm really getting tired of this."

Wow! What the hell is going on? Was Rock having a Deshawn moment? After some good sex, men started talking a bunch of bullshit that they wouldn't even remember twenty-four hours later. I wasn't falling for this.

"Rock, wasn't it you who warned on the first day when we hooked up, that you weren't looking for anything serious?" I waited for an answer, but he didn't say a word, so I continued. "When I thought I was pregnant last year, wasn't it you who told me if I was, I better get rid of it because you didn't sign up for this?" Again, I waited for a response, but he was speechless. "You know what I've been through with Deshawn, so why would you spring this on me? That's not fair at all," I argued.

"Look, I'm not sweating the issue right now, but at some point, I'm going to be ready to settle down. If you're not ready when I am, I'm moving on without you."

"We have something special going on. Let's not ruin the night with this serious ass conversation. You just said, at some point you'll be ready to settle down; you didn't say at this very moment." I gently lay my head back in his lap. "When the time presents itself, we'll both know it's the right time."

"I can respect that. When the time comes, we will revisit this conversation," Rock insisted.

After having such a major conversation, it was awkward just lying beside him. I didn't sleep a wink that night. I sat up thinking about important decisions I had to make, and for sure, this little stunt that Rock pulled tonight was one of them.

I didn't allow Rock's awkward ass conversation to affect me or my plans, and just as I shut Deshawn down when he attempted to put a leash around me, I did the same to Rock. The only difference was I took a different approach this time. Rather than cut him off abruptly, I slowly backed away, using reverse psychology and making him think it was his idea.

Months flew by after that weird night, and before I knew it, I was getting used to living on my own. It took some time, but I started to master being an independent woman. I wasn't waking up and working a nine to five job, but I was paying my rent and taking care of business. Life was easy and carefree until I noticed my stash was getting low. I still had plenty left, but I needed to preserve it.

The whistle of my kettle was blowing as I ran into the kitchen to turn it off. Myesha had me on the phone for so long complaining about her mother's drug habit, that I'd almost forgotten I put it on.

"I swear I don't care that she's my mother. This shit is getting out of hand. I'm finding crack residue everywhere around the house, and I don't need my sister accidentally eating that shit. Not to mention, the school has called me twice threatening to call Child Protective Services if she misses any more days. My aunt is helping out as much as she can, but she has her own life, too. Something has to give because I'm getting sick and tired of being sick and tired of this woman."

"You can always come and live with me. I have more than enough room. You and your sister can stay here until you get things situated at home."

"Thanks, Jamaica, but I have to stay here to take care of things. You know my father brought this house and worked on it for years before he died. I just can't walk away and make it go down like that," Myesha explained.

I understood. Her father really did work his ass off to purchase that house for his family and it was probably the only valuable thing she had left of him, since Mrs. Kendra had sold everything for crack.

"Okay, I understand, but remember the door is always open," I assured her. "I don't want you to ever feel stuck because if I'm good, you're good."

Later that night, I laid in bed channel surfing until I stumbled on a good murder mystery on the Lifetime Network. I was just about to dose off when a documentary came on about pimps and hoes that caught my attention. I was drawn to the diversity of women who were selling their bodies every night in exchange for money. They were walking up and down the street, promoting themselves like a sidewalk sale. From car to car, they walked up and asked the infamous question, "Looking for some fun tonight, baby?"

Now, I had watched the movie "Pretty Woman" on many occasions because it was one of my favorite love stories. It was romantic to see how Julia Roberts transformed from a street hooker to a stunning, classy woman with the help of her rich boyfriend. However, this documentary was completely different. There was no happy ending for these ladies. They had neither a promising future nor a handsome prince to save the day. The closest thing they had to Richard Gere were their pimps, who treated them like shit.

What blew my mind even more were the ones who worshiped their pimps as if they were God. These silly hoes actually gave these niggas all of their money and then had to turn around and beg them for shit.

"Daddy, can I get twenty-five dollars to get my nails done?"

I was like, 'bitch you just had one hundred fucking dollars until you gave it to that nigga!' I wished I would put myself in all that danger just to make another man rich. I wondered where were their family members and close friends? How did they end up in this fucked up situation in the first place?

These prostitutes weren't ugly drug addicts, turning tricks for a couple of hits. Many of these women were beautiful and spoke intelligently. However, they lacked guidance and self-love. They all argued they had a pimp in order to feel loved and protected.

I was wondering what kind of love did they have in their lives prior to make them confuse the sentiments of love with exploitation. They were brainwashed into believing this was the better road to take in life; how pathetic and sad!

The pimps flaunted their money, cars, and jewelry, and bragged about the power they had over these women.

"Bitch better have my money every night or it's trouble for her ass," one of them stated.

What got me was the bitch he was referring to was standing right beside him, grinning away and agreeing with his ass.

"My daddy don't fool around with his money. He can make a bitch as well as break a bitch, ain't that right, Daddy?" She looked up at her pimp with love in her eyes the whole time he called her a bunch of bitches and hoes. I shook my head in amazement.

The next thing that caught my attention was the blinged-out pimp cups. Every pimp had their street name or some kind of pimping phrase bedazzled on their cups.

I began fantasizing about my own pimp cup: *Jamaica Da Donstress* it sure sounded good to me. The more I thought about it, the more intrigued I became and after a while, I started wanting it for myself. If only I was a pimp with hoes working for me. I wouldn't have to worry about money for the rest of my life. I would make these bitches work and profit from their stupidity.

Pimping, now that was a career my business teachers neglected to lecture on. They grilled us on how technology was taking over the world. What about the fact that just as technology was taking over the world, so was poverty and crime! If we could make money from evolution and technology, why not bank off disparity? Suddenly a light bulb went off over my head.

If those men could make money off the sex game, why couldn't I? Women had fought long and hard for equal rights. We'd always stressed that we could do anything a man could do. So, if these niggas could be pimps, so could I.

I was onto something big. Now, sleeping was out of the question for me. It was around 1:00 am, and I was wide awake. I paced back and forth around my condo, constructing all sorts of ideas in my mind. I had to share this with my girl, and waiting until morning wasn't an option.

I drove to Myesha's house and waited for her ass to come home. When she finally pulled up in a cab, I greeted her on the porch. As soon as she walked up the steps, I jumped out on her. "Myesha, I'm so glad you're here. We're about to make money… BIG MONEY!" I screamed.

She stumbled back with her right hand over her heart.

"What the …. girl, you nearly scared me to death. I thought one of those fools from the club followed me home. What are you doing here this late?"

"I've finally found a solution to our money problems. It's been there all along, but we were just too blind to see it," I explained.

Myesha rolled her eyes and continued walking up the steps, not looking at me one time. "Jamaica, what scam are you cooking up now? I can't afford to fuck up what I got going on at the club because it's keeping a roof over my family's head. My mother is damn near balancing herself with one foot in the grave and the other in the crack house. I have to feed and provide stability for my family, okay? I don't have time to lose focus."

Lose focus? She was a stripper for heaven's sake. That right there told me that she'd lost focus a long time ago. This conversation could have gone completely wrong, but I stuck to my guns and continued to plead my case.

"Just hear me out for a second," I begged. "All our life we've been thinking of a way to make some serious money. We're beautiful girls with lots of beautiful friends. I got the money and you know the ins and out of the strip club. I say we put our brains together and take over the pimp game."

Myesha paused for a second, and then the next second, I heard laughter, and not just a mere snicker. The bitch fell to the ground laughing in my face.

"Pimp game? Girl, go home and take your ass to bed," she teased as she continued to laugh. "Now this crazy bitch want us to be pimps. You are hilarious."

"I mean it, Myesha. I'm going to put this shit down. Niggas are pimping bitches every day. Why not get in where we fit in and make some money, too? I know at least twenty bitches that's fucking everything moving for free. We can bring them under our wings and at least get them a couple dollars or two. Think about it. We could become Baltimore's first female pimpstresses. I got the cash and you got the experience, so let's do this, baby."

"Wait a minute; what kind of experience do I have? Are you calling me a hoe or something?"

Oh Miss Thing stopped laughing and became defensive when I said that. I wasn't calling her a hoe, however, the profession that she was in was a bit hoe-ish.

"I'm not calling you a hoe, but you work with plenty of them and you know how to get men to put money in your G-Strings. Let's face the facts, you're a stripper. Instead of taking off your clothes, why not make these bitches do it, and at the same time sit back and watch the money pour in," I suggested.

"You make this sound so easy but tell me, where are we going to find women who are willing to do this? Who's stupid enough to have sex with a bunch of men and then turn around and pay us for it? You always come up with these get rich quick schemes that never work out, and I got too much to lose."

"I'm going to put up all the money. All you have to do is talk to some of those girls from the club. I'm pretty sure you can find at least two freaks who would like to make some extra money. That's all you have to do. I will take care of the rest."

Myesha paused for a couple seconds to meditate on what I'd said. She zoned out while rubbing her hand over her forehead. Finally, she exhaled and said, "I don't know about this, Jamaica. This shit is dangerous, not to mention illegal. And how do you even approach someone with that kind of proposition? Do I walk over to a chick in the locker room and say 'hey, would you like to sell your pussy for me'," Myesha asked.

"If that's what it takes, yes, ask the bitch straight up," I responded. "Listen girl, I've thought this out, and if done correctly, we could walk away set for life in less than a year. I'm not saying we're going to make a career out of this. I'm saying is if all goes well, we could invest in something legit like the boutique we've been dreaming of opening. That's what my parents did with their drug money. Think back to when they were selling nickels and dimes to eventually selling weight. Now look at them. Their money is clean and they both have successful businesses."

I could tell Myesha was listening and she was slowly coming to grip with reality. I hadn't always been right, but this time I felt we could make this shit happen if we both played our parts. I had the money and Myesha had the connections.

I sat outside Myesha's house and reasoned with her for what felt like an eternity. I assured her that everything would work out. It was simple as one, two, three, if we played our cards right. I laid down all the reasons why she would benefit from coming onboard. One of the main reasons was helping her mother check into a good rehab as she always wanted. Then, being able to move out of the hood and offering a better life for her little sister.

"You could put money up in a trust fund so that Kiera could go to college. You don't want your sister being subjected to working in a strip club just to be able to hold down the family, do you? I'm not saying that what you're doing is wrong because you're doing what you have to do. But I know you want more for your little sister and if you don't make a way for her now, she'll be forced to take drastic measures just as you had to. Furthermore, your dad worked too hard to give his family a comfortable life. His dreams shouldn't die because he did." I told Myesha everything she needed to hear to join forces with me.

We sat on the front porch going over details of my masterplan until the sun smiled upon the sky and brightened up the world. After explaining and convincing Myesha that she had more to gain than lose, she said,

"Alright Jamaica, let's do this," she stated. "It seems like you thought this out so I'm putting my trust in your hands." Those were the words I'd been waiting for. It was no coincidence that we ran into Nina the other day and learned about her lifestyle, and then me stumbling on that documentary tonight. It was a sign and I wasn't going to ignore it.

"I think we need to holler at Nina and get her involved, too. She could plug us in with niggas or at least tell us where we need to be. Shit, she's already got a blueprint of locations where the ballers hang out so there's no need in us reinventing the wheel."

"That's fine with me. Let's call her now," Myesha suggested, as she whipped out her cell phone. She dialed her up and after about five attempts we finally got her on the line.

"What's up, Nina? This is Jamaica. I know it's pretty early, but Myesha and I were discussing a business venture that could make you a lot of money doing what you already do. I can't get into details over the phone, but if you meet up with us, I could fully explain."

"You said it's about me making money?" Nina questioned.

"Yes, lots and lots of money," I assured her.

"Okay, I'm on my way." I gave her Myesha's address and she was there in no time, knocking at the door.

"Damn you got here quick as hell," Myesha stated as she opened the door. Did you fly to this motherfucker?"

"Nah. I'm a NASCAR driver when I'm behind the wheel. Danica Patrick ain't got shit on me," Nina joked as she whipped her imaginary steering wheel from side to side.

"I know that's right." Myesha directed us to head to her bedroom so we could speak privately.

We tiptoed through the house to prevent waking up Mrs. Kendra. We walked into Myesha's extremely clean room and sat down on her neatly made bed. One thing about that girl, she was a clean freak who always kept things in order.

"So, tell me about this business idea that could increase my revenue. You know I'm about my money so I'm all ears," Nina stated.

I wasted no time explaining my reasons for calling her. I was super excited and knew for a fact, she was going to want to be on board. I mean, why wouldn't she, but if for some odd reason she didn't, I was going to hardball her ass and get whatever information I needed out of her and keep it moving.

"You basically told us that you juice niggas for money and do a damn good job of it. We want to take what you're doing to another level by roping in some other ladies, make them do all the dirty work, while we stack the money. We're going to run an upscale whore house and provide sexual services to an elite crowd of men. You already have a blueprint for the connections we need to get things rolling, so rather than reinventing the wheel, I think it would be wise to join forces. You can help us, and we can help you."

I was all excited and amped up about explaining the ins and outs of my plan to Nina, thinking she was going to get excited as well. But this bitch snickered in my face.

"No offense, Jamaica, but why would I need your help? I've been doing this since I was sixteen years old. I've gotten by fine by myself. Why would I need company?" Again, she snickered. How fucking disrespectful!

Don't get me wrong, the whore had a valid point, but being the business woman that I was, I was prepared for that question.

Of course, I was always ready to be petty, so I snickered back and stated the facts. "I agree you could continue doing this without us, but I assure you, you won't make a lot of money because my girls will be dipping in the pot. Plus, I'll cut out all the extra stuff you have to do to get in where you fit in. You won't have to pay your way into parties anymore, and you'll make way more money than you're making now. You see, we're going to take a business approach with this," I explained. "What is the most you ever made from a night of fucking?"

"What? A night of fucking," Nina repeated, sounding offended. "Jamaica, this is getting too personal and I don't go around telling my business."

"Nina, everyone knows how you get down. You said it yourself the other day, not to mention, niggas talk. I know for a fact you have given it up to niggas and walked away empty handed on more than one occasion. Now with us, your money is guaranteed. All we want is forty percent of everything. For example, I say a standard fuck is five hundred dollars. Out of that five hundred, Myesha and I only want two hundred, leaving you with three hundred. Let's say you get three dudes in that day. That's nine hundred dollars for you in less than twenty-four hours. At the end of the week, you could bring in almost sixty-three hundred. Be honest and tell me if you've ever made that much money in a couple months, much less a week."

Myesha, who was quiet as a damn church mouse the entire time, finally stepped in and added her two cents. "I was hesitant at first too, girl, but when Jamaica laid those figures out for me, it made a whole lot of sense. Like Jay-Z said, men lie, women lie, but numbers don't lie!"

I smiled at Myesha and then looked back at Nina who was thinking about the figures I just laid out. I could almost see dollar signs in her pupils. "Remember this, though," I added. "We're going to do this with or without you, Nina. If you don't jump on the wagon now, you *can't* hop on later," I warned.

After taking some time out to think about the odds that were against her, Nina finally gave in. "Look, I'll try this out for one month. If it's not working for me, then I'm out."

"Girl, in a month if I'm not making money I'm shutting the business down," I assured her.

For the next few hours, Myesha, Nina, and I discussed our new business venture. It felt like we were planning a huge bank robbery and I enjoyed every minute.

"We have to come up with a name for our business," Myesha suggested.

I looked over at Nina and we both busted out laughing. "You want us to name our business. I guess next we should get a website, too," I teased.

Everyone cracked up laughing.

"No seriously, we need a name for the girls who will be working for us," Myesha restated.

"Okay, that sounds about right," I agreed. "But what can we call the girls?" We brainstormed on a bunch of names, which were hilarious: Stardust, Lovely Ladies, Earth's Angels, and my favorite, Tongue Twisters were some of the names our silly asses came up with. Still after much deliberation, we could not come up with a decent name.

I looked over at some of Myesha's textbooks that she had stacked on her bookshelf. At the very top sat an old Spanish dictionary. I retrieved it, popped it open, and flipped through the pages. "I got it. I got it, girls," I yelled with enthusiasm. "We're going to call them, *Las Chicas*."

"Las who? Las Chicas? What the fuck does *Las Chicas* means?" Nina asked.

"*Las Chicas* simply means.... *The Girls.*" The name was simple, yet it had sex appeal.

"Las Chicas... Las Chicas.... Laaaaaaas Chicaaaaaas," Myesha repeated with a bright smile. "I love it. Las Chicas," she said it again.

"Hey, papi, come over here to Las Chicas and leave happy," Nina joked. "I love it, too. It has a nice ring to it."

From thereon Las Chicas was born. We all had our homework cut out for us over the next two weeks. I had monetary duties, such as finding a house to rent, paying all the bills, and once the girls were on board, then paying for their makeovers, including buying their clothes, shoes, manicure/pedicures.

Myesha's job was to go back to work and put in her two weeks notice. She also had to find girls from the club who were down for making extra money and didn't mind getting down and dirty for it.

Nina's job was to do what she did best and that was to mingle and get all the information on upcoming events. She was to keep her ears in the streets and lead us to the gold mine where our ladies would do all the digging.

We left that morning with an understanding that everyone had their job to do. We all agreed not to talk to anyone about our plan. For once I felt like I was on to something great and for me, there was no turning back. I had a dollar and a dream with much determination to succeed. Las Chicas had been born, baby!

CHAPTER 8

Dream Chasers

was out all day handling business and wanted a little company for the night, so I gave Rock a call. Honestly, I was reluctant to call him because of our last conversation, but I called anyway. I just hoped he left all that love and mushy shit with the last bitch he probably fucked this week, and didn't bring it my way again.

"Hey baby, are you busy?" I asked when he picked up.

"Yeah, but what's up?"

"I just wanted to spend some time with you tonight, that's all. Do you think that's possible?"

"Sure, I'll slide through tonight when I finish handling some business over here," he promised.

"Okay great. Be safe and don't forget to watch your back, front, and sides," I advised.

After finishing up my errands, I drove home and walked into the lobby of my condo. Mr. Pittman, our building security officer, called me over.

"You had a visitor earlier today, but he refused to show proper identification, so he was not permitted into the building."

I figured it was probably Rock, but didn't understand why he would refuse to show his ID when he had no problems showing it any other time.

I asked Mr. Pittman to describe the guy to me, however when he did, the description didn't match Rock whatsoever. I took into consideration that Mr. Pittman was an older white man who probably thought all black people looked alike, so his depiction of Rock might have been a bit off.

"I called upstairs, to get approval for him to walk up, but when you weren't home, he asked me to put an envelope in your mailbox and he left in a green fancy car. He sped off so I wasn't able to grab his license plate number, but I could always pull the security footage and get that information for you, my love."

"Okay, thank you. I wonder who that could be?" I questioned as I walked over to my mailbox, retrieved the envelope, and went on the elevator. I turned the envelope over on both sides — there was no return address. The only thing that was written in bold letters was "For Ms. Jamaica Johnson."

I walked into my condo, opened the envelope, and inside, there was nothing but a photograph. When my eyes finally absorbed the photo, I saw black. I collapsed to the motherfucking floor and began to cry.

It was an old picture of me sitting on Deshawn's lap when I was sixteen years old. He was the only one who had a copy of that picture. He kept it on his nightstand. That picture was special to both of us because it was taken during the time when we were both in love but had to hide our relationship because of my age.

I calculated in my head: Deshawn was sentenced to five years. I was eighteen years old when that happened and I was 23 now. That was five years on the dot. Deshawn had been released. *Oh my goodness he's home and I'm dead!*

I grabbed my pocketbook and headed to the door, but I was stopped abruptly by a knock at my door. My nerves shattered. I ran around like a lost child. Inside the kitchen, I grabbed the biggest knife I had and walked over to the door. I stood in silence for a moment. I was too afraid to make a sound. I wouldn't even look through the peephole out of fear the person on the other side would somehow see me.

As the knocking continued, I looked to see who it was and my fears were cast away. I opened the door, let Rock inside, and quickly slammed it shut.

"Wow, you're excited to see me," he stated.

I looked at him and began crying. I didn't have the strength to do anything else.

"Jamaica, what's wrong?"

"I think Deshawn's out of jail and he's after me. He came here today and left this envelope. He's going to kill me."

Rock knew the whole story behind Deshawn. He'd always told me that I didn't have anything to worry about because he would protect me. Rock had an army of niggas on his payroll, who got compensated to do whatever he told them to do. So, if he wanted a nigga dead, all he had to do was make one phone call and their momma would be creating a gofundme account just to pay for his funeral.

"Look, I'm not going to let anybody hurt you, and I'm actually offended that I'm here and you're crying like this. Deshawn is washed the fuck up and his time is over. You think that fool is still running shit out here? Did you forget who I am?"

"No," I answered. "It's just that I didn't expect him to have the balls to come to my house. How did he know where I lived? He must have niggas following me. Hell, he's probably following me. That's what scares me," I cried.

I knew Rock didn't like that, but Deshawn was the only person in this world I feared. I knew the consequences of being on his bad side. The thought of him and the gruesome night when he nearly beat me to death sent chill bumps up and down my arms.

"Stop crying, Jamaica, and stop letting that steroid looking weak ass nigga scare you. Besides, if he's out he's my problem, not yours. I'll deal with Deshawn ."

Rock had a way of making me feel safe and secure. The comfort of knowing that he had my back and was there for me put my mind at ease. Deshawn was far from a punk and I knew that he was pissed with me, however, a lot had changed over the last five years. He wasn't out here running these streets and his weak ass crew let the younger dudes on the block run them off.

Deshawn wasn't running shit no more, Rock was, so I was good. Besides, as Rock said, if Deshawn was home he was his problem because he damn sure was going to want his streets back.

"You know what? You're right, baby," I said, drying my tears. "I wasn't doubting you. I was just shocked that he was so bold to come to my home, that's all." Of course, I still had concerns but I wasn't going to let Rock know. I needed him to feel confident in knowing I had faith in him. I smiled and continued to pump his head up. "Besides, if Deshawn knows what's best, he would get the hell out of dodge. There's a new sheriff in town and he goes by the name of Rock and he just happens to be my baby," I praised.

"Now that's the Jamaica I know." Rock pulled me into his arms and planted a juicy wet kiss on me, reminding me why I'd invited him over.

He wiped the rest of the tears from my eyes as my gloomy frown transformed into a bright smile. "Thank you," I stated.

"For what?"

"For everything. I don't know what I would do without you." I looked into his beautiful bold eyes and returned the kiss. "Let me show you how much I appreciate you."

Before taking Rock into my bedroom and showing him the depths of my appreciation, I ripped Deshawn's picture into a million pieces. Rock was right. I was slipping and acting weak. It was time for me to put my big girl panties on, get on my grind, and show motherfuckers what I was made of. Besides, things were just beginning to look up for me and I had too much to lose to turn back now.

Rock stayed over that night and I slept like a baby in his arms. He left the next morning, but checked in periodically throughout the day to make sure I was alright. He even had two of his flunkies following me around for the majority of the day, until I told him that I needed some space to handle a private family matter. I still had to find a location for Las Chicas and I didn't need Rock's associates snooping around in my business.

I jumped in my car when the coast was clear and drove around looking for a decent house. I needed a single-family home, and was particularly searching for private landlords. My ideal landlord would be someone hard up for cash, looking for the opportunity to have their rent paid upfront for an entire year, and would stay the fuck out of my business just as long as my account was in good standing. But where would I find such a person?

I was on my grind, however, I kept running into minor setbacks. The houses I found in good neighborhoods were all owned by intrusive ass landlords who kept asking personal questions. They wanted me to provide my social security card and recent pay stubs. A couple even asked permission to run a background check. If they were this damn nosey now, I could only imagine how they would be later. On the other hand, the homeowners who were eager and willing to rent without asking questions had houses that were barely standing in the most drug-infested neighborhoods. I wanted to be able to run my business as freely as possible, but I wasn't about to put my or my friends' lives in danger.

This search went on for days, and by day number five, I started to feel physically and mentally drained. Doors were being slammed in my face, however, I never lost hope. I drove around on one particular day for so long that I actually forgot to eat. My stomach started to talk to me and it wasn't a pretty conversation, so I drove to a nearby sub shop to grab something quick.

"You wun cheesy steak sub with fries? It will be ready in fifteen minutes, okay?"

There she went with that fifteen minutes rule. No matter what the hell you ordered from a sub shop in Baltimore, the Chinese lady, who we all called Ma, always told you it would be ready in fifteen minutes.

After waiting only ten minutes, I paid for my food and was heading out the door when someone walked up behind me and tapped my shoulder. I spun around so quickly I nearly dropped my food. "What," I screamed out feeling annoyed.

"I'm sorry, I didn't mean to startle you. I was just admiring your beauty and wanted to get your attention."

I had a straight up attitude because dude was invading my space, not to mention that weak ass pickup line was for the birds. I was ready to let that motherfucker have it, but when I turned around and laid eyes on him I was like, *Damnnnn!* He stood roughly 6'5, had a dark chocolate complexion, with a ripped body that would put Tyson Beckford to shame. His thick dark eyebrows were positioned on his beautiful, not handsome, but beautiful face. The man was wearing a white t-shirt and a pair of straight leg skinny jeans that looked custom-made to fit his body. Dude was fine as fuck, and them tattoos all over his body made him look even yummier. I was very impressed but you know me; Jamaica Johnson showed no emotions. As much as I was feeling him, I had to make him work for it.

"Don't you know it's disrespectful to touch a lady without her consent?" I asked with a smile so that he knew this was a friendly read. "Why don't we start over and try this again. I'm going to turn back around and make my way out the door, and you're going to get my attention by addressing me properly." I turned around and walked toward the front entrance of the store. Just as I opened the door, Mr. Handsome approached me in a more respectable manner.

"Hello, my name is Brandon. I think you're a very beautiful woman and I would love to get to know you. Can I get your name and number so I can call you later? Maybe I can take you out on a date," he suggested.

Now that was much better. Brandon was fine and all, but a dude needed more than his good looks to approach a chick like me. "Sure you can. My name is Jamaica. but you can call me JJ," I responded. "I don't give out my number but why don't you give me yours and when I get through taking care of some business, I'll call you."

"That sounds like a plan. Here's my number." He wrote his phone number down on a napkin. "So what time should I expect your call?"

"Well right now I'm house hunting and it's reaaaaally time-consuming, but as soon as I get home and get settled, I'll give you a call."

It was like a lightbulb turned on over Brandon's head and I sensed that he got happy about something.

"So you're looking for a house? What if I told you I could help you with that?"

"Well, if you could help me that would be perfect. Can you?" I asked, thinking he was blowing smoke out of his ass.

"Would you believe me if I told you I was a realtor with many properties in Maryland and Virginia?"

"Okay…Yeah…Whatever," I replied as I laughed, figuring he was joking. "I wish my luck was that good, though," I added.

"Oh but it is," Brandon replied as he reached into his wallet and handed me a business card.

Ohhhhh ohhhh ohhh, I almost climaxed. His business card read: Brandon Harper, Realtor. God was surely blessing me today because this was too good to be true.

Not only was the man a dime times ten, but he was what the doctor ordered. "Wow, Brandon this must be fate. I need to find a place immediately, and I'm ready to move in like yesterday if you have something available, in good condition, and affordable," I explained.

"I'm all about my business so if you're ready and prepared to move into a house real soon, I can make that happen." Brandon began to ask all sorts of questions so that he would be able to find something compatible with my interests. He asked, "What's your price range? What side of town do you want to live on, and what features and amenities do you require?"

I sat down with him and answered each of his questions so that I could get exactly what I needed for Las Chicas.

After a brief conversation, which felt more like an interview, Brandon finally said the magic words, "I think I have a house you might like. We can actually go there now if you would like to take a look at it. Just drive behind me."

Of course I wanted to see the house, so we left. I admired how professional he was. Although he was flirting with me, as soon as he realized I was looking for a house, he went straight into business mode. Now that was my type of guy.

As we drove, I noticed we were very close to my condo. Brandon turned onto Brooke Valley Road and I was super happy because I literally lived about ten minutes away. If this house met my standards, I would be the happiest girl alive.

It was funny that I'd been living in this area for months, but I never noticed this small secluded subsection, with only five homes on the entire block. The houses were huge and the yards were spacious, looking like you could fit another small house in the backyard.

I parked behind Brandon, then followed him to the front of the house.

"I think you're going to love this one because it has just about everything you're looking for," Brandon stated as he walked up the steps and opened the door. "Check it out for yourself."

"Nice, very nice," I complimented as I walked in. The house had three floors plus an attic and a basement. It had four bedrooms on the third floor, two spacious rooms on the second floor, and the living room, dining room, and kitchen were on the first floor. Each floor had its own bathroom, not to mention the entire house was decked with rosewood hardwood floors, French-style chandeliers, and full mirrors on the walls.

"This is beautiful, so why is it vacant?" I asked, wanting to know why someone hadn't snatched it up already.

"The previous owners, my parents, recently retired and moved to Florida. I didn't want to sell the house, so I've been repairing and replacing little things here and there since they moved out. Now, everything is basically brand new so the rent is a bit high, but you're getting a lot for your buck."

"How high is high?" I probed.

"It's fourteen-hundred a month with no utilities included. You're responsible for gas and electric, water, phone, cable, those sorts of things," he explained. "Are you interested?"

I had to be dreaming. Did this nigga say the rent was only fourteen-hundred? Shit, my condo cost more than that!

"This is perfect and the rent is reasonable, so, where do I sign?" I asked.

"Slow down, sweetheart. I have other houses. We can look at some others so that you have choices."

"Ummm, why do I need to look any further when I see what I want?" I whipped out a stack of dead presidents so that he could see I was about my business. Brandon's eyes lit up like Time Square on New Year's Eve.

"And just so you know that I'm serious, I'm prepared to pay you a whole year of rent right now," I continued.

"You want to pay your rent up for an entire year?" Brandon asked.

"I never joke when discussing money and business, honey," I assured him.

My straightforwardness must have raised a red flag because from that point on, Brandon asked a lot of personal questions, getting all up in my fucking business. "What do you do for a living? Why does a single lady like yourself need such a big house? Will there be a co-applicant living with you? What exactly do you do for a living?" he asked again.

Uggggg. Why did he have to ask so many fucking questions? Why couldn't he just be a good boy and think with the head between his legs as most men did?

Think, Jamaica. Think quick and come up with something before this fool becomes suspicious and back out of this deal.

"My mother and sister are coming to live with me. They live in New York right now, but my mother just got a promotion and her new job is in Washington, DC. She's going to relocate to Baltimore to be closer to me and commute back and forth. I just want to have a comfortable house waiting for them when they arrive. And as far as where my money comes from my father owned a chain of successful Benz Dealerships. When he passed away last year, I received a very comfortable inheritance," I explained, not showing any signs of nervousness.

Technically I wasn't lying. My father was dead to me, and I did recently get a great deal of cash out of his ass, so why not maximize off our estranged relationship?

I could tell Brandon still had doubts. I had to get his mind occupied with something else and I knew exactly what to do. As he continued asking a bunch of questions, I walked closer to him, unbuttoned his shirt, and began passionately kissing his neck.

"Listen, you just don't know how much I need this house right now. I need it almost as much as I need you." I lifted my tank top over my head, revealing my beautiful melons. "I would do any, and I mean anyyyything, to get this house."

"When you say anything, what do you mean?" Brandon asked as he unbuttoned my pants, rubbed his fingers across my soft kitty, and felt the moist juices seeping through my panties.

As I stated, he was a very attractive guy so I was turned on and really not feeling bad about taking one for the team.

"I can accommodate you if you can accommodate me. Show me how bad you want this dick and I'll assume that's how bad you want this house."

Yes, I was about to smut myself out, but hey, he was fine as wine so at least he was worth it. The thought of him renting me this house, combined with his sexy luscious lips made it all worth it. I was enticed by him from the moment we met, so he would have gotten the pussy eventually.

For the first few minutes, we kissed passionately like we were deeply in love. He massaged my back, looked deeply into my eyes, and fucked me mentally. His foreplay was banging to the point that I was begging for it, and just when Brandon had me right where I wanted to be, the unbelievable happened. He pulled down his pants and whipped out what I believed to be about three inches of feather. You know, the type of dick that would tickle you into a coma. I had never seen a dick that small in my life.

Seeing how tiny my little friend was made me sick to my stomach. But, it did give me the upper hand. I could make this water gun squirt by just looking at it and as long as I had them door keys in my possession when it was all over it, I would have done my job. I took control of things. I pulled Brandon's pants and boxers off and without much resistance, I put every inch of his little ding-a-ling into my mouth. He moaned and groaned as I gave him deep powerful strokes with my mouth.

"Damn, you're good. You got the whole thing down your throat. Yeah, swallow this big dick, girl."

What? Was I missing something? This was the easiest head I'd ever given. At one point, I had his dick and both of his balls in my mouth at the same damn time.

After sucking on his peppermint for a minute or two, or three, (hell I lost track because my mind was somewhere else), Brandon ordered me to bend over. I smiled at him as I assumed the position, but as soon as I turned my back, that smile turned upside down. He grabbed my waist and hopped against my body like a fucking bunny rabbit. It was like I hit the speed button on this nigga. He had to be pounding at 100 miles per hour. And I wasn't feeling a thing. If it weren't for him asking me how good it felt, I wouldn't have known he was inside.

I had to tell Myesha about this, but words wouldn't be able to describe how fine and sexy this man was. Likewise, words couldn't describe the length of this man's *itsy, bitsy spider* dick. I needed to get that bad boy on camera, so I whispered, "Lay down so I can ride that sweet tasting cum out of daddy's big dick."

We switched positions, as I retrieved my cell phone. "Damn that juicy dick looks so good. I want to look at it later when I'm touching myself and thinking about him. I know I'm going to crave it later on, so let me take a picture." I looked into his sexy eyes and began rubbing and massaging his tender balls.

It was evident that Brandon was nervous about me capturing our little, and I do mean little, special moment, so to get him off his game, I lifted his balls and sucked and slurped them in and out of my mouth, before I deep throated him, while retrieving my cell phone. The idiot fell for it and allowed me to actually take pictures of not only his dick, but his entire body, including his face. Our kinky photoshoot turned him on even more because the next thing I heard was, "I'm about to bust," and he did just that. He exploded all over the place and the nigga had more nut than he had dick. He let off a puddle on my breast as he screamed in ecstasy, and just like that, the deal was sealed.

"Damn girl, you're the best I ever had," he complimented.

"Thank you. So, where's my set of house keys," I straightforwardly asked as I got dressed. I didn't have time for small talk with this fool, and I was too disappointed to be around him any longer.

"You can have this set right here. I have a spare at home," Brandon replied as he handed over the keys. "By the way, I need you to sign a lease agreement. I'll draft something up and meet you here tomorrow morning so you can read it over and sign it," he said.

"That sounds like a plan. Let's meet tomorrow morning at eight," I suggested.

We met up the next morning and Brandon handed over the lease. I signed it and kept my word by handing over a year's worth of rent. He kept trying to kiss and feel all over me, but I wasn't trying to play them games with him anymore. Knowing how most men worked, I decided to play Brandon's stupid ass out of position.

"You know, Brandon, after last night, I sat down and thought about something. I know you have a girlfriend." As soon as I said that he tried to interject, but I shushed him and continued to speak. "No need to explain, honey. I really don't care as long as you're honest with me. I need to be able to cover for us if she ever becomes suspicious. To be honest, I have a boyfriend, but I don't want to stop messing with you. I had a blast with you last night and I want to be able to get some of that good loving from my landlord from time to time. You don't have to worry about me being an issue," I assured him.

I put on a stellar performance, pretending as if I was sprung. Guess what? He, in fact, had a girlfriend, and my plan worked. My confession made Brandon feel comfortable and bold enough to confess a couple secrets.

"I'm glad we're being honest because I don't like playing games. Well, I do have a girlfriend. I actually have a wife, but we haven't been seeing eye-to-eye lately and to be honest, divorce is probably our next move."

"Thank you for your honesty, baby," I replied, feeling thrilled that this little dick, cheating bastard just gave me leverage. Talking about divorce is *probably* our next move. I bet his wife didn't know that. This nigga probably had the happiest home in America and was still cheating.

"So can I slide through and come spend some time with you tonight?" Brandon asked.

There was no way in hell that was going to happen tonight, tomorrow night, or any other night in this lifetime. My body felt more penetration while masturbating than it did with Brandon. I had to come up with a legitimate reason for staying away, however, it had to be executed in a respectful manner so that he would continue to rent this house to me.

"Listen, baby. I want to hook up with you like we did last night every chance I get, but I have to be extra careful right now. My possessive boyfriend is watching my every move and he claims that he sensed I was with someone last night. He said I had a sexual glow when I came home and vowed to get to the bottom of it. I really want to hook up with you, so how are we going to maneuver around this situation?"

Brandon looked at me like I was bat-shit crazy. He damn near pushed me off of him, as he eased away. "Look, I don't need this kind of drama. I'm a happily married man so if your man is following you, I think it's best to keep this relationship professional. We shared a very special moment, but that's about as far as I'm willing to take this. I'm not trying to get caught up in anything."

Brandon basically looked into my eyes and said, 'bitch, if your crazy stalker boyfriend comes after you, you're on your own.' Then, he had the nerve to say he was a happily married man. Really, bitch? I thought divorce was the next move in your marriage? Still, I remained calm and unbothered because my plan was playing out perfectly.

"I'm sorry we won't be able to kick it anymore. I guess I'll have to savor the special moment we shared and make it last," I replied, as I tried my best to refrain from laughing in this nigga's face.

"Yeah, I'm sorry, too, but I'm not for the drama. When you get your situation together, holler at me."

"Okay, baby," I replied as I continued to hold my laughter inside.

After wrapping up our mini soap opera conversation, Brandon hopped into his car and drove off. I called Myesha to let her know that I secured a house for Las Chicas. She was excited to hear the news because she'd found a couple of ladies from the strip club who were totally down with working for us.

I called Nina, who also had great news. She had inside connects to some exclusive events that were going down this weekend. After briefly speaking with the ladies, we hooked up later that evening and went shopping for furniture. We also hit up a popular adult store called, "The Love Zone" and purchased sex toys and DVDs. Trying to be cautious and two steps ahead of the law, I purchased prepaid cell phones so that we could keep in contact without using our personal phones.

Nina printed up business cards that read: "Las Chicas... Home away from Home!" My prepaid cell was listed on the cards as the primary number, which meant I would be in charge of scheduling all the appointments. Why would I take on this strenuous responsibility? Because I wanted to be in charge of my money and know everything that was going on with it! No ass shaking, no love making, and positively no bed breaking without Jamaica Johnson partaking!

It took some days to get everything situated, but we made it through. With everyone's input we got the house looking stylish and comfy for our male visitors. We had all sorts of sport themes and Playboy pinups on the walls. Our aim was to make the house look like a bachelor's pad, while keeping it classy.

Everything in the Las Chicas house catered to a man's needs, wants, and fantasies. All the bedrooms where equipped with Play Stations and a bunch of popular video games. Even the bathrooms had male-scented shower gels, deodorant, razors, shaving creams, and cologne. I made sure the refrigerator was stacked with beer, sodas, and steaks just in case they wanted a meal. These girls were going to cater to their every need as long as it was paid for. If the clients wanted a steak dinner cooked by a butt naked bitch with stilettos on in the wee hours of the night, somebody was going to get up and cook that shit for him. Whatever their wives, girlfriends, and even their mommas weren't doing at home, Las Chicas was going to deliver on a silver platter.

With the house secured, all we needed was to meet the official Las Chicas girls. I felt like Notorious B.I.G because it was all a dream, but now it was coming true.

CHAPTER 9

Pimpin Aint Easy

Nina and I were getting the house together and giving it some finishing touches when Myesha pulled up in a cab with the infamous ladies from the club. I'd been anticipating their arrival all week. Myesha assured me they were beautiful, but I wanted to be the judge of that. There couldn't be any flaws on these hoes because they all had price tags on their heads.

Nina made her way over to the window to take a peep. Her face was damn near glued to the glass. She was even more pressed to see these ladies than I was because she knew perfectly well they were her direct competitors. If she wanted to continue making money and being successful, she needed to be on our team.

I tried to make her feel comfortable about the situation because honestly, if it wasn't for her sharing her story, I probably wouldn't have come up with the Las Chicas idea. I needed to her to know she had nothing to worry about because my loyalty lay with her at the end of the day.

"You look nervous, girl. Loosen up and just chill out. We're about to make a lot of money," I reassured her. I gently patted Nina on her back to let her know everything was cool, but to my surprise, this bitch swerved on me.

Rather than embracing the kindness I was showing her, Nina gave me the coldest shoulder known to mankind. "Yeah, I hope you're right, Jamaica because I was doing just fine without company, you feel me? I hope helping friends don't come back to bite me in the ass."

It was obvious that she was firing shots at me and insinuating she only joined Las Chicas to help us out. Now that bothered me because here I was going out of my way to make her feel like she played a valuable role, when we really didn't need her. She practically gave us all the information we needed on the first day. I could very well drop this bitch right now and continue on with my plan.

As Nina continued to vent, the sound of multiple stilettos walking up the steps drowned out her irritating voice. I peeped out the window once again; Myesha was standing on the porch with the ladies.

Nina glanced outside and mumbled, "Oh… None of these bitches got shit on me, so I have nothing to worry about."

This was far from the truth because from my view, these ladies were banging. I knew Nina was trying to get a response out of me to see where my head was, but I remained unbothered. I didn't care about her feelings because this was not my battle to fight, not to mention she just tried me. I only cared about making sure this house brought in a lot of cash night after night. Whether these bitches got along or went to war was not my problem. As long as they brought that dough in, we were all good.

Myesha and the ladies walked in; I glanced over at Nina and gave her the "shame on you" look. Her slick comment about the ladies having nothing on her was incorrect. These chicks looked like video vixens. They were not only pretty, but they had body for days. I had to give Myesha her props. She did an excellent job with her selection.

To prevent the ladies from picking up on the tension, I introduced myself. "My name is Jamaica, but you can call me

JJ. I'm Myesha's best friend, sister, enemy from time to time, or whatever you want to call me."

The girls laughed and some of Nina's negative energy began wearing off, at least it did for me. The ladies introduced themselves. They already knew each other so since Nina and I were the strangers, they chatted with us.

There were five girls: Carlena, Rose, Samantha, Lashel, and Kelisa. We talked about fashion, our likes, dislikes, and of course, men. I listened attentively and took mental notes. The girls seemed cool and didn't seem to have hidden agendas, except that they wanted to make some extra money. I did notice some "extraness" coming from one chick, but I was not going to prejudge her yet.

After mingling for about a half hour, I decided to get down to business. We all showed up today for one reason and I didn't know about the others, but my reason wasn't for socializing.

I invited the ladies into the living room to sip mimosas and to start the conversation that needed to be had. I started off by asking, "So, what led you into the strip club?"

I knew the majority of females sliding down a pole had a story behind their G-strings, so if these girls were going to work close to me, I needed to know what I was dealing with. I learned a great deal about them and their struggles from asking that question. Carlena, who was biracial, shared that her white side of family wouldn't accept her because she was half-black, and her black side of the family hated on her because of looks and complained that she acted *too white*.

"Imagine going around your father's side of family and everyone is predominately white, and you have all of their features except, you have curves for days, breasts that looked like implants, an ass the size of the Big Apple in New York City, and full lips. They're listening to Barry Manilow and the only Barry you're familiar with is Barry White. I always felt out-of-place. If that wasn't nerve-wracking enough, when I took my ass down to Lafayette Projects around my mother's parents, all my cousins would jump me and whip my ass. It seemed like I couldn't be in the room with these people for five seconds without hearing the infamous phrase 'Just because you're white, don't make you right.'

"I couldn't take it anymore so I ran away at seventeen and started stripping to make ends meet. The money was good and the people I worked with became the family I never had. That's what led me into the strip club," she explained with sincere pain.

My heart became heavy as she told her story, but guess what, *Pimping ain't easy but somebody has to do it!*

"Well, as bad as they were, at least you were raised around your real parents," Rose interjected. "My mother sold me for crack to another crackhead who only wanted me around so she could claim me on her taxes to buy more crack. I was being bounced from crack house to crack house for sixteen years before the system finally realized I existed. I struggled all my life, until I started dancing and bringing home stacks on stacks of money every night," she explained, as she reached into her purse and flashed a knot of money in the air.

Again, her story moved me deeply, but guess what, *Pimping ain't easy but somebody has to do it!*

"So what's the deal with you?" I asked Samantha, the chick who was acting real extra earlier. Out of all the girls, I wanted to know her story since my "don't trust her" radar went off as soon as she opened her mouth. Everything on this chick was super-sized: titties, thighs, and ass. I suspected she had some work done because I didn't think God would ever put that much junk in any woman's trunk. As soon as she started to explain how she ended up in the strip club, her motives became clear as day; she was simply a fucking freak.

"I have no sad story to share because I was raised in a nurturing home. My mother and father are both lawyers in a successful firm they started together. My brothers and sister are doing big and exciting things. My two oldest brothers work with my parents at the law firm and my younger sister just graduated from medical school. I'm not one of the Cosby's kids and certainly don't wish to be a lawyer or a doctor like my brothers and sister. The only thing I want to do is party, live life to the fullest, and ride some good dick from time to time."

The other ladies laughed, gave her high-fives, and cheered her on, however, my radar continued to go off. The more Samantha spoke, the less I liked her. Although everyone else was buying her bullshit, I knew she wasn't being honest. She had a story to tell, she just wasn't telling it to us. Still, **Pimping ain't easy but somebody has to do it!**

Lashel and Kelisa both shared similar stories. Lashel explained, "My family didn't approve of me being in a relationship with a hustler much less an older man, so they gave me an ultimatum to either break up with him or move out. I loved my man, so I left. I was eighteen and my boyfriend was thirty-five at the time. We moved from Chicago to Baltimore after a drug deal went bad. When we moved to Baltimore, things changed. This nigga didn't just cheat on me with some random chick; he fell in love with her, threw me out, and then moved her into the home we built together. I was too ashamed to go back to Chicago, so I worked here and there to make ends meet until I met a friend who told me about an opening at the club and the rest is history."

"It's always a man behind a woman's downfall ninety-nine point nine percent of the time," Kelisa blurted out in anger. "Whether it's a boyfriend, husband, father, brother, uncle, pastor, whatever he is to the bitch, it's always a sorry ass nigga behind a woman's pain."

"Pastor?" I asked.

"Yup, pastors be on some bullshit, too. Trust me, I know; my father was one and he was a whole mess."

Kelisa was half Puerto Rican and half black. Her body was curvaceous and those pretty cinnamon colored eyes that matched her long sandy wavy hair gave her that extra exotic look men craved. "My man drove me from New York to B-more to start our new life together. The plan was to get settled in our careers, save money, get married, buy a house, and start a family; you know, the American dream type of shit. That was the plan, but as soon as we arrived, that sorry motherfucker took me out on Baltimore Street and told me to play my part in this relationship.

"For two years, I was tricking to keep a roof over our heads, and he had another bitch spending my money the entire time. One night while I was out on the strip, a silver Lexus pulled up with a group of girls inside. The driver called me by my government name, which was strange because only Rico knew my real name here in Baltimore. The streets knew me as Kristy. I walked over to the car with a stupid ass smile thinking she was an old friend from New York who recognized me. When I approached the window, she looked me dead in my eyes and said, "Look hoe, my payments are falling behind because you out here slacking. When you slack, he slacks, which causes me to slack and I'm no fucking slacker. You better get your shit together before I let my baby, Rico cancel your ass.' When I asked Rico about that shit, he told me to stay in my lane and to never ask questions about him and *his bitch*. So I moved out the house and became homeless until my friend Goldie introduced me to Paul, the owner of the strip club where she worked. I auditioned, got the gig, and been dancing ever since."

Kelisa's story sent the house into an uproar. Everyone had something to say. "I would have sliced him and his bitch,"

Samantha stated. "That shit right there is grounds for murder. Playing games with my pride will get a nigga killed. I can deal with a heartbreak. I can't deal with my pride being tested."

Although I wasn't feeling her just yet, I agreed with Samantha one thousand percent. Both of these ladies followed their men to Baltimore. After using them in every way possible, these niggas dumped them like trash. All I could do was think about Myesha's situation and how Marcus used her and married some random bitch after she stood by his side when he had nothing. Every one of these ladies had devastating stories, and we all had our share of issues. I had my own story about Deshawn, so who was I to feel sorry for these ladies when I had my own demons to deal with? But you know where my mind at with all this, ***Pimping ain't easy but somebody has to do it; Why not me?***

After our emotional discussion, I felt compelled to lay down some ground rules. I explained that I did not want anyone playing with my money, and if they did, they would see the other side of me that's not pretty and glamorous. I also warned them not to do anything beyond what was paid for.

"If someone pays for head, I don't want to find out they got some pussy, too. Don't get caught up in the hype and start enjoying yourself to the point you're giving yourself away for free. Also, please don't fall for the oldest trick in the book, which is let me just put the head in. If they only want to put the head in, there's a price for that, too. Nothing in this house is free," I explained. I asked everyone did they understand, and they all nodded so I continued. "Most importantly, every single penny that is made from this house will come to us first. Myesha and I will take our cut and pay you at the end of the night."

A couple of smiles turned upside down. They didn't like that rule, but I wasn't holding a gun to anyone's head. I was letting them know what was up from the jump, so they could make a conscious decision to stay or not. "You can walk out right now if you think I'm being unreasonable and I swear I'll have no ill feelings toward you. I'm being up front now so we won't have any miscommunication later, and I encourage you all to be just as frank and open with us as well," I encouraged. "Again, being here is voluntary. If any of you don't like our rules, you're free to leave." I looked around and no one moved an inch, so I assumed that we were all cool.

Once we discussed the basic rules, I gave the girls a tour of the house and explained how each room would be utilized. The bedrooms on the second and third floors were strictly for private sexual activities. The living room and den areas were our "man caves," where the fellows could unwind or simply have social gatherings, such as a bachelor party or game night. The "boom-boom" room was located in the basement. This was where all the stripping and lap dancing would take place.

Myesha's and my offices were located in the attic. I had video cameras and recording devices installed all over the house and the main switchboard was located in our office so we could monitor everything. The ladies seemed pleased with their walk-through and couldn't wait until our doors officially opened. We continued to hang out until the wee hours of the night. I became extremely tired and couldn't wait to get some sleep, so I ordered pizza and wings for everyone, and then sent their asses home in cabs.

Sensing how exhausted I was, Myesha offered to take a cab home as well, but I needed her to ride with me so that we could talk.

"So how do you feel about all this?" I asked while driving, barely able to keep my eyes opened.

"I'm excited and nervous at the same time. I think we're going to do great. It seems like for once in your life you actually thought out one of your "get rich quick" schemes and it looks doable. On the other hand, we are doing something illegal, so the possibility of getting caught and going to jail keeps crossing my mind. You know, it's not just me. I have my mother and sister to take care of."

"You don't have to worry about that. If anything goes down, I will take the rap for it. I would never let you go to jail, especially when this was all my idea in the first place," I assured my friend. "You know I've always had your back so there's no need to worry about what's going to happen if we get caught.."

Myesha didn't reply. She just looked at me and turned the radio up. I took her silence as understanding. She knew and trusted that I had her back. Besides, there was no need to ponder on the "what ifs". Too much time and money had already been invested; there was no turning back.

I dropped Myesha off and drove home. I pulled into my complex around 2:00 am, feeling completely worn-out. I couldn't wait to take a nice hot shower, slide my naked body between my satin sheets, and go off into dreamland.

As I walked up, I noticed an envelope with my name written on it taped to my door. My heart nearly fell to the floor. I didn't have to open it to know who it was from. It was identical to the envelope that he left before, the only difference was, this time it wasn't left in my mailbox, the sick bastard made his way to my door. How the hell did he get past the doorman? Did he know someone who worked here? Did he pay one of the tenants to tape this shit on my door? My mind was filled with a million and one questions.

I removed the envelope, walked inside, and turned on my shower just as I planned. Before stepping into the tub, I went into the kitchen and poured a glass of wine. I took a deep breath and opened the envelope to see what was on Deshawn's sick mind.

There was a note inside along with another old photo of the two of us. I walked back into the bathroom and began reading the very neatly written letter, when suddenly it hit me; these words were very familiar.

"Deshawn, I know that you may not be able to understand what I'm about to say, but I have to get this off my chest. Lately, I've been unhappy and I've tried to cope with it but I can't any longer. I feel like I'm living a lie and I want to do what's best for the both of us..."

Those were the exact words that I left on Deshawn's voicemail the night that I broke up with him. At the end of the letter, he wrote a short phrase: "Death before dishonor,". Deshawn was going to kill me for betraying him.

As I read my own words, I could see why he reacted the way he had. Leaving such a heartless message on someone's answering machine, while in the midst of planning a wedding was foul as hell. I was young and inexperienced back then, so I didn't know any better; however, as I sat and thought about it now, I saw the role I played in all of this.

I would be a liar if I told you that the note didn't shake me up, but I tried my best not to let it consume me. As expected, I had all sorts of questions running through my mind. Where was Deshawn? Was he following me? Did he really have it in him to kill me or was he just trying to intimidate me? God only knew the answer to those questions, so the best that I could do was pray and leave it up to Him, as my mother would say.

I showered and lay in bed until I finally dozed off around 3:30 am. I was knocked out to the world when I was abruptly awakened by someone strangling the soul from my body. The person was squeezing my neck in the most gruesome manner and within seconds, my airway felt like it was completely closed. The person then stopped choking me. I opened my eyes, after coughing and gasping for air, and there he was, the devil himself.

Deshawn stood over me with a gun in his hand. I tried to scream, but he kept a firm grip over my mouth so my cries went unheard.

"No one's going to save you now, and this time around, I'm not going to leave any evidence and that includes you."

I begged for my life but it was useless, Deshawn came for my soul and he wasn't leaving without taking it from my body.

"I told you I would come back and get you, didn't I?" he asked. "Death before dishonor, bitch." Before I could respond, Deshawn grabbed a pillow from my bed and placed it over my head. Again, I kept screaming but no one could hear me. Was this the end? Was I really going out like this?

The next thing I heard was the trigger of the gun being clicked back, followed by two shots, **_Boom! Boom!_**

Just as Deshawn shot me twice in my head, I jumped out of my sleep and realized it was a terrible nightmare. My entire body was covered in sweat and my heart was beating at 100 mph. Even after I realized it was only a nightmare, I was still horrified. There was no way I could ignore this. I had to take care of this situation. I knew that Rock claimed to have everything under control, but sometimes, it took a woman to get a man's job done!

CHAPTER 10

Scared Money Don't Make Money!

was scrambling around my bedroom, trying to get dressed so I could meet Myesha and the ladies. Las Chicas were making their debut tonight, and despite all the craziness going on with Deshawn stalking me and the recurring nightmares I'd been having of him killing me, I was excited to see how the girls would do on their first big night.

I grabbed my keys from the table and headed out the door when my phone rang. I was going to ignore it at first, but I saw the word "HOME" flashing across my screen, so I answered. It was my little sister, Rochelle.

"What's up, girl? I was just on my way out," I answered.

"Oh, I'm sorry. I can call you back later or you can just call me when you're free," Rochelle said.

"It's fine. I can talk while I walk. What's going on with you?" I asked. Initially, Rochelle was hesitant to open her mouth and when she did, she was talking about stupid shit. It was obvious she was pussyfooting around the real reason for her call. I tried to play along, but I was already running late and needed her to get to the point.

"Come on, Rochelle, spit it out. I know something's wrong and you're making me nervous. I have a real hectic night ahead of me so just spill the beans," I demanded.

"Okay...it's about Mommy and Daddy." Her words were simple, yet, it was enough to grab my full attention. "Last night I overheard them arguing because she found out he's been sleeping with Ms. Sheila for over a year now."

Wooooow! For a minute, I thought she was going to tell me she found out that Daddy slept with Aunt Pam, but she was telling me he was sleeping with another woman who was close to my mother. Ms. Shelia was the nail technician at my mother's salon.

I tell you, my father truly had no boundaries when it came to cheating. He would probably have sex with my grandmother if she allowed him to.

"Rochelle, there's nothing you or I can do about Daddy's cheating ways if Mommy continues to accept it. Until she finally says enough is enough, and actually means it, he will continue to fuck all her friends and co-workers."

"I can't stand living here. I'm tired of hearing her crying and begging him to stop. Look, I'm calling to tell you that I'm applying to all out-of-state colleges so I can get a one-way ticket out of this fucking house before it drives me crazy," Rochelle said.

This was not the news I wanted to hear. I may not have called and checked up on my sister regularly, but I hated for her to move to another state. This situation with my father was starting to affect me in more ways than one. His actions were breaking up our family and it was time for me to step up and show my mother and sister they didn't need him or his money anymore. I could hold this family down by myself if Las Chicas was as successful as I anticipated.

"Listen, I have a plan that will take care of everything, but I'm going to need some time. Mommy loves Daddy, but more than that, Mommy loves money. As soon as I save up enough, I'm moving both of you out of his house. I'm already working on this."

I continued to talk to Rochelle as I drove to the house. She broke down and told me how stressful it was living at the house, and said that things were getting worse. It was evident she was hurting and it made me furious. As her older sister, I felt like I failed her by leaving her behind to deal with the bullshit that I so needed to escape. I had to fix this problem and I had to do it quickly.

I pulled up to the house, sat in my car, and talked to Rochelle until I could calm her down. Just hearing the sadness in her voice weighed heavily on my heart. "I'm so sorry you're going through this, little sis, but just know I haven't abandoned you. I moved out for a reason, and I will tell you why soon."

"Why can't you tell me now?" Rochelle questioned.

"Just trust me, be patient, and please don't make any major decisions right now."

"I'll think about it, but I can't make any promises. It's easy for you to sit in your condo and tell me to stay home. If it was so easy to do, why aren't you here doing it with me?" Rochelle questioned.

She did have a valid point. I was telling her to stay, yet, I did the total opposite.

"Just give me some time," I pleaded. "If you still want to go away to college after I get my situation in order, I promise I will support you one hundred percent and will do everything within my power to make that happen for you."

Rochelle sighed. "I'm going to hold you to that, Jamaica. Please don't make me regret this."

"You won't," I reassured her.

"Well, I have a lot of studying to do for a big exam tomorrow."

"Okay, take care and talk to you soon, big head," I joked. After hanging up, I sat in my car to get my mind straight before heading into the house. I needed this wake-up call to remind me of why *Las Chicas* even existed in the first place. My family needed me now more than ever and I couldn't let them down.

After clearing my head, I went into the house. When I opened that door, it was complete mayhem. Wigs, make-up, clothes, and accessories were being thrown from hand to hand as the ladies went out of their way to outdo each other. Nina was standing in front of the mirror applying eyeliner and I patted her back to let her know that I arrived. We hadn't really socialized since our last catty conversation, however, I needed to put that to rest so we could focus on our goals and get this money.

"I hear there's going to be a lot of men at this party tonight," I stated to break the ice.

"Yup," Nina replied. "A bunch of ballers under one roof. It's going to be live as hell."

"Now that's music to my ears. That means if all goes well, this house should be flooded with niggas tonight," I predicted.

"I don't know about them other chicks, but when I attend these exclusive events, I never leave empty-handed. Tonight is no regular party. It's a bachelor party for this fine ass paid nigga, Michael Perison. He's a big-time kingpin and he has a lot of friends with crazy money. I'm not checking for his friends, though. Tonight, I'm going for the groom himself," Nina announced.

"What? You want the groom? But he's getting married!"

"Yeah, but not to me," Nina replied with no shame. "That's someone else's headache, not mine. I'm not one of the bridesmaids, am I? Nope, so I don't have a problem with fucking a nigga who wants to be fucked."

I looked at that grimy whore and shook my head because even I had to draw the line somewhere. I was no saint and yes I had slept with another chick's man before, but I refused to mess with a married man. I didn't play around with the Lord's union like that. Nope, that shit always came back to haunt you in the worst way.

"Well do you," I replied. "Just don't have his bride outside this house tomorrow morning trying to burn my shit down," I joked.

Nina snickered. "I can't guarantee anything, but I'll try my best to keep his boo away from here."

I glanced at my cell phone and realized we were running late, so I walked into the hallway and yelled, "Come on. It's time to go," loud enough for everyone to hear. When that didn't work, I opened the front door and demanded for everyone to get the fuck out of the house or else they had to find their own ride. That worked perfectly. Before I could get halfway down the front steps, Myesha and the ladies came running out behind me. Half rode in the car with me and the other half rode with Nina.

We pulled off with Nina following closely behind. I had my music blasting to the sky as we cruised down I-695. We were all singing along and getting into party mode when Myesha turned the music down, and asked, "So whose bachelor party are we going to tonight?"

"His name is Michael Perison," Samantha answered. "Nina has her dibs on him, but that bitch better pray I don't get to him first."

I looked at her through my rearview mirror to see if she was serious, and she was dead ass serious. These bitches were stunning, but their mentality was ugly as hell. I had never met a bunch of disloyal, down-for-whatever, spiteful bitches like this set of women in my life. You had one plotting to have sex with a man who was about to get married, and then you had another chick plotting to push her out of the way so she could get at him first. Meanwhile, they were smiling in each other's faces.

"Come on now, Samantha, I don't need any drama between you and Nina. She already has trust issues and feels that you girls might cramp her style. For years she's been working these streets on her own and doing very well, and she was nice enough to let us into her world so that we could all reap some financial benefits. If you go after the man she's going after, that's a recipe for disaster," Myesha explained.

"I don't mean no harm, but when you asked me to join this group, I told you I was coming to make money, not friends. Why should she get the Floyd Mayweather of the crew and leave the rest of the Money Team for us?"

Even I had to laugh at that one, but I kept my mouth closed and my eyes on the road. I had my own drama going on and wasn't going to add another to my plate; especially one that didn't concern me.

"We need to establish some kind of girls code to avoid this type of drama. I already see it's about to be a toxic situation between you and Nina tonight," Myesha warned. She was trying her best to reason with the unreasonable, but at the end of their conversation, nothing changed. Samantha had a goal and she wasn't going to let Nina stop her from achieving it.

When it was obvious Samantha wasn't going to change her mind, Myesha turned the music up and we went back into party mode.

I pulled into the jam-packed parking lot of the Martin's West ballroom about twenty minutes later, and was moved by the design of the building. It was huge and had tons of windows everywhere. The castle-like architecture and grand exterior of this building, combined with the many luxury cars parked outside, assured me we were among the big league tonight. I saw Benzes, BMWs, Porsches, Town Lincolns, stretch limos, and even two Bentleys, plus an entire roll of motorcycles lined up. All the heavy hitters were out tonight.

Nina and I parked beside each other, and together we all walked toward the front entrance. The line was long as hell, filled with the high-end THOTS and hood rats, who were taking off their two sizes too small cheap stilettos and standing barefoot on the ground.

"I'm about to go back home," one girl complained to her friends. "We've been out here for thirty minutes and the line hasn't moved."

"I know. I can't believe Michael has us out here waiting like this. We practically grew up together for goodness sake," her friend chimed in.

Oh, hell no! I was not standing in that long ass line. "Follow me," I demanded to my girls. I walked past the crowd, not caring about who was mad that I cut the line. We walked to the front, where a huge bouncer guarded the door with his life.

"Excuse me, ladies, but you have to wait in line just like everyone else unless you're on the V.I.P list." *Ugggggg*. There was always that one person who took their job too seriously.

Nina, who obviously thought her name rung bells, walked up to Mr. Muscles and said, "Hello my name is Nina; Nina Walters," she proclaimed as she extended her hand to greet him.

He was polite and shook her hand, but he also stared at her like she was crazy. Realizing that Mr. Muscles was about to send our asses to the end of the line, this dummy panicked and uttered the stupidest shit ever. "We were personally invited by Michael Perison himself. He's a good friend of mine and we're V.I.P although our names aren't necessarily on this V.I.P list if you know what I mean. I can tell you right now that Michael is going to be very upset if he finds out that you stopped us at the door."

Not the least bit moved by her words, Mr. Muscles nonchalantly replied, "If your name is not on this list, you're not as VIP as you think, sweetheart. Now, go to the end of this line or go home if it's too long and not moving fast enough for you." He folded his arms and opened his legs like a drill sergeant.

I intervened. "Can I speak with you privately for a moment please?" I asked.

"Sure," he replied. "But I meant what I said to your friend."

"Listen, I know you're doing your job, and a damn good job at that, but here's the thing. I need to get into that party and everything in this world has a price, so what's yours?" I asked.

I could tell Mr. Muscles thought I was bluffing by the way he blankly stared through me. Just as I did Brandon, I whipped out a stack and repeated my question because I didn't have time to waste. "So, what's your price?" Now, I had his full attention and he didn't waste any time getting down to business.

"I can let you all in for twenty-five dollars per head."

I quickly did the calculation, which added up to $200.00. I didn't want to spend that kind of money on these bitches. Not to mention, this was a free event! On the other hand, the men in that party would hopefully become valued customers, so this event could be written off as marketing and promotional expenses.

I counted out $200.00 and handed it over to Mr. Muscles with a smile. Although it killed me, I couldn't knock his hustle because I would have done the same. Shit, I would have doubled my price.

After conducting business, I went into my purse and handed him one of our cards. I liked the way he conducted business and something told me he could be good for Las Chicas. In our line of business, we were going to need some protection.

"Give me a call in the morning," I requested. "I may have a job for you I'm pretty sure you're going to love, and it pays extremely well."

"Sure thing, pretty lady. My name is Shanks. I'll most definitely give you a call," he assured me as he opened the door and let us in.

DJ Mark Bings from Jam Down Entertainment was on the wheels spinning and DJ Pork Chop, who was a radio personality from a very popular Baltimore radio station, was hosting the event. Everyone was on the dance floor, already turned up. The fun, vibrant atmosphere that filled the room would have made even the squarest person jump to their feet and have a good ole time.

Each table was decorated with indigo colored champagne glasses, blue and white rose petals, and personalized napkins that read, "Congratulations Michael Perison."

I'd never been to a bachelor party, but I could almost guess that this one was like no other. I'd always heard bachelor parties were strictly for men; however, this was co-ed and everyone was acting single as a dollar bill.

I was trying to strategize how my girls could fit in, while standing out at the same time. I decided it would be best for them to split up and work each area of the room in pairs.

"Okay ladies, you know what to do. We don't have time to waste so get in, handle your business, and let's roll the fuck out and make some money tonight. Myesha and I will be at the bar. Don't fuck this up because it's easy money," I encouraged.

Before going their separate ways, Samantha snickered. "I can't speak for everyone else, but I came here to leave with someone very special and I intend on doing just that." Her grimy ass winked at us to remind us of her plans to snatch up Michael Perison before Nina could get her paws on him. I was tripping because Nina was cheering her on, not knowing the joke was on her.

"You too, girl?" she asked. "That makes two of us because I plan on hooking up with someone special myself. Jamaica knows who I'm talking about." Nina smiled and I gave a half smile back, feeling phony as hell.

After the ladies parted ways, Myesha and I headed to the bar and ordered two glasses of wine. The party was lit as shit, so we were being entertained from the sideline.

My bestie and I were sitting back, sipping on our drinks, and enjoying the music, when Myesha said, "Come on, Jamaica. If we're going to be here, we might as well have some fun." She took the final sip of her wine and stood up. "I see a lot of cuties out there. Let's go rub up against two of them and get a quick fix before we head home," she joked.

I busted out laughing. "Girl, I'm not pants rubbing with none of these niggas. Either I'm getting the real thing or I'm going home to my best boyfriend that's waiting for me in my drawer."

Myesha rolled her eyes and walked to the dance floor. "Well, speak for yourself. I'm feeling my drink and hopefully I can feel a little something else tonight. All I need is some hard friction to get my juices flowing."

"Go and get your life, bitch," I encouraged. "I'll be right over here until you get back."

Myesha hit the dance floor and partied like she was the guest of honor. Just as she planned, Myesha found some random dude to boo-love and they locked down for three songs straight.

I continued to sip my drink and laugh at my poor sex-deprived friend, who was so desperately trying to dance an orgasm into her life, when my attention was stolen by a male voice who whispered, "Your next drink is on me, sweetie."

I had already turned away two or three guys since I'd been sitting here enjoying my own company, so I was prepared to send this bold motherfucker away, too. Just as I parted my lips to say, "No thank you," I turned around and I was face-to-face with this fine ass brother dressed in a designer suit. I knew it cost a good amount of money because it was like the ones my father wore and his shit was always top-of-the-line.

"Thank you. I'm drinking Pinot Grigio," I revealed as I faced him.

He motioned for the bartender. "Please send over a bottle of Pinot Grigio for this beautiful lady right here."

"A bottle or a glass?" the bartender asked for clarification.

"The bottle," he answered as he whipped out his credit card and handed it to him.

"Thank you very much," I stated, while trying not to blush too hard.

The next thing that happened shocked the hell out of me. After paying for my bottle of wine, he said, "No problem, sweetheart, just enjoy your night," and proceeded to walk away.

That sparked my interest real quick; I couldn't let him walk away like that. "So are you a friend of the bride or groom?" I asked in a desperate attempt to keep him in my presence.

"Well, I'm very, very close with the groom. Why do you ask?" he questioned as he took a sip of his drink.

"I'm just making conversation, that's all. Anyway, my name is Jamaica and you are…"

"Jamaica's a very tropical name. I can see why your mother named you that, though. You look like sunshine," he complimented.

"Thank you," I replied with another warm smile, to show off my dimples. "You know you still haven't told me your name, though."

"Oh, I'm sorry. My name is Michael."

"Well, hello Michael," I replied. "Are you enjoying yourself?"

"You know what? I really am. This party turned out just as I expected." After he made that last comment, an instant light bulb went off in my head. The light was so bright that it damn near blinded me.

"Wait a minute. You wouldn't be Michael as in Michael Perison, would you?"

He grinned. "I think I am, at least that's the name on my birth certificate."

Oh my God. I was sitting in the man's party and not knowing who the hell he was. I was mortified to the third degree, so I quickly commenced to doing damage control. "I'm so sorry. I was invited by a friend of yours who said it would be okay for me to come. Please forgive me for not knowing you personally."

"There's no need to apologize, sweetheart. This is more of a party for me than an actual bachelor party. If it makes you feel any better, I don't know half of the people here."

Michael was trying his best to make light of the situation, however, I still felt like a groupie. I wholeheartedly apologized to him about a million times, and he kept assuring me he wasn't the least bit offended.

"Listen, you're good, sweetheart. I swear everything is Gucci but I tell you what? You can make up for this by having dinner with me in two weeks when I get back from my honeymoon."

What? Did this fool just fuck up our conversation by asking me out on a date? And did he just say, 'when I get back from my honeymoon?' Is this the bullshit that women are subjected to these days?

I was stunned, but not to the point where I couldn't turn the situation around in my favor. Michael Perison turned out to be an asshole, but from the looks of this party, he was a very popular and rich asshole with a bunch of very popular and rich asshole friends. We came here tonight to leave with our first set of customers and that was what we were going to do.

"Oh, I don't deal with married men, but I have a few friends who do. A couple of them are here with me tonight and they would really like to meet you." I handed him a Las Chicas business card and added, "I sure hope to see you later tonight after you get finished partying. Be sure not to get too wasted so you can make your way to the after party at my spot."

In the midst of making plans to link up later, one of Michael's friends came over. "Yo, come get your brother, man. He trying to drive home and the motherfucker can barely keep his eyes open. You know he only listens to you, so come take his car keys away and call a cab for his ass."

"Man, where he at," Michael asked, sounding annoyed that our conversation was interrupted.

"Outside in the parking lot by his car, laid out on the ground like he's home in bed," his friend answered.

Michael sighed loudly and shook his head.

"Excuse me, sweetheart. I'm going to handle this situation, but I'll get back to you sometime tonight. Can I get your phone number just in case I can't find you?"

"No problem. I look forward to that," I replied. "My number is on the card I just gave you."

"Okay. Well, I'll talk to you soon." Michael smiled and walked off with his friend.

I peeped him reading our business card when he suddenly turned around and asked, "Las Chicas? What the hell is that?"

"Let's just say you need a little Las Chicas in your life tonight. Just call the number and see what it's all about," I assured him.

Michael put the business card in his wallet and walked away, still not fully aware of what the night had in store for him and his friends.

Myesha was still pants rubbing with the same dude and the rest of the Las Chicas girls were working. I continued to sit pretty much by myself, enjoying my bottle of wine when I heard an uproar coming from the other side of the room. People were running over to see the action. Being inquisitive, I made my way across the room to see what was going on, too.

"Rip her clothes off," a happy bystander yelled.

"Swallow her tongue, baby," another guy screamed as he began to roar like a lion, followed by the rest of his homeboys joining in and making the same animal sounds.

I guessed that was some kind of fraternity chant for their squad. Soon the entire room was filled with a bunch of hooting and hollering.

I fought my way through the rowdy crowd and when I finally got to the center of all the commotion, I fully understood what all the hype was about. I looked down to see Samantha and Kelisa going at it, damn near swallowing each other whole right there in front of everyone. They were kissing and touching each other in places that should only be touched in the privacy of the bedrooms.

Samantha was grinding on top of Kelisa, as she laid down with both of her legs wide open on the couch. Although their clothes were still on, it was wild and sexy. Their dramatization was so intense and seductive they didn't need to remove any of their clothes for people to feel the lust that filled their bodies.

"Let me see you eat that pussy."

"Can I join in, please?"

"This shit is turning me on so bad."

"This is the best bachelor party ever."

Both men and women were screaming out. From that moment, I knew we had this party on lock. Las Chicas came, Las Chicas saw, and Las Chicas conquered!

During the uproar, Nina began handing out Las Chicas business cards, and announced, "This is the censored preview. To see the full uncensored version of this girl on girl action, you need to call Las Chicas."

Perfect! That was great advertising and now the best thing to do was make our grand exit. I pointed toward the front door to let the girls know it was time to leave.

We left the party with everyone yearning for more. Before I reached the beltway, the Las Chicas phone was blowing up.

Before picking up, I asked the girls were they ready to get down to business tonight, and they all eagerly said yes. So, I answered the phone to take our first sale with my sexiest voice, "Las Chicas."

"Yes, hello, I'm looking for the girls who were just at Michael's party," the male caller announced.

"Yes, baby, you've reach one of them. What can I do for you?" I asked.

"Well my friends and I are trying to chill with you and your friends. Can you make that happen or what?" he asked.

"That could be arranged. How about you and your friends come over to our place for a little private after party. Of course, there is a fee."

"What's the price?" he inquired.

"Five hundred for each girl," I replied.

"Okay, what's the address?" he asked. The price didn't move the nigga one bit. It was as if I said $5.00.

I gave him our address and gave Myesha the thumbs up to let her know that we had a sale. When we pulled up to the house, Samantha ran over to Nina's car to let them know what was going on.

"This money is coming right on time," Samantha stated while twerking her oversized ass. "I have my eyes on this vintage Chanel bag, and now I can grab it this weekend and add it to my collection."

I listened to her and the rest of the ladies get all excited about their first sales and discussing what they planned on purchasing with their share of the money. All I could do was shake my head and thank God that we were not the same. While these fools were already planning to spend their money, I was planning on ways to make mine stack up.

The first thing I did when we arrived at the house was walk around to be sure everything was in order. I cleaned up the mess the girls made earlier. Next, I made all the girls take showers and get refreshed for their dates. I walked around the house to check the videos and recording devices to make sure they were working properly. I was in the attic, checking on our recording system when Myesha walked in and shut the door behind her.

"Oh my God, Jamaica. Is this really about to go down? You don't even seem the least bit worried, but here I am about to shit in my drawers," Myesha stated as she held her hand out to show me she was shaking.

"Why should I be nervous? If anything goes down, them hoes taking the fall," I joked, but really wasn't joking. "We're about to make some money by doing absolutely nothing. This is the beginning of our legacy, girl. I always tell you to trust me and that's exactly what I need you to do right now. Sit back, relax, and let's go make this money, honey!"

CHAPTER 11

Finance before Romance

I was trying to keep Myesha calm and collected, when two BMWs pulled into the driveway.

"They're here," I yelled as I stopped our conversation and jumped to my feet. I ran over to the intercom and made an announcement to the ladies. "Hey, the guys just arrived. We'll be in the office watching each room on the monitors, so if anything gets out of hand or looks suspicious, we got your backs. Collect payment upfront, get them in and out as quickly as possible to make your buck worth your while," I suggested.

I sat back and viewed the monitors, as Nina walked to the front door wearing nothing but a red thong with feathers in the front, and six-inch glass stilettos. She opened the door and five guys walked in including, Michael Pierson. I shook my head because I felt disgusted that he actually showed up.

Nina exchanged words with the guys and Michael handed her a stack of cash. She led them to the chill area where the other girls joined them. Nina and Samantha went into the kitchen and came back out with glasses of champagne.

"These are some good looking, successful men. Why would they have to buy pussy?" Myesha asked, completely confused. "Do you think they have girlfriends at home?"

"We know Michael's getting married in the morning, so he definitely has a fiancée and the rest of his friends are probably married. Where are you going with these stupid ass questions?"

Agitated by my response, Myesha rolled her eyes. "Oh, so my question is stupid? Just forget it, Jamaica."

"Yes please, let's forget it because I kicked out all the money to cover this business that's going to make you money. Let me at least recoup some back before you start acting all righteous on me," I snapped because this was not the right time for her to start having a conscience, worrying about these niggas' girlfriends. I knew that if I allowed it, she would eventually suggest that we find another way to make money.

"It's always about you and your money, isn't it?" Myesha clapped back. "Yes, you put the money up, but I found the girls, and I've been by your side every step of the way. Also, let's not forget that I didn't want to get into this business in the first place, but you convinced me to."

You know those sly comments got under my skin and set me off. I let out a few four letter words and maybe called her a bitch or two and she did the same.

Myesha and I were in one of our normal heated arguments when she looked over at the monitors. "Jamaica, shut up and look at the screen. Oh my goodness," she shrieked. We had been in such a deep debate that we didn't notice all the girls had teamed up with their dudes, headed back to their rooms, and were already getting it in.

Myesha and I put our debate on the back burner and began pointing and laughing like teenagers. My eyes kept moving from screen to screen. I couldn't stay focused to save my life. I was intrigued by everything I was seeing. The sweet juices in my body flushed to my clitoris. Watching multiple people having sex at one time drove me insane.

Rose was in room one giving this brother a dangerous blowjob. Both of her jaws nearly touched each other. As she gave him tender, slow, deep strokes, his toes curled up like curly fries. I busted out laughing. I couldn't make out everything he was saying, but I did know, "Ohhhhh Shiiiiiiiiit" was being repeated over and over.

Nina and Samantha occupied room number two and the steam that came from that bedroom fogged up the screen. I guessed Michael couldn't decide which one of them he wanted, so he fucked them both. Nina was on top of Michael thrusting and plunging on his erected penis as Samantha sat on top of his face. Every time Nina popped down against his manhood, he smacked her jiggly ass and pulled Samantha deeper into his mouth. The way this man was carrying on, no one would have guessed he was walking down the aisle to greet his bride in a few hours.

Myesha shook her head. "I wish I could send a picture to his soon-to-be wife. Like seriously, they're not only fucking these random ass broods, they're really doing the most with them. Check out this nigga right here." She zoomed into room number three.

This dude was straight licking Lashel's ass the entire time. It was like he had some type of shit fetish or something. She was on all fours, doggy style and he was too. Sitting up like his name should be Rover, with his entire face between Lashel's ass cheeks. You would have thought for the amount of money he paid, he would want to hit that. Nope! All he wanted to do was taste her ass. Meanwhile, his girlfriend was probably home alone with a vibrator under the blanket.

Carlena and Kelisa had their own fun going with their guys. They didn't go into separate rooms. They just had one big orgy. Carlena was fucking one dude on the top section of the bed, while Kelisa fucked the other at the bottom of the bed. At one point, Kelisa and Carlena embraced each other and began passionately kissing while the dudes hit them from behind. It was every man's fantasy. Hell, it was probably every women's fantasy, because I was surely getting aroused and I didn't have a lesbian bone in my body.

From room to room, all the girls were getting it on and working hard for the money. If these chicks kept up the performances they were putting on tonight, Las Chicas would be very successful in no time. Dick riding, clit sucking, ass licking, balls slurping, skin smacking, and climaxing, it was a night I would never forget.

Around 3:45 am, the worn out men staggered downstairs and out the door. I trained my bitches well. I told them this was no honeymoon suite. After the men *explored*, push them straight out the *door*, unless they paid for *more*!

As soon as the cars backed out of the driveway, I got on the intercom. "The coast is clear, ladies. Whoever wants their money tonight please meet me in the living room."

Within seconds, all the ladies were gathered downstairs, some didn't even bother to throw on clothes. They just ran down the steps buck naked.

Of course, the first thing I did was collect the money from Nina and counted it. Let's not get it twisted, these bitches weren't my friends, so business always came first.

After making sure everything was there, I asked, "So how did everything go? Were you guys nervous? Did it freak you out knowing that Myesha and I were watching the entire time?" I teased the ladies, trying to make sure everyone was relaxed.

"Didn't bother me one bit," Samantha answered. "I kind of enjoyed the fact that you two were watching. Hopefully you learned a thing or two."

I looked over at that bitch. *Yeah, I learned something alright, but not what you think I learned. I learned that it is important to handle my business and keep my paper right so I'll never have to live like you whores.* I faked a smile, ignored her dumb ass, and continued to speak to the other ladies.

We talked about the highlights of the night, starting from the party, down to the second the men left.

"I enjoyed myself," Kelisa explained. "Not only was the dick good, but I kept thinking about that five hundred dollars he kicked out. So, I basically got paid to have fun."

"Yeah, Michael had some bomb dick, too," Nina added. "As soon as he gets back from his honeymoon in Aruba, I have to look him up."

"How the hell do you know where the man is honeymooning?" I asked.

"Because Samantha and I asked him questions about his wedding, honeymoon, and his lucky bride-to-be while we were riding all over him, and it turned him on. He answered every question and right after answering them, he fucked the shit out of us and got extra aggressive. It was hot!"

Wow, what a loser. It was shit like this that made me say, "Fuck niggas, get money," in my Lil Kim's voice. Although the ladies were sharing stories and having their bonding moment, I knew they were sitting in my face for one reason—they wanted their cash.

I counted out the money, and started to disburse it. "Now this is only three hundred dollars, but you must remember you only had one client tonight. Just imagine if you had two or three in one day."

"Try four or five in one day," Samantha stated. "I'm all about making money and I don't mind putting in overtime. If a sale came in right now I would take it. Shit if my legs can open and I got some lubrication next to the bed, I'm good."

Although Samantha got on my last nerve, I appreciated her enthusiasm. I needed all of these bitches to have that kind of mindset. We stayed up and talked for another hour or so, and around 6:00 am, everyone was pretty beat. Nina had another event lined up for the ladies later in the day, so we said goodbye.

I drove my ass straight home, took a shower, and collapsed into my bed. I was knocked out to the world, snoring and drooling, when the Las Chicas' cell phone rang. Initially I ignored the call, but the person on the other line was very persistent.

"Hel-lo," I answered breaking one word into two.

Obviously, my obnoxious tone gave the caller a scare because he stuttered, "Ummm yeah ummm."

I cut him off, "Helllll-loooo," with more attitude, because it was too early in the morning for niggas to be playing over the phone.

"Umm yes, may I speak to the young lady who was at Michael's bachelor party last night with some friends?"

"Yes you're speaking to..." Oh shit, I almost gave out my government. I had to think of an alias. "Yes, you're speaking to Heather." That was the first name that came to mind.

"Hello, Heather? My name is Shanks. I met you last night at the party. You told me you might have some work for me."

Oh yes, Mr. Muscles.

"Hi," I responded in a more pleasant tone. "Please excuse my attitude. Someone's been playing on my phone," I lied. "I do have an excellent job for you. I know most bouncers work on the weekends until about two in the morning. I would like you to work for me during the week and after two on the weekends, if possible."

"That sounds cool. Exactly what do you need me to do?"

"The same thing you did last night. We need protection because our line of work is pretty risky, if you know what I mean." From the exit we made last night, I was pretty sure he knew exactly what I meant.

Shanks paused for brief second. "Oh, I understand, sweetheart."

"Good," I replied. I kept our conversation brief. I wasn't about to incriminate myself, but I said just enough for him to understand what I needed.

"So how much does a job like this pay?" Shanks inquired.

"We're pretty new to the business so we don't have a lot of money yet, but, I'll make sure you're compensated every night. I'll get into more details when I see you in person."

"No problem. When do you want me to start?"

"Are you available tonight?" I asked.

"I sure am. Just text me the time and location and I'll be there," he promised.

"Okay, I want you to meet me at my house. I'll text the address and location when we hang up. See you tonight," I said as we disconnected our call.

I texted Shanks the address and hadn't lay my head back down for two whole minutes before my phone rang again. I looked at the screen and saw Rock's name flashing. I'd been avoiding him all day because I didn't want him to send his flunkies to follow me around like he did the other day. I knew he meant well, and God knows I needed the protection from Deshawn, but there's no way I could pull off this business with Rock and his boys following my every move.

After sending him to voicemail four times, he finally got the memo. The next thing I received from him was a text that said, "Fuck you, Jamaica."

I smiled at the message and went right back to sleep to get ready for the event Nina had lined up.

This time we were going to an album release party. Some rich dudes had started a record label here in Baltimore. Of course, they were into other things, but the music was their front business. Las Chicas was making a grand appearance, so I didn't have time to entertain Rock's emotional text message.

I slept until about 8:00 pm. The only time I got up was to use the bathroom and grab a bite to eat. I woke up feeling restored and rejuvenated and couldn't wait to mingle with all the local "hood-rich" celebrities.

The rapper who was being featured went by the name of Black Scar. He was a very popular artist in Baltimore. All his singles were playing on the popular radio stations in the DMV and he even had two singles that were in heavy rotation in New York and Atlanta. From what I'd heard, he was next to blow.

Black Scar was signed to Blasfome Entertainment and they had lots of pull in the music game. You couldn't go anywhere in B-More without seeing, "Blasfome Ent." plastered everywhere. Their street team was on point and after tonight, I hoped to make Las Chicas part of their team.

I took a shower, got dressed, and headed over to the house to meet the rest of the ladies. I called Myesha to tell her that I was on my way to pick her up, but to my surprise, she was already at the house. Apparently, Nina had picked her up earlier and they'd spent the entire day together shopping and hanging out.

This didn't sit right with me because I didn't see any missed calls on my phone from neither one of them. The way my mind worked, I was looking at them both with the side-eye. When had they found time to become shopping buddies?

I could check Ms. Myesha, however, I just made a mental note and kept it moving. Maybe I was overreacting because Myesha was like my sister, so there was no need in second-guessing her loyalty.

I cruised down the road when I noticed my gas tank was damn near on empty. The orange light was beaming, so I pulled into the Exxon gas station. I paid for my gas and began pumping it when a gentleman walked up to me.

"What's a pretty lady like you doing pumping her own gas? Let me handle that," he offered as he extended his hand to take the gas pump from me. I wasted no time handing it over to him. I hated pumping gas away, which is why I was on "E" in the first place.

"Thank you," I replied and sat back in my car. I was chilling, looking for a CD to put in, when I heard an all too familiar voice.

"Look at my little girl all grown up."

Startled, I looked up and there he was. Deshawn in the flesh and in living color. He looked just as I remembered, except it seemed like he'd actually gained more muscles. His intimating presence scared the shit out of me.

"Deshawn, leave me alone. I'm going to call the police." I went to put my window up, but he snatched my cell phone out of my hand before putting his hands on the glass and preventing it from moving.

"Why are you being so mean? All I did was say hi. You would have thought I did some evil shit to you like send you to jail or something." He laughed hysterically, then abruptly stopped. "Oh, that's right. That's what you did to me."

I turned to the guy who was pumping my gas and screamed, "Please help me. This is my ex-boyfriend who tried to kill me. He's dangerous. Call nine-one-one, please."

He walked over and stood in Deshawn's face, who was not the least bit bothered. Deshawn looked at the guy, then looked back at me, and started to laugh again.

The guy turned around. "Yo, Dee, how much do you want me to put in the tank?"

Deshawn reached into his pocket, pulled out a gigantic knot of money, and said, "Fill it up. We got a long night ahead of us."

Oh my goodness. The guy…he was with Deshawn.

As the guy walked away, all I could do was shake my head and look down. I couldn't believe this was happening to me again. It felt like I walked around with a huge sign on my back: Trouble… Find me here!

"You know you've really grown into a sexy young lady. Keep up the good work," Deshawn complimented. He threw my cell phone on my lap. "By the way here's your phone, but I wouldn't call the police if I were you. You and I both know they're on my side."

What the hell did that mean? I guessed my expression showed that I was puzzled, so Deshawn enlightened me on some shit that I had no clue about.

"Think about it. With all those charges you put on me and all the evidence the police had against me, I only did five years. You don't think that happened by chance, do you?" he asked.

"Wait, what are you saying?" I asked.

"It's great to have connections in the State's Attorney office. I tell you, they always look out for a brother and although I'm still a little upset that I had to sit for five years, it doesn't compare to the twenty-five years I should have been facing."

Wow! So now it all made sense. Deshawn had this planned out from day one. The entire time that I was working with the police to bring down "Mr. Toe Tag Deshawn," he was already working out a deal with some crooked ass State's Attorney.

How was I supposed to compete with that? How could I stand up to a man who had a million men standing behind him? I felt defeated, but I wasn't about to let this bastard see me sweat. Not because I was some brave, courageous woman, but because I was just tired of living in fear.

"Leave me the fuck alone," I yelled. "Like seriously, what are you gaining from continuously harassing and hurting me?" These were questions I desperately needed answers to because I couldn't understand why this man was so obsessed with me. "God, why can't you just move on with your life and let me be?"

Deshawn said, "Really Jamaica, are you seiously asking me that stupid ass question? You think I still want you? Bitch, I was over you before you were probably over me, so don't flatter yourself. Please don't confuse me paying you back with me wanting you back. The two have very different consequences."

"Why do you want to pay me back? Don't you think you've done enough to me? You beat the shit out of me. You've emotionally scarred me for life. You've sexually assaulted and humiliated me to the point the act of making love itself has no sentimental meaning to me. What more payback do you want? If it's my life, then just take it and get it over with," I demanded.

I was speaking directly from my heart. I was so tired of looking my shoulder. I just wanted closure, whether it was him moving on with his life or taking mine.

I poured my heart and soul out to this nigga to make him see that he'd won, but it was as if I was talking to myself.

Deshawn simply replied, "See you soon, Jamaica, and trust me, I *will* see you *very* soon," as he walked away, hopped into a brand-new Porsche, and drove off with two other cars following behind him.

I was hit with a lot emotions. I was happy and relieved I was still alive, yet I was absolutely fearful of the unknown. This man had managed to get into my head once again. I wanted to turn back, drive home, crawl into bed and just cry, however, what would that accomplish? It felt like I'd been running from this man all my life and it was time that I stopped and fought fire with fire.

In the midst of my thoughts, Myesha texted, asking was I close by. I let her know that I would be pulling up shortly.

Determined not to make tonight's encounter break my hustle, I had to hop off the emotional roller coaster that Deshawn was attempting to put me on.

I pulled up to the house about ten minutes later and walked in like nothing had happened. As soon as I stepped inside, Nina ran over to me. "Okay, so the club we're going to tonight is called The Room. The VIP section has small circular beds positioned around a huge pool. There's three dance floors and spacious bars and lounge areas on each floor. Girl, I'm telling you, it's the bomb."

"Okay, that's what's up," I replied, not giving two shits about what she said. I brushed her off and walked over to Myesha, who was doing Kelisa's makeup.

"Myesha, I really need to talk to you about something important, but we'll talk later because it's private."

"No problem, girl. Is everything okay?" she asked.

"Let's just say I have a situation I need to take care of."

"Okay, well I got your back, whatever it is."

I didn't have to go into details with Myesha. That was what I valued about our friendship. All I needed to say was that I had a situation, and I knew she would ride with me until the wheels fell off.

I patiently waited for the ladies to get dressed and beautified, and about a half hour later, they were looking extra fabulous, as we headed out. We were walking down the steps yapping away, when I noticed a large Chevy Trail Blazer pull into the driveway. My heart damn near jumped out of my chest, and I wasn't alone. All the ladies stopped walking and had a look of suspicion on their faces.

"Who's that?" Rose asked.

"I hope it isn't one of those niggas from last night stalking the house already," Nina stated.

I retrieved my cell phone from my purse, dialed 9-1-1, and waited before hitting the send button. The driver hopped out, and as soon as I saw his face, my mind was put to ease.

"Ohhhhhh, I almost forgot. I told Mr. Muscles to meet us here." I put my cell phone back into my pocketbook.

"Mr. who?" Myesha asked.

"The bouncer from the bachelor party last night. I asked him to work for us so we could have protection at the house."

I walked over to Shanks and shook his oversized hand. "Gosh, you're a giant," I teased. "Thanks for coming out on such short notice. We're on our way to this album release party. We're going in, showing out, and leaving real quick like we did last night. I need you to stick by our side without being by our side," I explained.

"Well, let me know what's allowed and what's not allowed so that I know when to intervene," Shanks said.

"The girls are going to mix and mingle with a few men. They may create a scene like they did last night, and of course, some men are going to get rowdy, but that's okay. They can scream, throw money, and even dance with the ladies. However, they are not allowed to get too aggressive, and if you see someone going beyond the normal dirty dancing with the ladies, then you can intervene." During this time, I also took the liberty to explain my situation with Deshawn so that Shanks could fully protect us. He put my mind at ease and let me know he had my back.

"I will be here whenever you need me. A fool better not step out of line with any of you ladies." Shanks lifted up his shirt to show me he was strapped. "Don't worry about a thing because me and my girlfriend right here will see to it that everyone is safe."

"Say no more," I replied. "That's exactly what I needed to hear. And see!"

After our discussion, Shanks got back into his truck and followed us. When we arrived, the ladies walked into the party, but I asked Myesha to stay behind so that I could finally speak with her.

"So now that we're alone I need to tell you that Deshawn is home from jail and he's basically stalking me. He's been to my house already, leaving notes and pictures, and then tonight, he confronted me at the gas station. That's the real reason I was late."

"Oh my God," Myesha yelled out and her mouth dropped. "Jamaica, what are you going to do? He's like cancer. You go through remission, think you're out of the woods, and then boom, he pops back up and your life is in danger all over again." Myesha was all worked up, just as I expected her to be.

But for real, I didn't need her to panic because it was only going to cause me to panic. I just needed her to know what was going on.

"I'm trying not to stress. I'm just telling you so you know what's going on, just in case anything happens to me."

"In case something happens to you," Myesha repeated. You're saying that too calmly and you sound defeated. This is so unlike you."

"Myesha seriously, I have a lot on my plate. My father fucking my damn aunt. Rock is smothering the hell out of me, and Deshawn's stalking me. Yes I'm scared, but scared money don't make no money. I rather get this money and die a rich bitch than to live in constant fear."

Myesha looked at me with concern. "Jamaica, you have to take control of your situation before it takes control of you. But, I got your back regardless."

"I know you do, sis. Always have and always will. Now let's go make this money, because we're on a mission and no one, including bitch ass Deshawn, is going to stop us," I declared.

CHAPTER 12

Friends get <u>Less</u> with <u>Success</u>!

Myesha and I walked into the club and joined Shanks and the ladies, who were standing by the door waiting for us. Shanks gave me a hug and told me he was going to be outside helping his friend work the door, and to just call if I needed him.

The party was jammed pack, so I wanted the ladies to start working the room. I was just about to give the ladies my standard pep talk, but to my surprise, Myesha started before I could get a chance.

"Alright, you know what to do. Let's work the room and leave these niggas asking who the fuck is Las Chicas."

I looked at Myesha as if my ears were deceiving me. Was this Little Miss Sunshine? Was this my friend who was afraid of everything? I was happy that she stepped up to the plate. Typically, I was the one laying down the rules, while Myesha was on her Mother Theresa bullshit. However tonight, her attitude did a total 360 turn.

"I see money all around this room, so let's go get it and be out of here," Myesha added.

I'd never seen this side of her. She didn't even have this attitude at the strip club where she worked. I wondered if I should be worried? I mean, just last night she was second-guessing this whole scheme and tonight she was acting like... *She's acting like....* *She's acting like... Me!*

"We got you, Esha," Nina replied. She turned to the other ladies and added, "Come on. Let's go show out!"

Before I had a chance to add my two cents, Nina and the other ladies vanished into the crowd.

Again, I was puzzled. Esha? When did Nina and Myesha become so close and more importantly, why did she acknowledge Myesha and not me? Did she forget that I ran this shit, not *Esha*? Or better yet, did she forget that I was the glue holding this business together?

A million questions ran through my mind, however, I managed to keep my composure because this wasn't the time nor the place to address it.

Just as we did the night before, Myesha and I headed to the bar and ordered drinks while the girls worked. I used this time to have another conversation with Myesha. I needed to understand what was going on with her and Nina because Myesha was soft and a bit gullible. Bitches like Nina could sense that weakness and would prey on it. I wasn't jealous of their ben-ship, a friendship solely based on benefits, however I needed to warn my friend just in case she wasn't wise enough to see the bullshit.

"So what's up with you and Nina?" I asked, getting straight to the point. "You two seem pretty tight tonight." I took a sip of my Pinot Grigio and waited for a response.

"What do you mean?" Myesha replied sounding agitated.

"You two went shopping this afternoon. No one bothered to call and ask me did I want to tag along. Now she calling you Esha and telling you she got you, not once saying a word to me. I don't know, it just seemed a little shady."

"Jamaica, you're reading too much into this. Let's stay focused and worry about the petty stuff later," Myesha replied as she downplayed my concerns.

"So, you think I'm being petty?" I asked, both shocked and offended by her sly ass response.

"Yeah I do," she calmly replied as she took a sip of her drink and turned away from me.

Myesha not only dismissed me, but she threw hella shade my way. If I didn't know better I would say that I'd created a monster, or had this monster been around all along and I was just seeing it?

After checking me properly, home girl kept her back turned and engaged in everything and everyone else in the room except me. I sat in amazement, laughing on the inside because Myesha was not Ford-built like me. She wouldn't be able to handle the wrath of Jamaica Johnson if she dared cross me. There would be no boundaries I wouldn't cross to take her or any of them bitches down if I ever found out they betrayed me.

We sat awkwardly for a while, not saying much to each other. She was in her own little world and I was in mine. My thoughts were interrupted by the DJ, who got on the mic to announce that Black Scar would be on stage in less than twenty minutes. The crowd went wild. I noticed Nina walking over to the DJ and whispering in his ear.

I tapped Myesha and pointed to her new best friend. "What the fuck is she doing? She better not be requesting any damn music while her ass is on the clock."

Myesha looked toward Nina, threw her hands up, and replied, "I don't know what she's doing. I'm over here with you. Why don't you go ask her?"

"That's exactly what I intend to do." I put my drink down and headed toward the DJ booth.

As I was making my way through the crowded dance floor, the DJ got back on the mic. "Oh yeah! We got Las Chicas in the building. Men, if you don't know who they are, you definitely need to get familiar. Look around the club for the hottest women in here and you'll find them. If you get a card, you better hold on to it." He then turned the music back up and everyone continued to dance.

The smile on my face could have lit up the darkest room. I walked back to my seat feeling good about the free promo.

"Look at you over there cheesing like Ronald McDonald," Myesha teased. "You were getting all worked up for nothing. Nina wasn't doing anything shady. All she was doing was handling her business."

As much as I didn't want to admit it, Myesha was right. Maybe I was overreacting, but I came from a city known for having the best crabs in the world. Baltimore, Maryland is a great place to live, but it was filled with backstabbing, hating ass people who didn't like to see others doing better than they were.

"Okay, I'm mature enough to apologize when I'm wrong," I mumbled, because I really wasn't mature enough to apologize when I was wrong. I hated that shit.

"So what are you waiting for?" Myesha replied.

"Give me a chance to get the words out of my mouth. Damn!" I took a deep breath. "Myesha, I am sorry for overreacting and thinking something shady was going on with you and Nina. In my defense, my own aunt is sleeping with my father behind my mother's back so in my world anything is possible."

"Yeah but you can't hold us responsible for the things going on in your life. I mean, I don't act out on you and think you're stealing from me because my mother's stealing food out of our refrigerator. You have to learn to trust people."

Myesha had a valid point. With all the issues going on in my family, maybe I was applying them to the wrong people.

"Let's make a toast." Myesha raised her glass. "Here's to making money and doing absolutely nothing but counting it."

Again, this was a new attitude for Myesha, but I was going to try my best to ignore it. I smiled, raised my glass, and continued to sip on my wine.

Myesha and I were drinking and enjoying the music when the lights dimmed. A few moments later a well-dressed, caramel complexion brother walked out to the stage and announced he was the president and C.E.O of Blasfome Entertainment. Bingo! That was the man we needed to see. His beautiful brown eyes caught my attention.

"Welcome everyone and thank you for coming out tonight and showing love. If you don't know by now, I go by the name G-Sling and my little homie, Black Scar is dropping his album tomorrow. Every track is a banger. Trust me, you want to have this CD in your collection. With that being said, are you ready for Black Scar to hit the stage," he screamed.

The crowd went wild, but not wild enough for him. "I said are you ready for Black Scar to hit the motherfucking stage?"

Everyone screamed louder than before as the room became pitch dark. Seconds later, the stage lights came on and some half-dressed hoes were front and center, crawling around like animals. Some were dressed in cat suits while others had on nothing but jungle print thongs and bras. Some were swinging from ropes while others were sliding down poles. It was a real whore circus on that stage.

Suddenly, a burst of gunshot sound effects went off as Black Scar ran out rapping, "I got my pistol on my left and a bitch on my right. Either way you look at it somebody's getting fucked tonight. Yes I'm gonna kill that pussy!"

I swear you would have thought that Jay-Z hit the stage. Everyone had their hands in the air singing Black Scar's song word-for-word.

Kelisa, Samantha, and Rose were positioned in the middle of all the commotion, dancing like they did at the strip club. It was entertaining to watch how they used their stripper moves to seduce and lure in potential customers.

Nina, Lashel, and Carlena were back stage in an exclusive business meeting with G-Sling. I didn't know how they managed to maneuver their way back there, but they did. I was just happy to hear they got to the CEO, even though I kind of wanted him to myself because he was fine as hell.

With Las Chicas at the height of the night, I texted all the ladies and let them know it was time to roll. I had to get them back to the house and make sure everything was prepared for their night of fun.

We exited the club and headed back with Shanks riding behind us. As expected, the Las Chicas' phone started to ring within minutes. I picked up and answered seductively, "Hello, this is Heather. How can I help you?"

"Is this Las Chicas?" the male caller asked.

"Yes it is. How may I assist you?"

"Look, I'm pretty much aware of what's going on so we can cut to the chase. I threw the party you ladies just attended and I want to set something up for tonight."

Oh my goodness. It was my crush, G-Sling, Black Scar's manager. I wanted to kiss the phone, but the ladies were in front of me, so I held my composure.

"I have some important clients who need your services. Can that be arranged or is this too short notice for you?" he asked, sounding like a boss.

"We can accommodate your clients tonight," I assured him. "Let me tell you what we offer." I briefly discussed the price and all the accommodations that were available.

G-Sling sounded impressed. He asked me to hook his clients up because they were important investors who were putting up a large amount of money for Black Scar to go on tour. I promised him our ladies would take very good care of them.

"My girls are here to serve in any way. As I stated, they will cater to a man's every need, from throwing down in the bedroom to throwing down in the kitchen. There's not much that my girls won't do, for a price, of course," I reminded him.

"That sounds great. If all goes well, I'll be in touch with you on a continuous basis. I always have clients flying in from out of town and I like to keep them happy."

"That would be great. If you come to us on a regular basis, I'm sure I can work out a good deal for you," I stated.

"Cool. So Heather, are you a working girl yourself or do you just handle the business?" G-Sling asked.

"That's a clean way of putting it," I joked. "But, no I'm not a working girl. I'm just out here handling my business like you are."

"I feel you. So tell me something, what's your real name because I know it's not Heather. You sound too much like a sister to have the name Heather," G-Sling joked.

I busted out laughing again. This man had me cracking up on the phone like we knew each other for years.

"I can't disclose that information for my own safety. I'm not saying you're going to do anything, but I just don't need my government name out there in the streets." After making that statement, something hit me. "Hey, I don't know your name either and I'm pretty sure that G-Sling is nowhere on your birth certificate," I clowned. "So what's your real name?"

"Just call me Ghee for short. That's what my friends call me."

"Well alright, Ghee it is," I replied cheesing from ear to ear, boo-loving on the phone with a man that I didn't know from a can of paint. I became so lost in our conversation that I almost forgot I had Myesha and some of the girls in the car. I looked up and they were all staring at me like I was crazy, so I switched up the game and got back down to business. "Okay Ghee, I have to go, but as I stated, the price will be five hundred for each girl. Will that be a problem?"

"Let me explain something. The clients I have are very exclusive and low-key, so I need your business shut down for the night. I don't need anyone else in the house but them. I need a nice meal and a stiff drink waiting for them when they arrive. I want the whole nine yards. I know that's more than five-hundred apiece, so what's my new damage?"

I had to think about that one. Off the top, he was going to pay $3,000 for all six ladies. Adding the whole cater-to-my man package was another $500. Then, to shut the entire house down exclusively would be an additional $1,500. I was just going to throw these figures out and we could negotiate from there.

"I can shut my house down for you and your friends, provide six bad bitches who will do any and everything, cook dinner and the whole nine yards. That includes fucking, sucking, singing, hair braiding; you name it and it'll be done. That's going to run you five-thousand for the night." I waited for him to back out of the deal.

"Alright, give me the address and I'll drop my clients off in about an hour or two. I have to take care of some business here first, but we'll be over later."

It was just that simple. It was just that quick. After disconnecting with Ghee, I pulled up to the house and filled the girls in on the good news.

"Tonight's going to be a little different. Black Scar's manager is paying us five thousand dollars to shut the house down and cater to some important business clients. They want dinner and everything. We have about one hour to make this happen, so get in the house and get yourselves together. Leave all the cooking up to me and Myesha."

"What? Five fucking thousand dollars," Samantha yelled. "Now this the shit I'm talking about. Come on, ladies." The other ladies were equally excited. They ran into the house, took shots of Patron, and headed to their rooms to get prepared. Everyone was excited, however, Nina looked a little bothered. As a matter of fact, she was the only one sitting around with her lips poked out, giving hell of attitude. *Uggg, what the fuck is wrong now?*

"So what's your problem?" I asked.

"Is this some kind of joke? All of you are getting happy because someone called and said they're going to pay five grand tonight. How do we know this nigga is going to show up?" she questioned.

"Honey, let me do the thinking, okay? I'm not asking you, I'm telling you to go upstairs and get yourself together because these men will be here before you know it. That's all I need from you right now," I calmly replied.

I'd tried to treat Nina with a little respect because she did put us on, but she was irritating my soul and I needed her to play her role and stop trying to play mine.

If looks could kill, I would be as dead as Elvis. Nina couldn't hide the hate she had toward me. It was the same kind of look she gave me the first day the girls showed up. I was trying my best to keep things civilized between us, but something told me she was going to try me one of these days and I was going to have to give her the business.

"Please, just go shower and get pretty," Myesha interjected, trying to be the peacemaker. "Jamaica and I will handle everything else."

I could tell Nina wanted to say so much more, but she walked away and went upstairs. That was the smartest move she had ever made in her life because she literally had one more time to play with me before I popped off on her.

I was in the kitchen cooking up a quick meal. Around 2:30 am, I covered the last pot on the stove and walked upstairs to meet Myesha and the other ladies. I stood in the middle of the hallway so that everyone could hear me. "Okay the food is done and the guys should be pulling up any minute now. I don't think I need to talk too much because I've preached enough on how we all could benefit tonight. You see my ass in the kitchen cooking? You know it's serious when I cook for any nigga."

Myesha and Kelisa looked at each other and laughed. "Girl, we were just laughing about that a second ago. Kelisa was like, damn Jamaica is in the kitchen cooking. This is the most work I've seen her do since I met her."

"Oh when five grand is on the line, you better believe I'm going to put that work in. There's no shame in my game. If a nigga wanted lobster to go with his steak tonight, I would have found a way to have it on his plate," I joked. "We're going to head to the office now and Shanks is downstairs so you all are safe."

Myesha and I went up to the attic and began talking about Nina's attitude, when Shanks buzzed in over the intercom and announced that the guys had arrived. I looked down on the monitors to see Nina escorting the men into the chill area as she did last night.

Four dapper, well-dressed businessmen walked into the room with Nina. Two other guys were with them but they didn't look as important. I suspected the four dudes were Ghee's important investors from New York and the other two were his flunkies who were there to drive them around and assist them.

The rest of the girls came downstairs to join the group. They were mingling and getting to know the guys when two other men showed up moments later. I remembered their faces from the party. It was Black Scar and Ghee.

Ghee walked through the door looking as sexy as I remembered. There was something about that man that turned me on. Some women love light-skinned dudes. Some women love dark-skinned dudes. But me... I looooove bosses, of all shades, and Ghee was a boss for real.

Ghee handed Nina a stack of money, took a seat on the couch, and whipped out his laptop.

As I was obsessing over him, my thoughts were interrupted by Myesha. "Girl, I want to holler at that one." She licked her lips like she was sitting in front of a Thanksgiving plate, and couldn't wait to dig in. "He can get it for sure."

"Which one?" I asked, knowing she better not be referring to Ghee.

"The dude, G-Sling," she replied with her eyes still locked on him. "Black Scar's manager. I like his demeanor, you know. I want to get with someone like that. He got money, yet he's humble."

"Okay rule number one, never mix business with pleasure. G-Sling is a client and he needs to stay that way. Furthermore, when did you start digging guys like G-Sling?"

Myesha looked at me like I said something out of the way to her. "Forget about it, Jamaica. If you say he's off limits, then he's off limits. I'm not about to get into it with you because I can tell this conversation is about to go left."

"I didn't know we were getting into anything," I replied. "I asked you a simple question. Why are you making this an issue?"

"It's an issue because any time I try to do something on *your* level, it's like you kick me back."

"What the fuck is that supposed to mean? It's only been two days and you already making this little petty ass money change you. Get some act right in your life and come back down to reality. I've been carrying you since we were little ass girls and now you think I want to hold you back?"

As I was talking, this immature bitch began tuning me out by humming some song and acting like I was invisible. I couldn't believe it. Who was this girl?

"Keep humming, bitch. After tonight we're going to reevaluate a couple of things because if this business is getting to you now, it's only going to get worse when we really start making money. So enjoy your little song but we will have a sit down later on," I warned.

I turned back to the monitors just in time to see Black Scar making his way down the basement with Rose, as the others ladies paired up with their dates for the night. Ghee was still in the living room chilling when Samantha walked over to the couch and began giving him a massage.

Just seeing her hands on him made me a little tense. I had to keep reminding myself this was business and Ghee was a client who was off limits, as I told Myesha.

Samantha wrapped her hands around Ghee's neck and massaged his muscles. He closed his eyes and leaned his head back. She began kissing his neck, as she made her way to the front of him. She stood up for a couple of seconds doing absolutely nothing so that he could focus in on her curvaceous body. With lust in her eyes, she sat on his lap and kissed his neck again. Then she swerved her tongue down the side of his chest to his rib cage. She moved from his rib cage and made her way to his pants. She began massaging his aroused cock, as she continued to kiss his chest.

Ghee kept his eyes closed as Samantha slowly pulled his pants and boxers down to his ankles. She pulled them off and his supersized dick stood up in the air. I actually saw Samantha smile as she wrapped her hands around his big shaft and made her tongue explore the premises. Slowly, but with much power and effort, Samantha tried to deep throat Ghee's cock but it was impossible. He kept filling her mouth before she could get it all the way to the back of her throat. Still, she was persistent. I could tell he was enjoying himself because he kept moaning and pulling her hair back to look down at her face.

"Do you like it, baby?" she asked in a soft voice.

"Yeah, don't stop until I stop," he ordered as he pushed Samatha's head back down to his cock. She continued to suck and slurp until he released himself into her mouth. She swallowed every ounce of him.

I must admit, I was jealous. There was no other way to put it. I was jealous because I wanted him for my damn self.

I guessed I was wearing my emotions on my sleeves because out of nowhere Myesha blurted out, "You want him, don't you? That's why you shot me down when I said I wanted him. It's written all over your face."

"I don't know what you're talking about." I quickly turned away from the monitor and started to fidget with my cell phone to draw my attention from Ghee.

"Oh you know damn well what I'm talking about. He's too good to be with me because you have to have him, don't you?" she asked again.

"Look, go for what you know. You're a grown ass woman. Why do you need my approval anyway? If you want him, go get him. I want his money and connections. You can have his dick after these hoes get finished with it tonight."

"Like I said earlier, you want everything that's good in life for yourself and I'm supposed to settle for the leftovers. Everything that's good is only good for Jamaica. You're the queen sitting on your throne. I salute you, boo."

Where was all of this coming from? Or better yet, when did Myesha start having these type of feelings toward me? I didn't have anything else to say to her because she had already said a mouthful. I didn't know if she knew it yet, but we might never recover from the bullshit tonight and even if we did, I might never fully trust her again.

"It's evident that you feel some kind of way toward me and I don't know where all this animosity is coming from. But like I said earlier, we're going to reevaluate a couple of things. Let's just leave it at that."

For the remainder of the night, Myesha and I sat in silence. About an hour or two later, the freak show ended and the men got dressed and made their way out the door. Shanks escorted them off the premises and came back into the house and announced that the cars had pulled out of the driveway.

I met the ladies in the chill area as we did last night, however, tonight Nina did some weird shit. Rather than hand me *my* money, the bitch walked past me, handed the money to Myesha, and said, "We just made five grand in less than three hours, girl. We some bad bitches."

No she didn't just hand *my* money to someone else. What was even more disturbing to me was the fact that Myesha took the money and started counting like she was the boss bitch up in here. Then she did the unthinkable. The bitch began distributing money out to these bitches without it even touching my hands. She even handed me my share like I worked for her.

Typically, this wouldn't have bothered me, but after the conversation we just had, it struck the last nerve I had in my body.

After handing everyone their cut, Myesha said, "Okay ladies, you see how easy this shit was? Let's keep up the good work and keep business rolling in." I just stood there, taking it all in.

"What if we book our own clients? Do we have to split our money with you two or could we just rent the rooms out?" Nina asked.

Before I could answer, Myesha jumped in. "Well, I don't think you have to give us anything for the client because technically…"

"Hell fucking yes you have to pay *me*," I interrupted. "I don't know about no one else but I want my share because I put up money for all of this. I'm the one paying rent and utilities bills in here. No one else has paid for anything out of their pockets but me, so yes Nina, I want *my* money. And for the record, the next time you collect *my* money, hand it to me and no one else." I was livid. Myesha knew me well enough to know that I was in beast mode so she kept her mouth shut.

"Well I'm sorry. I didn't know I was doing anything wrong by handing the money to your best friend… your sister… your partner in crime. I didn't know that you wanted me to hand you the money specifically," Nina sarcastically replied.

"Well now you know, and it better not happen again," I clapped back as I gathered my belongings, walked away, and left the house without saying another word.

Later that night, I laid in my bed thinking about the situation. I kept asking myself was it really worth all this drama? It was only day two and my friendship with Myesha had changed. Even my relationship with Rock had ran its course. The last message he sent me was pretty self-explanatory:

"You know what, Jamaica; I've been calling you and you've been avoiding me. Fuck it. See you around. I took it that he was through with me and to be honest, I didn't care.

The next couple of weeks flew by. Business was booming and we were making a lot of money, but my friendship with Myesha never recovered. Every conversation we had since our big blowup was business-related.

Las Chicas had new clients consistently rolling in, but Ghee kept our lights on. He continued to shut down the house for his business affiliates and label mates on a weekly basis. It was to the point where the ladies didn't have to go out to promote anymore because anyone who was anyone knew who they were. This allowed me to be able to separate myself from the house, only stopping by in the mornings to collect my bread and then dip. Myesha, on the other hand, still hung out with the whores like she was one of them. It was a damn shame how money changed her so quickly, but as my mother always said, friends get *less* with *success!*"

CHAPTER 13

Wolf in Sheep Clothing

My phone was sounding off all night long. I hadn't spoken to Rock in weeks and the last message he texted basically stated that we were over. I was going to ignore him, but something inside of me said to pick up phone.

"Hello," I answered, trying to sound half sleep.

"Jamaica, what's the problem? Did I do something to push you away," he asked without wasting any time.

Oh God. *Here I go again dealing with a thug who didn't know how to control his emotions. This pussy was driving these niggas crazy.*

"No, you didn't do anything, Rock. I'm just trying to get settled and get my life together. Nothing personal toward you. I just need some time to myself, that's all."

"So basically, you're saying you want your space. You're not rocking with me anymore, am I correct? If that's what you want I don't have a problem with that, as long as you make it clear to me. Later on down the road, I don't want to hear you getting upset if you see me with someone else."

That wouldn't bother me one bit. He could date my mother right about now and I wouldn't give two fucks.

"Rock, you're free to date anyone your heart desires. Right now, I'm dealing with some issues that are more important than worrying about who you're sleeping with. And it's not about me being with anyone else either, so please don't take this personally."

Rock was calm at first, but after he had time to process what I'd just said, he went off. "Lately all I've been hearing from you is bullshit, Jamaica. I've seen you do some cruddy shit to people over the years and then act like they did something to you. You're a fucking user and once you get all that you can get from a person, you leave them and move on to the next victim. No wonder that nigga tried to kill you. I understand why he did it, because honestly, if I was a weak-minded nigga like him, your ass would be dead by now."

"Is that right," I asked, feeling alarmed that he would even go there knowing the nightmare that Deshawn put me through. That statement got my full attention and I needed clarification. "So, are you saying you want to hurt me, too?"

"I see you only hear what you want to hear. Goodbye, Jamaica."

"Wait a minute, explain to me what you meant by my ass would be dead by now. Are you planning on doing something to me because if you are…"

"Check this out. I may have feelings for you, but I'm far from a weak nigga. I'm not losing sleep, money, or my freedom over no bitch." Then, Rock went on a rant. He told me I wasn't shit and a bunch of other bull crap that I could care less about.

In the midst of his outburst, the Las Chicas business phone started to ring. I looked down and saw that Ghee was calling.

"Look I have to go," I interrupted. "We can continue this conversation some other time."

"No, this conversation is over and so are we. Have a good life." He slammed the phone down.

This man had some nerve acting up with me like he didn't warn me not to catch feelings for him. All I did was follow his instructions and now that he was the one who caught feelings, I was supposed to change my life around.

I missed Ghee's call fucking around with Rock, but luckily, he called right back. This time I picked up on the first ring.

"Hello, friend," I answered.

"What's up, Heather? I'm just calling to confirm the usual for tonight."

"Okay, you want the house shut down and a delicious meal prepared, correct?"

"You got it, sweetheart," Ghee answered.

We flirted with each other all the time. Sometimes, I thought he kept locking the house down so he had a reason to talk to me.

"Okay, I got you locked in. Is there anything else you need from me?" I asked.

"Actually, I do have one more request."

I scrambled to get a pen and notepad off my dresser. "Okay, what do you need?" I inquired.

"I need you to meet me for breakfast tomorrow morning."

I started to blush so hard I swore he could have seen it through the phone. God knew I not only wanted to meet him for breakfast, but would have loved to stay for lunch, dinner, and a nightcap, but my luck hadn't been good with men lately. Revealing myself to Ghee could only come back and haunt me.

"Boy, I'll be home in my bed tomorrow morning, and besides, you know the drill. We could never meet because business and friendship don't mesh well. It's like oil and water; no matter how hard you try, you can't mix the two." My lips were talking, but my heart wasn't feeling anything I was saying. I would have loved to have a cup of coffee, and engage in stimulating conversation with Ghee because he seemed so wise and intriguing, but it would never work out. He would only connect me to Las Chicas and probably never truly respect me.

"One day I'm going to see the face behind this sexy voice of yours. I don't know what it is, but I feel that we have a lot in common. I feel we can make good money and love together."

"Making money, yes. Making love, maybe," I flirted.

Ghee laughed, probably thinking I was just joking. Little did he know I was serious. "One day you will meet me, but I'll never tell you who I am," I added.

"I'm a very powerful man, you know. I always get what I want. Right now I'll allow you to continue to play your little game, but sooner or later you'll be laying in my bed getting your beauty sex."

"You mean beauty *rest*," I corrected.

"No, I meant what I said."

"Well everyone's entitled to aim high and dream big," I joked. We flirted some more and discussed business before disconnecting our call.

I was chilling, watching TV when my phone rang again. This time it was my mother. I swore, it was like someone put up a billboard sign that said: call Jamaica Johnson, because everybody wanted a piece of me today.

"Hello, Ma," I answered.

"Hey, baby," she replied in her warm Jamaican accent.

Hearing her voice was soothing to my ears. "I'm having a dinner party tomorrow evening for Rochelle's birthday. You have to be there, so if you have plans, break them."

Oh Lord, I almost forgot my own sister's birthday. I always did something special for her every year. With all the drama going on in my life, I didn't remember.

"I wouldn't miss it for the world. What time does it start?" I asked.

"Dinner starts at five sharp so don't be late. We haven't sat down as a family in God knows when. Rochelle really misses you and I think she would appreciate a family dinner for her special day."

"Okay, Ma. I'll see you tomorrow," I assured her.

"Great! I love you."

"I love you more," I answered before hanging up. After taking calls from Rock, Ghee, and my mother, I put my phone on silent and went back to sleep.

Later that evening, I got myself together and made my way over to Las Chicas to get the house prepared for Ghee. About five minutes after walking through the door, I noticed a shiny navy-blue Benz pull into the driveway. No one was scheduled to be here and I didn't recognize the car. I whipped out my phone and had my fingers ready to dial 9-1-1.

The car door opened and out hopped a chick wearing a bad ass pair of Gucci pumps that I'd had my eyes on for months now. The last time Myesha and I were out shopping, I told her I was coming back to get them. My vision was a little blurred because the sun was beaming through the window, but I did see the woman with the bad ass pumps had a banging ass body to match. She had on a clinging dress that highlighted her curvaceous body, and her weave, which fell to the brim of her ass, was slayed for days.

Who could this be? As the female walked up the steps and whipped out a house key, it became evidently clear who the bitch was.

She walked in, threw her hands up, gave me a quick hi, and kept it moving. My mouth nearly fell off my face.

I was livid, but I tried to keep my cool. "Good evening, Myesha," I calmly greeted. "Ummm, when did you get a spare key to the house? I thought I was the only one with a key," I asked, confused.

"I had this key cut when we first got the house just in case you lost yours."

Wait, did this bitch say when *we* first got this house? Was she speaking French? When did *we* get anything?

"Is there a problem?" she continued.

"Yes, especially when shit is being done behind my back. You could have just asked me for a copy. It's not a big deal. I just need to be informed."

"First of all, I didn't do anything behind your back that I wouldn't do to your face. Secondly, if it's not a big deal, then why are you bringing it up, asking me crazy questions?" Before I could even respond, she cut me off. "As a matter of fact, I don't feel like getting into it with you today, so do us both a favor and keep your anger to yourself." She picked up remote control, turned the TV on, and tuned me out like she normally did when shit hit the fan between us.

"You know what, Myesha; you're getting above yourself and I'm not for the bullshit. You need to calm the fuck down and ..."

"Look," she screamed. "I just told you I wasn't going to have this conversation with you and I mean it." She turned off the TV, walked out of the room, began walking up the steps, but stopped and turned back. "I'm glad to know how you truly feel about me, though. So, I'm getting above myself because I'm finally standing up for myself? I guess you're so use to sitting on top of the world you can't stand to see another bitch climb up there with you. Well, I am getting above myself and I don't plan on coming back down any time soon."

I didn't know if it was anger, jealousy, or resentment that made me go off, but I ran up those steps and jumped in her face to the point where I was practically on top of the bitch. She truly believed she was on my level. Whatever the case may be, the bitch was going to learn today.

"Bitch, you're my echo. You repeat everything I do. There's levels to this shit and trust me, you're nowhere near mine. You couldn't possible walk in my shoes, boo, but it's nice to know that you aspire to. I guess that's why you ran out and purchased the pumps I told you I was getting." I looked down at her shoes and busted out laughing so hard I almost passed out. "Girl, those pumps, your new weave, and this new profound attitude will not make you Jamaica Johnson. You need to be humble and remember who you are."

"And who might that be?" Myesha asked.

"You're a stripper who I raised because your mama was too cracked out to do it herself. I've been carrying you since the day I met you, and now you want to bite the hands that literally fed you for all these years? That's a big mistake," I warned.

Myesha kept this sly smirk the entire time I was reading her. Nothing I said got under her skin, the way it normally did. Still, I continued to curse her ass out because my emotions were flowing and I couldn't control them to save my life.

"You pulls up in someone's Benz, wearing some old ass Gucci shoes that came out months ago and think you're doing something big? Girl bye!"

Myesha laughed. She was laughing so hard she almost tumbled down the steps. "So, I'm driving someone's car and wearing some old ass shoes. That joke would actually be funnier if it was accurate. Honey, go look at the registration. That shit says Myesha Thompson. You drive a 2000 and what Benz? Never mind don't answer because mine is newer and my daddy didn't buy it. I saved my money and paid for my own shit unlike you. You see, Jamaica, you can talk all that good shit, but I know the real you. You don't have money, your parents do, and it's a fucking shame how you blackmailed your own father and aunt to get what you got now. I don't have to scheme to get my cream, boo!"

I stood speechless. I wanted to say something to hurt her, but I couldn't find anything. She had me stuck on stupid.

"Oh, by the way, tell your mother thanks for the employment verification and fake pay stubs and tell your father thanks for the great deal on my new ride. He helped me out tremendously. I guess I should thank you too because he did it on the strength of you." Then, Myesha laughed in my face again.

"You went to my parents behind my back and used them to get a car?"

"That's a harsh way of putting it, but yes, I guess that's exactly what I did," she replied as she walked up the steps, leaving me standing there in total shock.

I didn't have the strength to pursue her. I just fixed the house up for Ghee and took my ass home to have a drink and reflect on what just went down between Myesha and me.

I thought things were bad before, but now I saw that I had a serious problem. Myesha knew all my secrets and without a doubt, she would use them to get at me and if I tried to kick her out of Las Chicas. Hell, the bitch might even go to the cops. I felt betrayed and defeated, however, if Myesha truly knew me, she should have been prepared for what was coming her way. I didn't take disloyalty lightly. If I got even with my own father and aunt, God only knew what I would do to Myesha. No one played me for a fool. As of today, my bestie had made her way to my shit list, and when I say it was about to hit the fan, trust and believe me, it was about to hit hard.

CHAPTER 14

Guess who's coming to Dinner?

Despite my encounter with Myesha, I still managed to keep my word and showed up for Rochelle's birthday dinner the next day. I pulled into my parents' driveway around 4:00 p.m., but I didn't physically walk through the front door until 4:30. I sat in my car contemplating about whether I should turn my black ass around and go home or attend this dinner and sit around people who I despised. After weighing my options, my mother's happiness meant more to me than anything else, so I decided to go through with the dinner.

I stepped into the living room and was greeted by the familiar smell of vanilla scented candles. Then, the aroma of my mother's home-cooked Caribbean meal took hostage of my nose and made my stomach smile. I walked over to the wall and looked at old family photos that showed the happier moments of our lives and thought about how life was so much easier back then. I was strolling down memory lane when Rochelle ran into the living room.

"Jamaica, you made it. I can't believe you're here." She gave me the biggest bear hug, nearly lifting me off the ground.

"I was not missing your birthday dinner. Do you think I would miss Mommy's brown-stew chicken, rice and peas, and steam cabbage?"

"Damn, how you know what she's cooking?" Rochelle asked.

"My nose is always on point when it comes to food. I could probably tell you what the next door neighbor is cooking," I joked. "So, what else is on the menu?"

"Well, on top of all of that, Mommy cooked oxtails, fried chicken, jerk chicken, mac and cheese, potato salad, and cornbread."

My mouth watered just thinking about all the delicious food I was going to smash. I couldn't wait because this life as a bachelorette often ended with a chicken box at night. I couldn't remember the last time I had a home cooked meal, especially since I'd been caught up with Las Chicas.

"You know Mommy gets out of hand when she plans a dinner. Plus, Aunt Pam cooked a few dishes, too, so it's going to look like Thanksgiving in this bitch," Rochelle bragged.

Ugggg. Why did she have to go there and say that name? My mood switched from hot to cold. "Aunt Pam? Is she coming to the dinner, too?"

"Yes. This is a family dinner, you know. She's here every Sunday for dinner. Don't you remember how it used to be before you moved out?" Rochelle asked, while giving me the 'duh' look.

I couldn't believe the bitch had the balls to still come and sit at the dinner table with my mother and father. How could she even feel comfortable stepping foot in this house?

"I only asked a simple question, Rochelle. Calm your nerves boo-boo," I replied.

"Is there something going on with you and Aunt Pam that I don't know about because you seem really blown that she's going to be here today?"

I'd always been bad at hiding my feelings. I should have known that Rochelle's ass would catch on to even the tiniest detail. "There's nothing going on between me and Pam. So, what you been up to?" I asked trying to change the subject.

"Pam? When did you drop the word aunt?" Rochelle asked, with an astonished expression.

"Pam, Aunt Pam, whatever. Why are you making a big deal out of nothing?"

"Because you've never…." Just as our conversation started to get intense, my mother dashed into the room.

"Hey, baby. I'm so happy you made it. Come over here and give your mommy a hug."

I hugged my mother feeling relieved that she interrupted my sister's interrogation And I was even happier to see my mother because I really missed her a lot.

"Thanks for coming. It really means so much to me," my mother added as she squeezed me in her arms.

"I told you I wouldn't miss it for the world. Not to mention it's been awhile since I've eaten some delicious authentic Jamaican food. As a matter of fact, can I sample something until dinner is ready?" I pleaded, hoping to walk away with a drumstick at least.

"Dinner will be served shortly so there's no need to ruin your appetite. Go upstairs to your room and chill out until I call you down," my mother instructed, as she guarded the pots like a correctional officer.

"Okay, but I'm warning you, my stomach has a mind of its own, so don't be shocked if I make my way back down in this kitchen to snack on something," I joked, as I headed upstairs to my room. I opened the door, turned on the light, and was literally taken aback. Everything was in the exact same place. My bed was neatly made, my teddy bears were all lined up on top of my pillows, and my mail was piled up on the corner of the nightstand. Even the clothes I left behind still hung in my closet.

I laid down on my soft queen-sized bed and let out an extensive sigh of relief. The comfort of laying my head down on a familiar pillow made me feel warm and fuzzy. I closed my eyes and reminisced on all the time I spent doing good and bad in this room. Myesha and I had sat up many nights and made plans to get rich together. Now our dreams had finally come true and we were not even speaking.

I turned on the television and watched old reruns of the Golden Girls.

I was laughing my ass off at one Sophia witty *picture-it* stories, when my mother stood at the bottom of the steps and yelled, "Dinner will be served in less than ten minutes."

Rochelle rushed to my doorway. "Girl, you better get downstairs before I do. I know you love the chicken neck and Mommy said it's only one in the pot. Guess who's going to put it on her plate and devour it if she gets to it first? Me." Rochelle took off running like a bolt of lightning, nearly tripping over her own feet.

"You better not touch my damn chicken neck." I jumped from my bed and ran behind her. I caught up to Myesha halfway down the hallway, pushed her to the side, and took the lead. We both ran down the steps and into the kitchen, laughing and play fighting like two four-years olds. It had been awhile since my sister and I acted silly like this. I was truly enjoying my time home with my family.

I looked over at my mother and saw the happiest expression on her face as she transferred her salad into a huge serving bowl.

"Look at my two baby girls. I miss this so much. It really feels good to have both of you here with me." My mother became teary-eyed, but she was able to keep her composure. "Everything is already set up in the dining room so let's go eat." She picked up the salad bowl and led the way.

We walked into the dining room, where my father was already sitting at the head of the table like he was king of the castle. I should have known this pleasurable moment wouldn't last. I didn't even hear this motherfucker come through the door. He must have snuck in here trying to avoid me.

I entered the room and barely spoke to his ass. "Hey," I nonchalantly greeted, not looking his way.

"Hello," he mumbled.

He didn't have much rap for me and I damn sure didn't have a drop for him. From thereon, we both sat silently, which made the moment even more awkward. The tension in that room was thicker than a 1960's afro, and there was no combing through the bullshit. Rochelle and my mother tried their very best to break the ice by engaging in small talk and telling a few corny jokes, but it didn't lighten the mood.

"This sure feels good," my mother stated as she smiled and looked around at our dysfunctional family.

I thought she must be in denial because I didn't know what the hell felt good about any of this bullshit.

"It's been awhile since we all sat down as a family. I'm just so happy to have everyone here for Rochelle's special day," she added.

I nodded but continued to keep my mouth closed because I didn't have nothing good to say, at least not with my father sitting a few seats away from me. Again, the room became uncomfortably silent.

"I agree," Rochelle blurted out, desperately trying to remove the cloud of tension. "Thank you all for being here for me today."

"I love you, sis. I will always show up for you… and Mommy," I replied, throwing obvious shade at my father.

"Well, okay, let's say our grace. Bow your heads," my mother ordered. I guessed she sensed the shade I was throwing, too. "Dear Father in Heaven, we want to take this time to thank you for your love and mercy this evening. Please bless and anoint this meal that we're about to receive. Thank you for blessing my wonderful baby girl to see another year. And Lord, I especially want to thank you for my family. No matter the condition we're in right now, we're still a family. Thank you for my kids and my wonderful husband. Amen!"

"Amen," we all repeated as we began passing the food around. Of course, my plate was stacked to the brim, and I planned on eating every drop of food. Everything I put to my lips was seasoned to perfection. I was enjoying my food like a fat girl, when my mother hit the side of her glass to grab our attention.

"I have some great news for you girls. Your father and I are thinking about renewing our vows and going on a second honeymoon within the next few months. It's nothing big. It'll just be us, Pam, and a few close friends."

I heard the words coming out of her mouth, but I tried my best to block them. I felt sick just seeing how excited she was and knowing that I knew the ugly truth and was keeping it from her. My mother happily looked at Rochelle and me, waiting for our reactions. I didn't want to respond because I knew I wouldn't be able to control my real emotions. So, instead of saying anything, I continued stuffing my face.

Rochelle jumped from her seat and hugged them both. "I'm so happy. Did you pick a date yet because I can't wait to go shopping for my dress?" She was thrilled about the news, which was puzzling to me considering that she'd just called my phone a couple weeks ago crying about our father's cheating ways.

"Did you hear that, Jamaica? Mommy and Daddy are renewing their vows," Rochelle said.

"Yes, I heard. I hope it turns out well," I replied as I ripped into my jerk chicken.

"What do you mean by you *hope* it turns out well? Are you insinuating that you're not going to show up or participate?" my mother asked. Before I could get a word in she followed up with another question. "Aren't you happy for us, Jamaica, because it seems that you're not."

Again, I stuffed a spoonful of mac and cheese into my mouth. I was desperately trying to be on my best behavior.

"Ma, Jamaica's going to be there," Rochelle interjected, trying to be the peacemaker. "Did you guys forget this is my birthday dinner? Let's talk about me for a change since it's technically supposed to be my day."

During the commotion, guess who came strolling in? Yes, my dear Aunt Pam. She sashayed her ass into the room, took one look at me sitting at the table, then looked at my father, and tried to get the hell out of there.

"Umm. Hello, everyone. I'm sorry I'm late but I can't stay for dinner. Something came up but I wanted to drop off the stuffed salmon that you asked me to cook, Mary."

My mother looked up at Pam like she was crazy and totally disregarded everything she'd just said. "Pam, don't be ridiculous. You cannot miss your niece's birthday dinner. We planned this together and now you want to back out? Sit your butt down and make a plate."

I glanced at my father, who had the most uncomfortable look on his face. He was sweating profusely and Aunt Pam looked like she was about to wet her pants. The horrified looks on both of their faces was priceless.

"Okay, I'll stay for a little while, but then I'll have to leave to take care of something important," Aunt Pam explained as she took a seat.

My mother picked up a plate and began putting food on it for Aunt Pam. I wanted to grab the dish and go upside my aunt's head with it. I couldn't fabric how she or my father could sit at this table, knowing I knew what had been going on between them.

After making my aunt's plate, my mother sat back down and we all kind of just ate our food, not saying much to each other. It was beyond awkward. I was getting ready to take my plate to go when Rochelle decided to spring some interesting news on us.

"Well now that everyone is here, I can finally tell you guys about my wonderful news." Rochelle stood up to face us. Her words became muffled and her face turned pale, which made me know that this news wasn't as wonderful as she proclaimed.

I knew my sister better than anyone at this table, so I knew that she was nervous. "Ummm, well I recently applied to three colleges and so far, I've received two acceptance letters."

My parents had to stay on top of me and damn near bribe me with $30,000 to stay focused enough to graduate from college, but Rochelle was the total opposite. She loved school and always kept her head glued to her books.

Everyone was happy and we cheered and congratulated her. Well, almost everyone. My mother's demeanor went from merry to monstrous. She sat quietly, looking at the rest of us like I was looking at her earlier.

"Which schools? Is it University of Maryland? No, I bet its Loyola or Towson University?" I asked. With Rochelle's good grades, she could pick, choose, and refuse whichever college she wanted to attend.

"Actually, I didn't apply to any of those colleges," Rochelle answered, with a weird expression.

It was hard to explain, but at that moment I knew something big was about to go down. From my mother's body language to my sister's facial expressions, it was apparent this dinner was about to go all the way left. "I've been accepted by Temple State University and Spelman College so far. I'm still waiting on Ohio State to make their decision, then I'll make mine."

Whoa, I wasn't expecting that answer, especially since I asked her not to apply to any out-of-state colleges until I got my financial situation together, and she said that she would.

Before I could respond, my mother jumped into the conversation; or should I say dived because she went all the way in. "Ohio? Temple? Spelman? Where the hell are those colleges located?" she asked.

"Temple is in Philadelphia. Spelman is in Atlanta and it's obvious where Ohio State is located. Out of those schools I'm leaning toward Spelman. I've heard some great things about the school and I also heard that Atlanta is a great place to live. They say downtown Atlanta has…"

My mother pulled the plug on Rochelle. She wasn't trying to hear all that bullshit. "You're leaning towards Spelman, huh? Spelman that's in Atlanta? What's wrong with going to a local school here in Maryland?"

Rochelle attempted to answer, but my mother cut her microphone completely off and wouldn't allow her to get a word in.

"Let me enlighten you on something. I do not support this decision and as long as you're attending an out-of-state college, I refuse to pay for it."

"Mary, calm down and let's talk with Rochelle about this privately. Today's her birthday. Let's not ruin it. She's been accepted to two great colleges and you're behaving like she just announced that she was dropping out of high school. Let's just enjoy our evening and work this out tomorrow," my father said.

God knew I couldn't stand my father's guts, but I was happy that he intervened. My mother was acting selfish and overbearing.

It was a side of her that I'd never seen before. In fact, the only time I'd ever seen her get this upset was when someone fucked up her money.

Rochelle slammed her glass down, nearly shattering it into pieces. "Thank you, Daddy but we're not having this conversation later. I want to discuss this right now so everyone could hear how my own mother plans to stand in the way of a great opportunity for me."

"Fine, let's talk about it. I don't have nothing to hide. I repeat, I'm not paying for shit If you leave Maryland, you're on your own," my mother fired back.

"I already have a partial scholarship that covers my tuition and room and board. All I need help with is my books and personal expenses. I can find a part-time job and take care of that. So I really don't need your support."

Jesus Christ! I wanted to get the hell up from that table and moonwalk my ass out the front door because I knew it was only going to go downhill from this point.

My mother forcefully moved her chair back and I swear on everything that I loved, I ducked, thinking she was about to start throwing plates, cups, and anything else within her reach. She didn't get physical, but she did get petty. "Well, let's see who's going to sign off on that paperwork and those documents you'll need your parents to sign. I'm not signing them and your father's not going to sign shit either."

Rochelle and I both looked at our father and he simply shook his head and looked away. He didn't feel like getting into it with my mother. At one point, it even sounded like Aunt Pam was about to speak up but as soon as she parted her whoring lips, I gave her a dirty 'bitch, I wish you would' look that made her close her trap as fast as she opened it.

From that point on, things got out of control as Rochelle and my mother argued. Then finally, my father spoke up, once again on Rochelle's behalf, but that made matters worse. My mother wasn't backing down for nobody, and although she was typically passive to my father, she gave him a piece of her mind as well. At first, I tried to stay neutral, however, I saw the pain in my sister's eyes, looking ultimately crushed, so I did what came natural to me.

"Rochelle, I'll give you the money for your books and expenses. Just let me know when you need it and I'll put it into your account." The words came out of my mouth faster than the actual thought.

Oh my goodness, what made me open up my big mouth? My mother's anger turned from Rochelle and fell straight into my lap.

With a bolt of fire in her eyes she said, "I should have planned my motherfucking dinner without you. It's not like you being here today has made a big difference. You're the one who put these thoughts into your sister's head and now she wants to move out and leave, me too. This is all your fucking fault."

I couldn't believe it. She was really putting the blame on me? "How am I responsible for Rochelle wanting to go away to college?"

"It's all your fault. You act as if living in this house is so horrible and that's why Rochelle wants to leave now. Why don't you just go back to wherever you call home and stop trying to ruin mine!"

"Rochelle wants to go away to college and it's because of me? Wow! You got to be kidding me."

"I'm dead ass serious. Do I look like I'm fucking kidding? Why don't you just leave?" she screamed.

Those words turned the argument into something that changed the dynamics of our family forever. I thought this dispute was already out of control, but boy was I wrong.

I tried to explain my reasons for helping my sister. Rochelle jumped in and tried to explain to my mother that it wasn't my fault, but of course she didn't want to hear that. Instead, she began to verbally attack both Rochelle and me like we weren't her children. I mean, she was going in and calling us a bunch of ungrateful bitches. Then my father tried to calm her down and she went off on him, too. It was complete mayhem at the dinner table. Things especially intensified when Aunt Pam opened her mouth.

"Your parents know what's best for you, Rochelle. Rather than argue with your mother, you should sympathize with her. She loves you, that's why she's trying to hold onto every moment she has left with you."

I didn't remember what I was saying or to whom I was saying it to, but I remember cutting my thoughts short to address that whore. It was like someone had lit a match under my ass. I hopped out of my seat.

"Pam, you need to mind your fucking business. This does not concern you so do not say another word about being sympathetic to my mother." The nerve of this bitch. My hands were shacking.

Pam attempted to part her lips to say something, but she quickly succumbed to them urges. I was two seconds away from whipping her ass and she knew it. Most importantly, her little secret was two seconds away from being revealed, so she shut the fuck up. My mother, however, had a lot to say about that. She jumped to defend her sister the same way I was defending mine.

"Wait a minute, that's my sister you're talking to, little girl. Pam is a grown ass woman, not to mention she's your aunt. Have you lost your fucking mind?" my mother screamed. "Who do you think you are, Jamaica? You know what? This dinner is over and you have to go."

My blood pressure elevated so high, it almost shattered my brain. My mother was yelling and screaming all types of hurtful shit to me and putting me out of the house, while the whore who was fucking her husband got to stick around. This wasn't going to fly with me.

"You know what? I'm about to leave this house for the last time. I can't believe how you're talking to me right now. I've done nothing but love you and this is how you repay me? I'm never going to step foot back in this house, ever," I screamed, while trying my best to hold back the tears.

"Get the fuck out then," my mother screamed back. "You say you're not coming back here again? That's your damn business. I'm not kissing your ass anymore. If you don't want to come back here that's fine with me."

I took one good look at my mother to see if she was serious and she looked at me like I was a curse from her womb. I couldn't take the hurt anymore. I had to get away from this hell house.

"Good night everyone," I calmly stated as I made my way toward the front door. "Rochelle, this was your birthday, however, this was a very memorable evening for me. And thank you so much for revealing how you truly feel about me, Mommy. Let me remove my devilish presence from your sanctified house."

"Oh, just leave already," she replied. "I'm tired of kissing your ungrateful ass, and you know what, your father will no longer kiss your ass either. None of us will! Ever since you moved out, we have been praying and hoping you come back home. Every night I watch your father walk past your bedroom and get sad. All that stops tonight. Goodbye!"

That was it. I had the front door open and could have very well just walked through it, hopped in my car, and went home. However, the evil Jamaica shut that door and fed my ungrateful ass family some of my delicious homemade petty spaghetti.

"Well, Daddy doesn't have to kiss my ass because he's too busy kissing your sister's. Ask him how Aunt Pam's ass taste? Go on and ask him," I insisted.

I had everyone's attention now. You could tell my mother was trying to comprehend what I just dropped in her lap. Her fucking eyes squinted so hard she could have changed her name to Ching Mang Ling. I didn't want her to think too hard, so I spelled it out for her.

"Yes, ma'am. Your husband, the piece of shit nigga you keep defending, is fucking your baby sister, the slut bucket who's sitting over there damn near peeing on herself right about now. You wonder why I moved out. You wonder why I have a nasty attitude toward your *husssband* and your *sisssssster*? It's because I caught them fucking in your bed. But wait, I guess that's my fault, too. So, should I apologize for that?"

The entire house became silent. Everyone, including me, needed time to process my words. Once I threw the truth out into the universe, a part of me wished that I hadn't, but the other part said fuck it; she needed to know what was going on.

Aunt Pam burst into tears and my father simply held his pathetic head down. They didn't even try to deny my accusations.

"You caught your father and who having sex in my bed?"

I looked at my mother and shook my head. She needed to speak with her husband and her sister. Rather than answering her question, I looked at my father and aunt. Of course they remained silent and so did I.

"Somebody better say something," my mother demanded. "Delroy... Pam... What the hell is she talking about?"

After an awkward pause, Aunt Pam finally attempted to explain herself. "Oh God, I'm so sorry, Mary. Please forgive me. I swear I didn't mean to hurt you. I was lonely and vulnerable and

Delroy showed me some comfort. I guess we went too far and I've been regretting it ever since."

My mother's lips moved but nothing came out of her mouth. She was trying to speak, but her emotions clogged the words. Even Rochelle sat stunned.

Finally, my father got the courage to speak up. "Mary, please let's talk about this privately. I can explain everything, honey. Just hear me out for a…"

Smash!

Before he could finish his sentence, a crystal vase went flying toward him, missing his head by an inch. It hit the wall and shattered. My mother picked up another vase and this time, she threw it directly at Aunt Pam. She hit the target. The vase landed in her chest. The impact was so powerful, it knocked her down to the ground.

"What the fuck could you explain to me? You really think you cwaan bloodclat explain anything to me? How could you possibly explain that you, my husband, took your rotten, dutty dick and stick it inna mi sista nasty stinking pussy," my mother screamed in her Jamaican dialect, as she punched the wall. "This is who you choose to cheat on me with this time around? My fucking little sister? *Me ah go kill de both of you.*" My mother dashed into the kitchen, grabbed one of her biggest knives, and rushed down on the closest victim, which was Aunt Pam.

I wanted the bitch dead myself, but I didn't want my mother to go to prison, so I ran over and wrestled the knife out of her hand. I pinned her down to the ground, which wasn't an easy task. Aunt Pam realized how serious my mother was so she began crying and screaming for dear life.

"Mommy, please calm down. No one wants to see these two get what they deserve more than me, but this is not the way. Don't allow them to ruin your life. The best thing you can do is to leave them alone and let life deal with them. Please let the knife go," I pleaded.

My mother didn't budge; she gripped the knife even tighter.

"Mommy, let go. They're not worth it." It took about five minutes, which felt like five hours. I repeatedly reminded her about the possible consequences, before she loosened her grip.

Rochelle took the knife out of her hand.

Aunt Pam fell to her knees. "Mary, please, please forgive me. I'm so sorry. I swear, I didn't mean to hurt you."

Rochelle yanked Aunt Pam up from the ground. "Bitch, get out of this house before I kill you myself. I can't believe you did this to my mother. I confided in you when I found out that Daddy was cheating on Mommy. I came to you for advice and you were sleeping with him all along. Get the fuck out of my house now," Rochelle screamed so loud it echoed throughout the house, as she opened the front door for Aunt Pam.

"Yes, bitch, it's time for you to go," I added as I grabbed my aunt by her arm, and escorted her through the door. "Leave while you still have a choice."

Aunt Pam shamefully walked through the front door with a face full of crocodile tears. My mother wasn't buying that crying shit and neither was I. She wasn't sorry for what she did. She was only sorry she got caught.

With a tight grip around her arm, I leaned in and whispered, "This isn't over. You will see me later." I pushed the bitch through the door and slammed it behind her.

My mother sat on the steps crying in disbelief, while my father stood across the room, tearfully shaking his head. Rochelle and I sat with my mother and tried to console her, but there was nothing we could have said to make the situation hurt any less.

"Please hear me out, Mary. I swear, I will do anything to make this right. Just talk to me and tell me what I need to do," my father pleaded.

Moments later, my mother wiped the tears from her eyes, walked over to my father. "Delroy, you said you would do anything to make this right."

"Yes! Mary, I promise I will do anything," my father answered.

"I want you to stay the hell away from me. I'm going to leave this house for two days and when I come back, have all your shit out of here."

My father wasn't expecting that response. This was not the first time he cheated and got caught. The difference was this time, he went too far and wasn't going to be able to buy my mother's forgiveness with a Chanel bag or Versace pumps like he normally did.

My mother walked over to Rochelle and me and kissed us on our foreheads. "I'll call you both within a day or two and tell you where I'm staying. I need some time to myself right now, so please respect my space and don't try to stop me from leaving."

"Are you sure you want to be alone? You can come stay with me," I offered.

"I'll be fine, honey. You have nothing to worry about," she assured me.

My mother went upstairs, packed a small bag, kissed me and Rochelle once again, and walked out of the house without telling us where she was going. As much as I wanted to follow her, I respected her wishes.

Rochelle wanted to talk, and I knew she had a million questions. However, I wasn't in the mood, not to mention, I didn't want to be in the same house with my father, so I left shortly after my mother.

The ride to my house was emotional as hell. I didn't expect the night to end the way it had but that was the story of my life. I'd grown accustomed to expecting the unexpected. On a brighter note, I no longer had to walk around with the burden of my father and aunt's nasty secret weighing my shoulders down, and could focus on tying up loose strings on my end. By loose strings I meant Deshawn, Myesha, and maybe Rock. Once I get them squared away, I could focus on stacking my paper and getting my family back in order.

CHAPTER 15

"Mission Payback"

woke up with a serious headache but I had business to take care of. As much as I dreaded dialing this bitch's number, I had to call Myesha to let her know about the sale I had booked with a new client for this afternoon. Also, Ghee was scheduled to come through with some business affiliates later, so the house would be locked down again. Although my mind had been on my mother since last night, I had to concentrate on my business.

I called and Myesha's phone went straight to voicemail. I called back two more times before some strange woman answered sounding young, dumb, and filled with cum. "Hello. You've reach Myesha's hotbox. This is her personal assistant. How may I direct your call?"

"Who is this?" I asked, annoyed. I hated it when someone picked up another person's phone and played games.

"Who is this?" the person yelled in my ear. "You called my manager's phone. Nobody called your ass so we'll do all the questioning. Like I asked the first time, how may I direct your call?" The person started to snicker and I heard giggling in the background, which made me know that I was on speakerphone.

A couple seconds later, Myesha came on the line, still giggling. "Yes, Jamaica, what's up?" she casually asked as if some chick didn't just answer her phone, playing games with me.

"Look, tell that bitch I'm in no mood to play games. I'm calling to discuss business."

"Jamaica, chill out. That's Nina's sister, Halley. She was playing with you. It's not that serious, love."

It's not that serious, love!

When did Myesha start talking like that? Money had changed this hoe completely. Now she was not only hanging out with Nina, but also hanging out with her sister. Something had to be done about this.

"Look, a client is coming to the house today, and Ghee is locking the house down tonight. I'll text you the information, but be sure to erase it once you read it." I couldn't sit on the phone with the bitch any longer. I needed to stay focused to handle my business, and entertaining these hoes today would only distract me.

As I was hanging up, I overheard the girl who answered saying, "Come on, Easha. Let's go make this money real quick."

Then I heard "Shhhh," as if someone was shushing her to be quiet.

"What money are you going to make real quick?" I asked. Myesha never answered.

Instead she hung up knowing she heard me.

I redialed her number, but she didn't answer. I called back until my fingertips became numb, but she never picked up. As a matter of fact, she began sending me to voicemail. Now getting smart with me was one thing, however, fucking with my money was another. I wasn't at the Las Chicas' house as I should have been, but I was supposed to be the only one booking clients. I made that perfectly clear from day one. If the girls were using the house or the Las Chicas name to make side money, I wanted my share and if I found out that they were doing otherwise, there was going to be hell to pay.

I threw on some clothes and my tennis shoes and headed out the door to confront Myesha and whoever, when my phone rang.

I looked down thinking it was her dumb ass calling back, but it was my sister. I'd been expecting this phone call all morning.

"Jamaica," Rochelle began as soon as I picked up, "I couldn't sleep last night. How did you live with that secret for so long without going crazy? Daddy has done some foul shit, but this is the worst."

"It was hard, but I had to hold it inside until the right time. Your birthday dinner wasn't the right time, but it just came out under the circumstances. I'm happy it's all laid out on the table so Mommy has to make a decision. Is she going to finally walk away from this unstable marriage or will she continue to stay with him for the money?"

"I guess we all have to wait and see. I've seen her upset before, but never to the extent that she was last night."

"I agree. She was furious."

"So, tell me everything that went down and don't hold out on me," Rochelle insisted. "If you can handle it, so can I."

I really didn't want to tell her. God knew I wished I didn't know myself. I was haunted by the thought of my father sleeping with my aunt, and I wouldn't wish this type of pain on anyone, much less my sister. But she was an adult, and I had to start treating her like one.

"Okay, well one day I came home early…" I explained how I found our father in bed with our aunt. We talked for hours, discussing issues we used to avoid. Rochelle told me some dirt on my father I never knew.

She told me about the women she'd overhead him talking to on the phone when our mother was at work, and even found hotel receipts in his gym bag when she borrowed his yoga mat one day. She went on to tell me, "Girl, Daddy even stooped as low as paying for pussy from real prostitutes."

That one caught me off guard. I knew my father was out in the streets doing dirt, but buying prostitutes was something I didn't think even he would stoop to.

"Daddy's screwing prostitutes? I don't believe that one, sis. Daddy is a freak, but he got too much integrity for that. Besides, he got women throwing ass at him all day long. He's not going to pay for something he can get for free."

"Well, he did," Rochelle insisted. "You're thinking about downtown hookers on the strip of Baltimore Street. I'm talking about something totally different. I don't know if you've heard about these bitches who go by the name Las Chicas or some Spanish shit like that. They're some high priced whores who surfaced recently. These girls are not your average street corner prostitutes, from what I hear. They live lavish and got mad money. Men are paying them as much as five thousand for sex."

As Rochelle continued to ramble about these *Las Chicas* prostitutes, I blacked out for a moment. No, I didn't physically pass out, but I mentally checked out. No way did I hear my sister correctly. My father paid the Las Chicas girls for sex?

"I don't mean to cut you off, but why are you linking Daddy with them Las Chicas girls? I heard about them, too, but they don't run in Daddy's circle so how would he have linked up with them?"

"Well you know my homeboy, Ronnie's father works with Daddy at the dealership. Ronnie told me his father saw three of the Las Chicas girls having a private meeting with Daddy in his office."

"But that doesn't mean he paid them for sex. Maybe they were buying a car or something." I was trying to come up with excuses because there had to be some explanation. Myesha said she got her car from my father so maybe that was why they were linking him to Las Chicas.

"Ronnie's father said when they were leaving, he overheard them bragging about making five thousand a piece, and one of the girls got on the phone, called someone and said, 'Thanks for the plug, girl. You were right. He was an easy sale."

I could actually smell the fumes coming out of my ears. That was how livid I was. So they were doing side jobs, just as I suspected, and I could bet Myesha sent them in my father's direction. She knew his weakness and knew it would be an easy sell.

Enraged was the only word I could use to describe how I felt. I couldn't talk and I didn't want to hear another word from my sister. I didn't want to hear or see anyone. I just needed to lay down until my migraine faded away.

"Rochelle, I have to call you back, okay? I'll talk to you later." I didn't wait for a response. I hung up, turned my ringer off, and went to sleep. No exaggerating, I literally went the fuck to sleep.

I woke up two and a half hours later feeling a bit vulnerable. I was helpless to point where I felt the need to be held, and the only arms I wanted around me were Rock's. As much as we argued, I knew that he was always there for me and would always have my back when I needed him. Hey, it was the nature of being human. It was the nature of being a woman. It was the nature of running to your comfort zone when there was nowhere else to run.

I took a deep breath and dialed Rock's number and just as I anticipated, Rock picked up on the first ring.

"Hello," he answered, sounding unbothered. Men were so phony when it came to showing their true feelings. Rock knew damn well he was happier than RuPaul in a wig store to hear my voice, but he had to put on this act to prove that he was over me. Honestly, he didn't have to do all of that because I was the one crawling back. He'd won the war, yet he was still in battle mode.

"Did you really mean it when you said you weren't going to call me anymore and that you were moving on with your life without me?" I sadly asked, as I laid down the bait to reel him in with a good old lie.

"I don't make idle threats, Jamaica. If I said it, I meant it."

"You claim to love me so much, yet it's so easy to leave me alone. I knew you were no different from the other dudes. That was why I tested you and you failed with flying colors."

"You tested me?" Rock asked. "I don't hear from you in God knows when and today you call talking about some fucking test like I'm a little ass boy? Shorty, you got me all the way fucked up."

Wait, this was not how the conversation was supposed to go, but he wasn't falling for the bullshit. I had to go to plan B.

"Okay, let me be honest with you. Baby, I really like you a lot. I'm just dealing with some issues that I plan to take care of by the end of the month. I need you to support me and not give up on our relationship," I pleaded.

I was being honest, speaking from the heart. However, in the process of being honest, I had to remind Rock of the part he played in all of this. "Baby, you're no saint yourself. In the beginning, you gave me an ultimatum. 'Keep this strictly fun, or I'm going to run'. Those were your exact words. You preached over and over that you weren't looking for a girlfriend and if I planned on catching feelings, I needed to get a grip. All I've been doing is following *your* orders so please don't punish me for that." For some reason, I became emotional and started to cry, not fake cry, but really crying. I guess I did have strong feelings for Rock. Maybe, just maybe, I did love him.

"Look, I never treated you like…"

"No," I interjected. "Hear me out. When I met you, you were just starting to see some real money coming in, so you were feeling yourself. I opened up to you and told you about my situation with Deshawn, and you explained to me you were no rebound type of dude, so if I was looking for someone to save me, you weren't that guy. At the time, I accepted that because I was reluctant to jump into a new relationship myself, not to mention I had trust issues. Now years later, you catch feelings and get upset because I did exactly what you asked me to do. That's not cool at all."

Crickets!

Rock had nothing to say after that because he knew I was telling the truth.

For a minute, the line was silent. I had to say hello to check if he was still there. "Look," he began, "when I reached out to you the other day it was for a reason. I needed to know if this relationship was going somewhere because I sort of met someone and things were getting serious with her, too."

What the hell? Did this bitch ass nigga wait until I spilled my guts to tell him to tell me he's fucking with someone else…. Already?

"Wait a minute. Meeting some random bitch and kicking it is one thing, but what do you mean by things were getting serious? Who is this bitch and where did you meet her?"

"These questions are irrelevant because it's done. I gave you the opportunity to be with me and you chose to do whatever it is that you're doing. She's no one you know. She's a registered nurse, who works at nights, which fits perfectly into my world. She don't want or need anything from me but love. We've been kicking it and I actually like her. I like her so much that I proposed to her two days ago and she accepted. It's a bit fast, but I'm willing to take a chance with her."

POWWWW! About thirty bullets shot through my chest. This nigga sat on the phone as I poured my heart out, just to have him tell me he proposed to some random ass bitch he just met. He fucked me for years, but met this bitch and put a ring on her finger within months.

"Wow! Engaged, huh? That was quite easy for her. You made me work for your heart and you hand it over to another woman. Well, I wish you both the happiness you never allowed me to get. Have a great life and God bless you and your significant other."

I disconnected our call and just stared at the wall for hours. I felt betrayed. The sad part was I was starting to get used to the feeling of betrayal, which said a lot about my life. Rock's engagement was just what I needed to jumpstart mission payback.

Deshawn, my father, Aunt Pam, Myesha, and now Rock; god damn my shit list was longer than the New Jersey Turnpike, however, if it was the last thing that I did, I would even the score with every one of them, starting with Little Miss Sunshine.

Rather than drown in my sorrows, I decided to fight. People were smiling in my face and stabbing me behind my back so I needed to do the same. The greatest way to fuck someone over was to do it when they least expected it. For years, Myesha had sat in my face playing the loyal best friend role, when all along she was my biggest enemy. That was the route I needed to take.

I called my dear old pal Myesha to check on some business matters. As usual, I had to dial her number a million times before she picked up, but when she finally did, I didn't speak to her dry and short as I'd been doing these past weeks. I spoke to her in the most pleasant and fake way that I knew.

"Hey, Myesha I wanted to swing by and pick up the money from last night," I stated. I was so consumed with the drama at my parents' house last night that I never made it to the Las Chicas house to collect my money in the morning as I normally did..

"Ummm...yeah... ummmm well, I'm at the house right now if you want to stop by."

Okay, I'll call you when I'm close. Thanks for holding things down. See you soon."

"Ummm… ummm…when you get here, we need to have a talk," Myesha suggested.

"About what?" I inquired.

"Well, I was hoping we could talk about this whole childish feud between you and me. I don't like how things went down. You're my best friend and I know you like a book. You miss me just as much as I miss you. I could hear it in your voice."

Wow, it was super easy to con this idiot. That was why her ex-boyfriend was able to get over on her stupid ass. One cordial conversation, and now I had her right where I wanted her.

"Myesha, you know that I love you, too. I've been down with you like a car with four flat tires. I've always had your back. So yes, naturally I was hurt by how close you became with Nina. It felt like you replaced me and was being loyal to her and disloyal to me. It really hurt my feelings." I spoke in a soft tone to make her think I was crying. I put a working on her pathetic ass. She fell right into my trap.

"Jamaica, hurry up and come over here so we can talk this out face to face. Maybe we can grab a bite to eat and have a drink or two for lunch. I miss you so much and had wanted to reach out to you but didn't out of fear of rejection. You know how evil your crazy ass can get when you're mad at someone." She snickered at her own joke, but little did she know, she was right on target.

I snickered right along with her dumb ass because the thought of the joke being made on her made the moment even more enjoyable. "I can't tell you how much it means to have you back in my life. I don't know how the universe made it work, and I have no intensions on trying to figure it out. All I know is my sister is back," Myesha proclaimed.

"You can say that again," I cosigned. "We are a dynamic duo. Like Ne-Yo said, 'I'm a movement by myself but I'm a force when we're together.'"

"Yes indeed, sis. You make me better. You make me better," Myesha sang. I joined in and sang with her until we both laughed. "Girl, hurry up and get over here. We have some catching up to do. A lot of stuff have been going down behind the scenes of Las Chicas, girl."

Bingo. That was exactly what I needed to hear. I grabbed my keys and purse off the table and headed out the door.

With my cell phone pressed to my ear, I said, "I miss you, too, and you know with this crazy life of mine I always have some news to share. See you soon, best friend."

"Okay, bestie. I love you. Please drive safe."

I hit the end button and gave my phone the middle finger. I didn't even respond to her last statement. Girl bye with all that phony shit and while you're at it, fuck you! This bitch was literally stealing money from me and smiling in my face. Then she brought my father into our beef and violated my entire family. I sure hoped Little Miss Sunshine was suited and booted because the games had just begun!

CHAPTER 16

Let the Games Begin

pulled into the Las Chicas driveway and saw Myesha's luxurious ride parked outside. Flashbacks of our argument replayed in my head. Most importantly, I remembered that the bitch was rocking the Gucci pumps. Out of everything that bitch did to me, running out and buying those pumps behind my back hurt the most. If I didn't get her little prissy ass back for anything else, she was going to feel the wrath for purchasing those pumps.

Although we just had a civilized conversation and said our fraudulent apologies, I could tell Myesha was still a tad bit apprehensive. I knew her well enough to know she was nervous as shit. She knew me well enough to know she needed to proceed with caution.

I quickly defused the situation by giving her the biggest hug I had ever given any human being in my entire life. She smiled and hugged me back, falling for the ookie doke.

"Where's my damn money," I joked, in attempt to keep things normal.

"Your money? I thought this was our money," Myesha replied.

"You know your money is my money and vice versa, girl. So, when I ask where's my money that's just like me asking where's our money," I assured her.

She handed over the cash and I counted it. I took my cut and handed back over the rest for her to distribute.

"I was just about to watch TV to kill time. You staying here or you're leaving back out," Myesha asked.

"I don't have any plan, but I also don't feel like being cooped up in the house. Let's have lunch and a cocktail or two," I suggested.

"I'm always down for a good meal and a nice drink. Let's roll," Myesha replied.

We grabbed our pocketbooks and headed out the door. As we approached my car, I stopped. "How about giving me a ride in that shining new car of yours."

"Okay, girl." Myesha took out her remote key pad and handed it to me. "Why don't you drive?"

"Sure." I took the key from her and smiled, but as soon as her back was turned, that smile turned upside down. I opened the door and was hit with the new car scent that I loved so much.

The inside of her ride was decked the fuck out. It had a sunroof, leather interior, voice-activated navigational system, reclining seats, hands-free Bluetooth interface, TVs in the headrests, and some more shit. Myesha showed me every feature like she was a damn sales representative. I knew she was showing off, but as bad as my blood was boiling, I continued to play the game. "Very nice," I complimented with much envy in my heart. "This had to cost you a couple of pennies."

"It did, but when you work hard, you should play harder," she replied.

"I hear that. I feel like I'm driving one of the Jetson's cars. You got all the latest features." I was being super extra, but she was playing right into my hands.

Myesha snickered. "You know you can borrow this anytime you want, girl."

"I'm going to hold you to that," I replied, knowing that shit would never happen in this lifetime. I would rather ride the bus. "So, where do you want to go to eat?" I asked, changing the subject.

"I'm in the mood for some shrimp and grits. How about Stone Cove."

"Oh I love that spot, too. Let's go." I jumped on the highway and headed to Owings Mills.

During our ride over, Myesha filled me in on everything that had been going on in her life.

"Jamaica, I've been able to save a lot of money thanks to you and your brilliant idea of starting this business. I saved so much that I was able to sign my mother into a rehab center last week, a real exclusive upscale one in Georgetown. My little sister's still living with my aunt, but I enrolled her in a private school, so she's good, too."

"Myesha, I'm so happy to hear that. I really hope your mom gets herself together because I still remember how fierce she was back in the day before your father died." Although I'd been gaming Myesha, I was actually happy to hear about Mrs. Kendra and her little sister because I loved them both.

"Guess what else, Jamaica?" Myesha asked.

"What?" I replied.

"I moved out of my parents' house and have an apartment of my own. I'm still paying all the bills for my mother, but I needed to get out of that toxic environment." What? When did she find time to pull this one behind my back? How much more information was this bitch withholding from me? "I wanted to tell you so bad when I first signed the lease but we weren't on good terms. I thought it would be best to wait until we were speaking again."

So, she had a new car and a new house. She checked her mother into some fancy rehab and enrolled her sister into a private school. I knew how much Las Chicas was bringing in, and from my calculations, Myesha shouldn't be able to afford all of this so quickly. My suspicions were on high alert, however, I kept my game face on while Myesha unraveled the rope that would eventually be used to hang her.

Myesha talked my ears off as we drove. She raved over how much her life had changed for the better and even enlightened me on how things had been on the up and up with the other ladies. I smiled, listened, and put on my best acting face, all while plotting their demises. I allowed her to yap away until I pulled into the parking lot. That was when I took control of the conversation to initiate mission payback.

"Myesha, I thought about all that went down between us. You may think it didn't bother me but it really did. We don't need to argue over money again, because what's mine is yours and what's yours is mine. We're both equal partners of Las Chicas but right now everything is in my name. I want to change that to make you feel more secure in your position so that we never have this misunderstanding again."

"What you do mean by that?" Myesha asked, as she leaned forward to give me her undivided attention.

"Well, right now I'm on a month-to-month lease with Brandon. I called him before I came over here today and told him to change the lease into your name. Also, I plan to put all the utility bills into your name, too. I'm still going to make the payments just as I've been doing. This way, you know that I could never kick you out of Las Chicas nor make any major decisions without you. I'm going to hand over the main cell phone and house keys to you, also. I know you have your own copy, but you can give one to Nina. She worked hard to build this empire with us so she should have some ownership as well."

Myesha's face lit up brighter than Rockefeller Center. She didn't ask who, what, when, where, nor why. All she heard was ching- ching and she was sold. "Are you serious, Jamaica? You know you don't have to do this to prove anything to me. I mean, I'm happy you're doing it, but I want you to know you don't have to on my account."

"I know, but I want to," I assured her. "If I don't do this, I will never forgive myself for treating you guys the way I did. Plus, I'm trying to work on some other business moves for us, so I need time to myself. A good businesswoman must be a visionary for the company and I can't do that by sitting up in the house. I trust you and Nina to hold Las Chicas down even when I'm not there. Of course, I still want my cut," I replied.

"I will handle all the money coming in and out of the house and make sure your cut is always secured. Are you sure you want to sign over everything to me?"

"I've never been so sure of anything in my life. It's time for you to get your shine on. I need this break from Las Chicas."

"Is there anything I can do to help?" Myesha asked. Although I knew she was being a two-faced liar right now and had no intension of actually helping me, I could really use her help.

"As a matter of fact, there is something you can do, but we'll talk about that later. Right now, I'm ready to eat so let's go get our grub on." I removed the key from the ignition and exited the car.

Myesha and I dined, drank wine, and swapped gossip. Actually, she did the majority of the talking while I took it all in.

We ate every drop of our food and ordered some to go. After our brunch date, we made plans to meet up the next morning so that I could see her new apartment and sign over the paperwork for Las Chicas to her and Nina and then, she dropped me off to my car and I headed home to chill for the remainder of the day.

After showering and getting ready for bed, I made one important phone call to a very special friend.

"Hello, Jamaica." Brandon answered. "What's up?"

"Hello, Brandon. Nothing's up. Well, actually something is up. I need you to do me a huge favor?"

"A huge favor," he repeated. "I thought I made myself clear when I said we can only have a professional relationship. Tenants typically don't call their landlords asking for favors," Brandon said.

"Look, I'm not calling to borrow money or anything like that. I just need you to sign over my lease to my friend, Myesha Thompson because she's taking over the house. I can give you all of her information right now so the paperwork can be ready for her to sign tomorrow morning when we meet with you."

"What? I don't even know this Myesha person, not to mention our lease is a legal agreement between you and me and no one else. Furthermore, I have something to do in the morning," Brandon stated.

"Myesha is my best friend and as far as you meeting with me tomorrow morning, it would be wise of you to be on time."

Brandon snickered in a cocky manner. "And if I don't?"

I began texting photos to his phone; you know the ones of us getting down and dirty when we first met.

"Well, if you don't show up on time tomorrow these photos will be sent to your wife, who by the way, you failed to tell me about until you wasted my time tickling me with that little ass dick of yours. One minute you said you two were heading toward getting a divorce and in the same breath you said you're a happily married man."

"Bitch, you kept those pictures?" Brandon furiously asked.

"I sure did because I knew they would come in handy one day. And you might want to censor that bitch word when referring to me," I warned.

"Why are you doing this? I rented you a house when you were in need. I don't pop up and do random checks at the house. I pretty much allow you to do you. And as far as us sleeping together, you came onto me and I had a moment of weakness, and now you're using it against me and blackmailing me?" Brandon, who was cocky before, became humbled and started to beg like a little bitch. My beef wasn't with him so I tried to reason with him so that he could give me what I needed, and be on his way.

"Look, I'm not trying to mess your situation up. I promise in a little while, you won't have to deal with me ever again. I will destroy every photo that I have of you and leave your life for good, but I need you to cooperate first. So, I need you to draft a lease dating back from the first day that I moved into this house and put Myesha Thompson's name on it. While you're at it, also add Nina Jones as a subtenant and destroy all paperwork with my name."

"What are you up to?" Brandon asked.

"I'm not up to anything, but I will be if you don't cooperate. I'm asking nicely for you to destroy the old lease and to create and backdate a new one with my friend's name. It's that simple. Remember, if you try to fuck me, I will fuck you and so will your wife when she divorces your cheating ass. I wouldn't want to see you lose all of your properties over some dumb shit that could have been avoided had you followed simple directions."

"I can't believe this is happening to me. I wish I never laid eyes on you," Brandon stated, with pain in his voice.

"I'm not trying to ruin your life or bring drama your way. Just come to this meeting tomorrow morning with the paperwork completed so the girls can sign it. I'll be out of your life very soon."

Brandon tried to say something, but I disconnected the call. I felt bad for putting him in this situation, but he was just a casualty of war.

The next morning, I woke up bright and early. Not only was this the day for me to give Myesha and Nina exactly what they'd been craving for, but I would also get to see where Myesha lay her head.

Around 6:30 am, I took a shower, cooked breakfast, and washed it down with a glass of Merlot. I knew that wine was not a typical breakfast drink, but I needed to clear my mind. By 7:30, I was on the phone with Myesha getting directions to her apartment, which to my surprise was directly around the corner from me. I was parked outside of her apartment within ten minutes. I walked up to her building and dialed her code on the phone pad.

"Who is it?" she asked over the intercom.

"It's me, Jamaica," I pleasantly answered.

"Okay, take the elevator and come up to the top floor. My door number is fifteen-fifteen."

I took the elevator up to the 15th floor and knocked the door. "Welcome to my pad," Myesha greeted after opening the door.

I crossed the threshold and was stunned. Goosebumps appeared on both of my arms. It was the weirdest shit ever. Myesha's entire apartment was damn near identical to mine. Our couches were the same style and color. She had the same flat screen TV and had placed it in the exact location of her living room as I did. From the oversized black and white paintings of Marilyn Monroe on the walls, to the overall décor of her bedroom and bathroom, Myesha copied the entire scheme of my condo. Although I felt like I was in some creepy ass Lifetime stalker movie, I remained composed so I wouldn't blow my cover. But it was hard. I was a fighter and I had a mouth on me that could cut a bitch cleaner than any knife. But when it came to this "Single White Female, Hand that Rocks the Cradle" type of obsession, I was a straight up punk. I wanted to run out of that damn apartment faster than I walked in.

"I love your place, Myesha and I absolutely love how you decorated everything. Your style is chic and very unique." I hoped she would mention that I influenced her.

"Thank you, Jamaica. You know if you want me to come over and decorate for you, I don't mind at all. When I'm at the mall or furniture shopping, I'll start looking around for you, too."

What the fuck? Okay, now Myesha had climbed to another level of crazy. Why would I need her to decorate for me, when she knew damn well she stole her entire concept from me? I wanted to slap sanity into this bitch. I couldn't believe she was sitting in my face ignoring the big fat copycatting elephant in the room.

"That'll be great, Esha. I'm going to hold you to that," I replied as I noticed her brand-new Tom Ford handbag with the matching sunshades sitting on the table with the price tags still attached. Now, either Myesha left them out for me to see, or she'd just purchased them and didn't have time to put them away. My bet was she purposely left them out for me.

Once again my head started pounding because the bag alone cost $3,000. All I could think about was the fact she more than likely used my share of Las Chicas to purchase it.

"Nice bag," I complimented. "I see you've been shopping without me. Let me see what else you got up in your closet. I may need to borrow something." I walked into the master bedroom. Little Miss Sunshine had now turned into a label whore. From one end of the closet to the other, I saw just about every designer hanging up with price tags still on them. There was a $2,000

Chanel dress, $1,500 Kate Spade pencil skirt, and a $900 Marc Jacob blazer. Myesha's closet looked like a mini Saks Fifth Avenue. The headache I had turned into a massive migraine.

As I scrolled through Myesha's closet admiring all her exquisite pieces, she walked up behind me. "I guess you see I've been doing a little shopping."

"Yes ma'am. It appears that you've been murdering the malls. I'm about to nickname you "The Mall Murderer.""

Myesha smiled. "The Mall Murderer? Yesssssssssss, I love the sound of that. I'm the Mall Murderer and you're the Boutique Bandit."

"Oh my goodness, that is so corny," I teased.

"Leave me alone. You know I am not the witty type," Myesha stated as she softly punched my shoulder. "Let's get out of here and get our day started. We have to stop at Starbucks first. I'm a moody bitch if I don't get my coffee in the morning."

"That's fine. I had two big ass cups at home, but there's always room for Starbucks," I replied.

Myesha and I grabbed our pocketbooks and headed out the door. At Starbucks, we ordered our drinks, and then made our way over to the Las Chicas house. Brandon's car was the first thing I saw when we pulled up. His ass knew better than to play with me.

"Who's that?" Myesha asked as she stared Brandon down.

"That's our landlord. The nigga with the pussy-sized dick."

"Damn, what a waste. He's too fine for his dick to be that small."

"I said the same thing when he whipped that tiny ass grape out of his boxers. I wanted to use my index finger to pluck that little motherfucker back inside."

Myesha laughed so hard tears rolled down her cheeks.

"I swear fucking that nigga was the worst experience of my life. I would never have sex with him again even if it was to save my damn life. I would actually take a bullet before taking his dick."

"Oh no, bitch. You didn't just say you would rather get shot than to sleep with him?" Myesha asked while laughing hysterically.

"That's exactly what I'm saying."

After getting all our jokes out of our systems, we exited the car.

"Hello, Brandon. Thanks for making it on such short notice. This is my best friend, Myesha. We're still waiting for one more person, but you're more than welcome to start working with Myesha signing the necessary documents until the other young lady arrives."

Nina pulled up just as we were heading into the house. She parked and rushed to meet up with us on the porch. "Sorry I'm late. There was a terrible accident on the interstate so I had to make a detour."

"No need to apologize. It's all good," I replied as we all stepped into the house and headed toward the kitchen. I pulled out a chair, sat down and everyone followed.

"Brandon, this is Nina."

Brandon nonchalantly looked over at her and nodded. I guessed that was his way of saying hello. It was apparent he had an attitude and I didn't want his mood to make the other ladies suspicious, so I got the ball in motion.

"Well, I don't want to waste anyone's time so let's get down to business. We're all here because I've made the decision to turn my lease over to you two ladies. I'm also putting the bills in your names as well, but I will continue to pay them. All I ask is that you both keep Las Chicas up and running."

"You know we got you," Nina replied.

"Yeah, we're going to hold everything down," Myesha added, sounding like Nina's hype man.

"I have another meeting to attend, so can we hurry this up?" Brandon asked as he cut into the conversation and took paperwork from his briefcase. "Here's the new lease with both of your names. All I need now are your signatures."

"No problem," Myesha replied, and without hesitation, both she and Nina retrieved pens from their pocketbooks and signed their lives away. Not one time did any of these fools stop to read over the lease or even question my motives. Greed overpowered their better judgment.

I remembered a time when Myesha would sit and think before making rash decisions; however, right about now, all she thought about was money. It was heartbreaking to see how a few thousand had changed her. I wondered how she would act if she was seeing some real money?

Within minutes the leases were signed, sealed, and delivered. Myesha and Nina handed their copies over to me, and I handed them to Brandon.

"Well, that's all I need from you two. I'll file them at my office and send copies to your emails once I get them notarized. Have a great day, ladies." Brandon got up from the table and headed out the door.

"Let me walk you to your car." I excused myself from the table and followed him. "I want to thank you for everything. You really helped me out in a major way and I sincerely appreciate you." I was being nice, but Brandon had his guard up like we were in a boxing ring.

"Jamaica, what are you up to?" he snapped. "Like seriously, what the fuck are you really up to?" Brandon pointed to the house and continued, "Those nitwits in there may be oblivious to your bullshit, but I'm not. I just hope whatever the fuck you're doing doesn't involve me. To be honest, I only showed up here this morning because you said if I did this, I wouldn't have to deal with you ever again, and I hope you keep your promise."

Brandon stormed off to his car. I walked over to him, looked deeply into his eyes, and said, "Brandon, I am a woman of my word. You can erase me from your memory. As a matter of fact, we have never met. If anyone questions you about me, simply say that you don't know me," I demanded. "Also, I need you to keep this conversation that we're having between us. You do that, and you will never have to worry about me again."

"That's it?" Brandon asked. "Keep this conversation between us and you're out of my life for good? No more threats about showing my wife the pictures?"

"Yes, that's it," I promised. "Don't tell anyone about this conversation, especially not Myesha and Nina."

"Consider it done. What about the photos?"

"What photos?" I asked. "Oh wait, you mean *those* photos. Well, if we've never met, how could I possible have any photos of you? Get it? If you open your mouth and let anyone know that you know me, then I'll be forced to show them exactly how we're acquainted."

Brandon gave me the all too familiar look that I'd been receiving from a lot of people lately. It was the stare of death. He reached into his briefcase, handed me the original lease, and said, "Well, I think it would be best if you destroyed this. I want you to have it so that you can't come back later and blame me for anything."

I took the old lease and ripped it into a million pieces. "Well, goodbye Brandon. It was a pleasure not knowing you and not doing business with you," I joked.

I laughed, however, Brandon wasn't a bit amused. He drove off without saying a word.

I watched his car until it vanished. I shook my head and said, "Another one bites the dust," under my breath. With my name finally off the lease and the original one destroyed, I could jump straight into the second part of my plan. I walked back into the house, and put on a Colgate smile for Myesha and Nina. Let the games begin!

CHAPTER 17

This is Chess...Not Checkers!

Myesha and Nina sat at the kitchen table arguing about two parties they were scheduled to attend tonight. Nina felt that she and Myesha should split the girls up and half should attend one party, while the other half attended the another. Myesha didn't like the idea of splitting up. She wanted everyone together to hit both parties.

"Look, if you want to split up, then Shanks is rolling with me," Myesha insisted.

"And why the hell does he automatically go with you? We need protection, too," Nina clapped back.

I laughed to myself because I literally had just given them ownership and they were arguing already.

I walked into the room with one finger in the air like a church usher excusing herself from the sanctuary. "Don't mind me," I stated. "I have some business to take care of, so I'll be in the office."

Their petty argument was so intense that neither of them even acknowledged my presence. They kept right on bickering.

I eased out of the room and headed to the office. I immediately got on the phone and cut ties with every company that had my name associated with Las Chicas. Within a half hour, I had our cell phones, Comcast cable, and gas and electric all scheduled for turnoffs. After making about a million phone calls and sitting on hold listening to elevator music for what seemed like eternity,

I finally separated myself from all of Las Chicas' affairs. I went back downstairs to fill the two airheads in on their next moves.

"Okay, so the lease has been turned over to you and I just called and requested all utility bills, including the cell phones turned off. This means unless you two quickly call them back and make preparations to cut them back on in your names, Las Chicas will be closed temporarily. Is this too much for you or do you need me to cancel those requests and keep them in my name until you feel comfortable enough to handle business on your own?" I asked, knowing damn well they weren't going for that shit. Once niggas got a tip of power, they wanted it all.

"No, we're fine," Nina quickly answered. "Come on, Myesha, let's go handle that right now so there won't be any hiccups. We can't afford to have Las Chicas closed even for a minute. That's like flushing thousands of dollars down the toilet."

Myesha and Nina began calling up companies and scheduling services to be restored in their names.

"Well ladies, hopefully this is a new start for us. You can fill the other ladies in on the changes that have been made so they're in the loop. While you two are handling business, I'm going to go ahead and clean the house so it's perfect for Ghee tonight."

The cleaning story was just a cover up so the ladies wouldn't become suspicious of me walking around the house, checking every nook and cranny, making sure there was nothing to link me to Las Chicas. I destroyed every receipt and paperwork with my name on it. I literally spent over two hours dusting, vacuuming, and destroying everything that could connect me to this house. By 4:00 pm, the only drop of evidence that could associate me with Las Chicas was my physical body itself. After cleaning, I loaded the trash bags into my trunk so I could dispose of them myself.

I stayed in the office for the remainder of the day just to make things look normal. I wanted to go home, chill out, and have a few glasses of wine, but this was a job that needed to be carried out strategically.

The rest of the ladies came to the house around 8:00 pm. Both events they were attending were in Washington, DC, so they had to hurry and hit the road early because the commute was at least forty-five minutes to an hour long.

Although I didn't want to see nor speak to any of them bitches, I knew I had to continue to act like I fucked with them. I went downstairs to say hi; however, they didn't hear me coming, which was evident in the side-conversation they were having. I didn't take it personally. I laughed at how stupid they were to always get caught.

"Her back was against the wall and she did exactly what I told y'all she was going to do. She crumbled and came crawling back to us," Myesha whispered. "She even signed over the lease and all the bills to me and Nina."

"Bitch, you lying," Samantha replied with a mischievous laughter. "So we don't have to deal with her ass at all? This is almost too perfect now."

Nina was on the sideline cosigning and bragging right along with Myesha, while the other girls laughed and clowned me for being pushed out of Las Chicas. Now, I understood the other hoes falling for this bullshit, but I couldn't believe how naive Myesha was being. She knew me well enough to know that a bunch of bitches, including her, could never make me crumble. But hey, as I said before, all she was hearing was ching-ching, so her mind was clouded.

I tiptoed back up the steps and made a great deal of noise coming back down. I strolled into the room and was affectionately welcomed with bright smiles from all the ladies.

"Hello," I greeted as I walked into the lion's den. I returned their fake smiles, and gave them all compliments. "Wow! You all look amazing. Las Chicas is going to be the life of the party tonight," I stated.

"They are going to shut shit down as usual," Myesha added. "Are you sure you don't want to join us? You and I could chill at the bar and have a few drinks while the ladies do their thing. You know, just like old times."

"I'm sorry but I have to pass. I have a hot date tonight and God knows I'm overdue for some good-good in my life," I lied.

"I know that's right," Samantha cheered. "Go on and get you some, girl. You work hard enough. It's about time for you to play hard, too."

"I hear you, girl," I replied, feeling super phony for even engaging in conversation with these fake ass broods.

"Okay, ladies I have to go. Remember, leave the party with every man asking about Las Chicas, but be sure not to book anyone for tonight because Ghee has locked the house down already. Be safe and watch each other's backs."

"Be safe on your date as well. I'll meet you sometime tomorrow to give you the money," Myesha replied.

I said my goodbyes to the other ladies and left.

I drove back to my condo feeling thirty pounds lighter. As much as I enjoyed racking up Las Chicas' money, it wasn't worth the burden and headache that it was causing me. I stopped at 7-Eleven and tossed the trash bags in their dumpster. With that last task completed, I went home, showered, and took my ass to sleep, feeling satisfied that my plans were coming along fine.

I was sitting in my living room, sipping a mimosa and enjoying a delightful breakfast the next morning when Myesha called. As much as I wanted to ignore the call, I had to keep the ball in motion. So I picked up and put on my best Oscar performance.

"What's up, sis?" I answered as I took a sip of my mimosa.

"Nothing much. I was calling to see what you were up to. We had a ball last night. The only thing missing was you."

"Trust me, it's not that I don't want to hang out with you guys. I really do, but I have so much to deal with right now. Let's not forget that Deshawn is out of jail and he's been making his presence known."

"Fuck Deshawn," Myesha screamed. "I'm so tired of his weak ass. Are you sure you can't call his parole officer and file a report for harassment? There has to be something we can do or someone who could help us deal with this bitch ass nigga."

Wow, once again Myesha was acting outside the norm. She was always the walk away, live to see another day, peacemaker type of broad, but now she was down for getting someone to deal with Deshawn. Although she sounded faker than a three-dollar bill, she was barking up the right tree and I had her right where I wanted her.

"It's funny you say that. I do have something planned for Deshawn, but I'm going to need your help. Next Saturday, I'm planning to shut the house down and lure him over. That's about all I can tell you right now, but I promise if we do this right, Deshawn will never be an issue for me."

There was moment of silence over the phone. I could almost hear Myesha's heart beating. She was just talking all that gang-gang shit; now that I said let's get it popping, it was crickets.

"You want to bring Deshawn to where we do our business? That sounds crazy, Jamaica. I'm down for doing just about anything with you, and you know that I have your back one-thousand percent, but this has to be one of the craziest plans you've ever cooked up. This seems more like a death wish than a plan."

"Myesha, you've questioned just about every plan I've had since we were in kindergarten. You even questioned Las Chicas, and now you have more money in your account than you can count. It's about time you to stop questioning me and trust me. I've never steered you wrong, and I don't ever plan to," I stated.

There was another awkward period of silence before Myesha sighed loudly. "I got your back. Let's finally get rid of this big mutant ass nigga for good."

"Okay, great. I'm going to call you later today to fill you in on the details," I advised. I was able to make Myesha feel secure by the time we got off the phone. It was important for me to keep her and the other girls focused enough to successfully carry out my retaliation against Deshawn, yet confused enough to successfully carry out my retaliation against them. Every move I made had to be carefully executed.

With my plans already in affect, I could now focus my attention on more important matters. Deshawn, Myesha, and them raggedy ass Las Chicas whores were one thing, however, dealing with people who I genuinely loved and cared about was another.

Since I'd spilled the beans about my father sleeping with Aunt Pam, I'd been trying my best to avoid the drama. I'd been in contact with my mother since then, however, we'd avoided speaking about the situation. The only thing we spoke about was her saying she was going to file for divorce. I hadn't spoken to my father at all, so I didn't know what kind of mind frame he was in. Dealing with this situation was much easier when it was still a secret.

I texted my parents telling them I needed to speak with them. My mother texted back and said she took the day off and was home. My father said he would be at work all day. I got dressed, headed out the door, and drove to Harford County to see my mother.

I pulled into my parents' driveway and took a deep breath. This used to be the house of joy and comfort for me, but it had turned into the house of horror and pain. My heart raced as I opened the front door and stepped inside. I didn't know what to expect. My mother could have had an Angelia Bassett "Waiting to Exhale" moment and cut off all her damn hair or burned all of Daddy's expensive suits in the front yard. My family had been extremely unpredictable, so I'd been handling our issues by praying for the best, while preparing for the worst.

"Jamaica, is that you?" Her soft mellow Jamaican accent resonated down the hallway.

"Yeah, Ma," I answered as I walked into her bedroom.

"Hey, baby. Give me hug," my mother said while giving me one of her infamous bearhugs. "It seems like I haven't seen you in years." To my surprise, she was in a cheerful mood. Had I found out my husband was cheating with my sister, I would be sitting in someone's jail cell or psych ward.

"Well, I see you're feeling and looking a lot better. You're practically glowing," I complimented.

My mother smiled. "Thank you, baby. I'm just finding myself and learning how to love me unconditionally. I could sit and be upset and lash out at the world, or I could use that negative energy to find positivity in my life. If you don't remember anything I tell you, remember this. In all you do, you have choices. You can make the choice to be happy or you can make the choice to be sad. I choose to be happy."

"I'm happy that you're happy. That's all I ever wanted for you. That's also the main reason why I didn't tell you about Daddy and Aunt Pam. I didn't want to see you cry, not even for a second. I hope you understand and can forgive me."

"I don't have to forgive you because you didn't do anything wrong. You're not responsible for your father or Pam's action.

You're not responsible for my actions either. I understand you tried to protect me. I would have probably done the same for you," my mother explained.

Hearing those words made me feel much better about where I stood with her because I honestly didn't have a clue. She could have hated me for keeping this secret, yet she took full responsibility. She knew my father was unfaithful. She'd known for years and ignored it.

"When we last spoke, you said you were going to file for divorce. Are you still going through with that, or do you need more time to think this over before making such a major decision?"

"I thought I made it perfectly clear this marriage was over. Didn't we talk about this the other night?" my mother asked as she looked at me like I had two heads on my shoulders.

"We did talk about it, but I wanted to make sure you thought this over completely. If you know for sure without a doubt there's no room for reconciliation, then by all means move on. However, if you still have love for Daddy, then maybe you should postpone this divorce and see if you guys can seek counseling."

I laid the pros and cons out on the table for my mother. I understood that she wanted this divorce because she was hurting right now; however, later down the road, this decision could kick her in the ass. So I got on her nerves a little bit by probing and asking a lot of questions she was trying to avoid, but it was for her own good.

"What about your sister? She's still living in the house you purchased for her and reaping the financial benefits of having her restaurant in your building. Why is she still around if you want Daddy gone? It takes two to tango and let me tell you, they were both tangoing."

"The only reason Pam is still in my building is because she signed a lease and if I evict her without probable cause she can sue me. As soon as her lease is up, I am not renewing it. As far as the house goes, I put everything in her name so I can't legally take it back. A gift is a gift in the United States. If this was Jamaica, I would have already had her out of the house and out of my building."

"I can get rid of Aunt Pam if you really want her gone. Just give me the word and she'll be out of your building and your house. I've already torture her once, believe me I can go it again," I stated.

"I don't need you to do anything. God is going to deal with your father and Pam in His own way. I don't want you involved anymore."

"Okay, Ma. As long as you understand that I don't want anything to do with Pam and don't want you changing your mind later down the road. Once a traitor, always a traitor!"

My mother and I spoke for a long time, which is something we'd been avoiding. I expressed how I felt about her allowing my father to cheat in the past and told her her choices were a part of their problems. She explained her motives for staying and said it had nothing to do with the money, but with keeping our family together. She said she stayed with him for me and Rochelle. I left feeling optimistic about her future. So, I hopped back in my car and headed over to visit my father.

The drive to his dealership was the longest I'd ever had in my life. I pulled into the parking lot and just stared at the building. So much had gone down between us. I really didn't know if our relationship would ever be repaired, but at least I could say I came here today to get closure. Although my nerves were on ten, I took a deep breath, calmed myself, and walked inside.

"Is my father in his office," I asked one of the salespersons.

"Yes, he just walked back."

"Thank you," I replied. His door was slightly open so I didn't have to knock. I just pushed it open and stepped inside.

At first my father didn't know what to do when he looked up and saw me. He stood up and started to walk over, but stopped suddenly. It was like he wanted to embrace me, but didn't know how. I decided to make the first move to make him feel more comfortable.

"Hello, Daddy. Thank you for seeing me today," I said.

"Hello, Jamaica," he replied as he stared into my eyes, probably trying to read me to see if my visit was sincere or not.

"How have you been?" I asked. I knew it was a stupid question, but that was the first thing that came to mind. I'd been angry with my father for so long I didn't know how to communicate with him without being confrontational. I was not mad at him anymore, but I didn't know how to feel around him.

"I'm hanging in there. It's not the life that I want but it is the life that I've been dealt. I want you to know that I love you, your sister, and your mother very much. I'm sorry for all the pain that I've caused, but I'm paying for it now. Your mother won't even answer the phone, and I think this time it's really over."

"I love you, too, Daddy. No matter what I've said or done, I do love you. That's why you hurt me. Only the ones you love could hurt you the most. Do you remember you told me that when I was mad at Myesha for befriending Kyra Blakes in elementary school?"

My father's eyes lit up as he smiled. "I can't believe you remember that. Kyra Blakes was that little girl that Myesha started to hang with at lunch. You would come home crying and upset. I had to explain that people are allowed to have more than one friend and your feelings are only hurt because you love her so much. Only the ones you love could hurt you the most, is what I said. It's nice to know that you were listening."

"I've always listened," I replied. "Life was much easier then. I was too young to understand the good from the bad. I'm grown now and damn sure know the difference. What you and Aunt Pam did was bad. Our lives are changed forever and it's nothing we can do about it."

"We can't change the past, but we can navigate the future. You're my baby girl, my first born. I love you more than life itself and I'm sorry for hurting you and putting you in that predicament. I would do anything in the world to make up for what I've done."

"Daddy, you had a lot of time to stop doing what you were doing, but you take it to the next level every time you get caught. It's like this is a game to you," I stated.

"You think I enjoy cheating on your mother? At first I was faithful to her, but all she ever cared about was the money. When I wanted to take romantic trips with her, she always used that opportunity to make drug connections and turn our trip into business. I came home from work many nights just wanting to hold your mother, but she was always too busy. For Mary, it was always about money, money, money, as if my love alone couldn't make her happy." Tears fell from my father's eyes, but he quickly wiped them away. I could see he was hurting deeply. "I loved your mother, that's why I worked my fingers to the bone to give her everything she wanted, but the problem was she wanted everything but me. So, I stopped reaching out to her and started filling the void in our marriage elsewhere."

This was the first time that I'd ever heard my father's side of story. I wished he would have opened up to me a long time ago. Maybe, just maybe, I would have handled the situation differently.

I spent the next forty-five minutes listening to my father telling stories that I'd never heard before. By the end of our visit, I felt compelled to let my father know that if he wanted to work on his marriage, he had to be quick.

"Daddy, I have to tell you something. Mommy got a lawyer and is in the process of filing for divorce. If you want to work things out, you have to do something and do it like yesterday."

"I figured she contacted her lawyer already, so I contacted mine as well. I know how your mother operates, and right now all she's worrying about is losing money, property, and investments. She's not worried about losing me. I will not fight her dirty because I take responsibility for the part that I played, however, I can't sit back and let her take everything from me because she needs to take responsibility, too. I'll try to reach out to her once more and if I can't, then it is what it is. I have to live with the consequences."

My father and I talked until we ran out of things to talk about. The topic of me extorting him never came up. I was happy about that because this was the first time I actually felt bad about taking the money from him.

Although the future of my family was still up in the air, I felt like I had a little piece of closure by speaking with my parents. With that task crossed off my list, I could now focus on the smaller issues I had going on in my life, like getting rid of Deshawn and paying back them ungrateful ass Las Chicas bitches.

I came home and laid in my bed for the remainder of the day, however, I didn't have the urge to sleep. So, I did something that was out of the norm; I logged onto my dry ass Instagram page that I hardly paid any attention to. I looked at pages of random famous people like Kim K and Rhianna to see what they were wearing and read some of the funny comments underneath their pictures. Then I went to Dance Hall King Chrissy's page because this guy always gave me life with his self-confidence and funny videos. Somehow, I stumbled upon a page of a party promoter in Baltimore. The page was filled with hundreds of people partying at random events in the DMV area. I didn't know if it was fate or the devil, but I ended up pulling up a picture of two people hugged up and boo-loving at a party. I clicked on the picture to enlarge it, because I had to see if my eyes were deceiving me. There before my two eyes were Rock and Nina, hugged up and kissing at a party.

I scrolled down some more and they were in more pictures. Rock, *my Rock*, and Nina were standing side by side like a happy fucking couple.

"What the fuck is going on," I blurted out.

Nina didn't even run in Rock's circle. She was not even his fucking type. How the hell did they hook up? Suddenly, it hit me like a bag of bricks. Was this the girl Rock told me about? Was this the nurse who worked at night? Did Nina steal my man from under my nose? This had to be some kind of mistake. There was no way Rock fell for a piece of trash like that.

Of course, my first instinct was to call him up and drop a dime on her, but I was no snitching type of chick, not to mention, telling on her would slow my money up. Besides, he called himself shitting on me for her. He was actually bragging about her career and how successful and established she was as a registered nurse. Karma alone would be payback enough when he found out the truth.

Then I wondered, was Myesha behind this? Did this bitch set Las Chicas hoes up on my man like she did with my father? At this point, it didn't even matter if she was involved or not. I wasn't taking this sitting down and if I had a drop of second thought about seeking revenge on them, it just went flying out the window. Everyone who crossed me was going to pay in the worst way.

CHAPTER 18

For Every Action... There's A Reaction."

called Myesha to meet up to collect my money. We agreed to meet at a cozy little bistro in Fells Point. I was waiting for her when she walked in rocking her oversized sunshades, printed t-shirt, and some body-hugging ripped jeans. Homegirl looked like a one of those paid models strolling the streets of New York City.

"Hey girl. I hope you weren't waiting long," she stated as I stood up and gave her a hug.

"No, I was just seated about ten minutes ago."

"Oh, that's good. I was burning rubber trying to get down here. For some reason, I've been sluggish all morning." Myesha sat down and the waitress came over to our table to take our orders.

I stared at Myesha as she placed her order and thoughts of strangling her ass played out in my head. Every time I tried to push the negative thoughts away, the photos of Nina and Rock popped up in my head and I would get angry all over again.

"So how does it feel to handle the business side of things?" I asked, after the waitress left our table.

"It's cool. I do see that it's a lot of work that I didn't notice before, so now I understand why you were always so tense, but for the most part, I think Nina and I are going to do just fine."

"There's no doubt in my mind you two got things covered. You were always the business-minded one who planned and thought things out. You were born to be your own boss," I stated, gassing

Myesha's head up and her dumb ass was falling for it. She sat, smiling, totally clueless that I was playing her like a fiddle.

"Trust me, we got this. All we need you to do is continue to cover the financial parts, and being available to step in if we need you," she replied.

"That won't be a problem," I assured her, as I steered the conversation in another direction. "Do you remember the favor I asked you? About Deshawn?"

Myesha nodded. "I sure do. You said you would get back to me with the rest of the details."

"Yeah, I didn't want to talk over the phone. I have a task for you. I want you to take the girls to Club Mansion tomorrow and make them lure Deshawn back to the house," I said, as I pulled out an old photograph of him. "Show the girls this picture so they know him. He always conducts business at that particular club, and is there almost every night between eleven and one-thirty. He keeps his car parked in the rear between the dumpster and the fire escape. Tell the ladies to get him white-boy wasted because he gets sidetracked when liquor is in his system. He's a fucking rocket scientist when he's sober, so please make sure he's drunk out of his mind," I explained.

Myesha was down. "You know our girls can get a man to do just about anything. I'll make sure they look extra sexy tomorrow to keep his mind occupied. That nigga won't know what hit him," she promised.

"One more thing. These girls cannot know that Deshawn's my ex. I don't want them to know my business. If they ask why they're targeting him, tell them it's a private matter that you'll explain later. Also, make sure that Deshawn does not see you because if he does, it's a wrap. I'll be at the house by the time you guys get home. Tell the girls to fuck the dog shit out of him and don't charge him at all."

Myesha looked at me like I was out of my mind. "Girl, you know these bitches ain't doing shit for free. They'll want their money for sure," she stated.

"Ghee is locking down the house tonight so take my share and split it among the ladies. As a matter of fact, pay Lashel and Kelisa for this job, and tell them to invite Deshawn back to the house again on Friday. If he questions why, tell them to act like they're super sprung over the dick and can't get enough of him."

I knew Deshawn very well and one thing I remembered about him was that he loved to feel like the man in charge. All these bitches had to do was show him a little attention and make him feel like a king. That special attention mixed with alcohol was enough to catch him slipping.

"What's going down on Friday when he comes back?" Myesha asked.

"After Lashel and Kelisa get him drunk and passed out, they can go home. Don't worry yourself, I have this all figured out. All I want him to do is come back to the house, sip on some liquor, and get comfortable."

I laid all the rules down for Myesha as we continued to eat. Thinking back on the photo of Nina and Rock, I had to do some investigating to see just how much Myesha knew about the situation.

"Hey, didn't you mentioned that Nina's dating some new guy on the serious tip? How's that going with her being missing almost every night," I probed.

"Yes girl," she answered as she busted out laughing, almost spitting out her juice. "She's dating this guy who thinks she's a registered nurse working the night shift at the GBMC hospital. The nigga hustles, so his time is always occupied anyway. At first, it was just a money thing for her, but she claims to really like him a lot now. He was dealing with some chick when they first met, but Nina said he cut the other bitch off for her, so now she's super sprung."

I wondered if Myesha could see the steam coming out of my ears. I wondered if she knew how close I was to stabbing her with my fork.

"So, they pretty serious?" I asked.

"I would say they are because they're engaged. Nina said she's going to stack up some bread and then lay off Las Chicas to settle down with him."

"So, you've never met this mystery man?" I asked.

Myesha took a deep breath, leaned toward me, and put her hand over my hand. "Jamaica, I know what you're thinking and you're completely wrong."

What the fuck? Why would she say that? Is this bitch on to me? "Nina did not meet this guy with Las Chicas. She met him through a mutual friend. Her cousin is dating his cousin or something like that."

"Girl, I didn't think anything like that," I replied, feeling relieved that she was barking up the wrong tree. "I'm just being nosey because my life is dry and boring right now. So, what's the dude's name?" I continued to probe.

Myesha stared out into space. "It's funny, his name never came up. She always calls him Boo or Boobie. I never even thought to ask his real name. I just know she wants to keep him as far away from Las Chicas as possible so he never finds out her real occupation. I mean, she's taking care of people but not the way he thinks she is."

"Oh my God. You're a mess," I replied as we laughed so hard the people sitting at the table next to us looked over like we were disturbing them.

After drilling Myesha, I felt comfortable in saying she didn't know that Rock was Nina's mystery guy. It didn't change my feelings toward her; in my mind, she's still guilty.

"Speaking of Nina, I wonder where she's at?" Myesha asked as she pulled out her cell phone. "She was supposed to call me this morning to let me know about some new girl who wanted to join Las Chicas."

"Wait, you're going to bring another girl on? Is that a wise decision? We don't even have enough rooms to accommodate all the girls we have now."

"That's true, but Nina and I were thinking maybe we could have an afternoon shift and a night shift. That way, we're consistently bringing in money and the girls don't have to spread themselves thin."

Once again, Myesha was proving that she lacked street smarts. The secret to this game wasn't quantity, it was about quality. Sooner or later, too many girls were going to lead to too many problems.

"I guess you have this all planned out. If you think that hiring more girls will be better for business, then go right along and do it," I encouraged.

Myesha smiled and continued to call Nina. As they spoke over the phone, I couldn't hear what Nina was saying, however, I sensed that Rock was there because Myesha said, "I knew there was a reason for you not calling me this morning. You're all booed up, huh?"

As Myesha and Nina joked around, my heart shattered. I felt like a fool because I had something special and I let it slip away. Yet, if it was so special, why didn't he fight harder to keep me? I hated the fact that Nina was in such as great space. She had money, a man, and joy in her life. Damn it, she had the life that I'd been longing for. Being the bitch that I was, I decided to play a little game with Rock, while fucking with Nina at the same damn time.

"Girl, hearing that Nina is all snuggled up with her man makes me want to go lay up under Rock. I'm about to set up a little date of my own," I whispered to Myesha. I dialed Rock's number and as expected, he sent me to voicemail. So, I did what any spiteful female would do; I pressed redial until my fingertip turned red.

Ring… Voicemail. Ring… Voicemail. Ring… Voicemail. I didn't expect him to pick up anyway, but I did expect Nina to see that someone was blowing his phone up.

My plan worked because as I continued to call, I overheard Myesha say, "Girl if his phone keeps ringing, then answer that shit. That's your man, and if you suspect something fowl is going down, don't be afraid to call his ass out on it."

I chuckled because within moments, I heard Nina screaming at Rock. She was super mad.

"Why is she yelling like that?" I whispered to Myesha.

She pulled the phone away from her face, covered the receiver, and whispered back, "Nina's boyfriend's phone keeps ringing and he's ignoring the calls. He just put the phone on silent so she's wilding out."

"Put your phone on speaker so I can hear too," I jokingly demanded.

Myesha put her phone on speaker and Nina was laying into Rock. "You're being disrespectful as hell right now. Why can't you answer the phone? Obviously, it's someone who really wants to speak to you because they keep calling back to fucking back. You know what, I'm about leave."

"I'm a grown ass man. I don't have to hide shit, and how the fuck am I disrespecting *you* by not answering *my* phone. Bitch, you're disrespecting me by invading my privacy. If you want to leave, then get the fuck out," Rock yelled back.

"Fuck you, then," Nina screamed.

"Fuck you, too and your friend on the phone who you're showing your ass off for."

Myesha and I busted out laughing. That was my baby handling his business and not taking any shit from no one.

"I'm about to hang up before he grabs the phone and starts cursing me out for no reason," Myesha stated as she disconnected the call while we continued to laugh our asses off.

Right before I called, Nina and Rock were happily cuddled up in bed. Now, they were beefing. Damn, I was good.

I drove back to my place after lunch and as expected, I received a phone call from Rock. I knew he was going to call. Of course, I picked up with an attitude. "So now you want to speak to me?" I asked.

"I was in the middle of something and couldn't answer the phone. What's up? Why were you calling like it was some kind of emergency?"

"I tell you one thing, I'm glad it wasn't an emergency because I would have been dead by now." I had to think of a quick lie. I needed him to feel like I was worried about him. It had to be something to make him feel like shit for sending me to voicemail. "Look, I didn't want anything. One of my friends called and told me that someone around your way got robbed and shot so I was just calling to make sure it wasn't you. Well, now that I hear your voice I see that you're okay, so goodbye."

"Wait a minute, Jamaica. Don't hang up," he demanded. "Do you still love me?"

"What type of question is that? I wouldn't be worried about you if I didn't care about you," I replied.

"That's not the question I asked. I asked do you still love me?" Rock repeated.

I held back for a second before answering because I didn't want to say something that would allow him to have the upper hand. On the other hand, it was this type of game that caused me to lose him in the first place. "Yes, I still love you, Rock, but I don't appreciate how you carried me. You made me feel bad for not giving you one hundred percent, yet you were sharing fifty percent of yourself with another woman the entire time. Then, you basically left me for her and called yourself bragging about her education and credentials like I give a fuck."

"So it's safe to say that you still love me," he asked again, not acknowledging anything else I said.

This brother played too many games for me and I wasn't about to make him cloud my head up today. Had I not just heard him all booed up with Nina, I probably would have fallen for the bullshit, but I knew better.

"Like I said, someone got shot around your way so I was making sure it wasn't you. Have a good day." I quickly hung up before he could ask me more stupid questions.

Rock didn't call to work things out. He called to play mind games with me and that wasn't going down today.

About five minutes later, I was chilling in my bedroom, watching TV when I heard a knock at the door. I looked through the peephole and Rock was standing there, looking extra scrumptious. Knowing his ass, he was probably parked outside of my house the entire time we were talking on the phone.

"What are you doing here?" I asked as I opened the door.

"Jamaica, you want me to be here so don't act like that," Rock stated.

I frowned at him and walked back into my bedroom, not responding to his cocky ass comment. He followed me, then stood in front of me. "You wouldn't have opened your door if you didn't want me here. You know you miss me, so why you fronting?"

"Is that right," I nonchalantly replied as I sat down on the bed, not looking at him. It was funny that he was over here talking all this bullshit, like he wasn't just laid up and all in love. I wondered if he would be standing in my bedroom had I not instigated an argument between him and his bitch. Probably not. He would still be up under her slut ass, playing house during the day, while she *works at the hospital* at nights.

"Why can't you just be a good girl and stop playing around with me? I want to be with you, but I'm not standing for your games." I turned up the volume on the television and started surfing the channels. This nigga sounded stupid. Talking about I was playing games when his middle name should have been Monopoly.

"You called me today because you wanted me to come through. I'm here, so just stop fronting."

"You really need to get a grip," I replied. "I called you today because I thought your ass was laid up shot somewhere. We're not together, but I still care about your well being. You can save all that other shit for Nurse Betty."

"Who the fuck is Nurse Betty?" Rocked asked.

"Your new bitch. The nurse you told me you loved. The nurse you proposed to."

"Engagements aren't permanent, baby. They can be cancelled at any time." Rock pushed me on the bed, and stood between my legs. "I settled for her but we both know who I really want you." My body began to tremble as he gently kissed every inch of my neck, and whispered, "Damn you smell so good. I miss you so much. I just want to feel the inside of you one more time," he whispered as his warm breath hit my skin and made me hot.

I tried to stop Rock from touching me but the truth was, I wanted him more than he wanted me, and he sensed that from the moment he walked through the door.

I didn't have to say much because my body was talking up a storm. Within a matter of seconds, the both of us were completely naked, caressing and kissing. The sex was always good, but it was thrilling and exciting this time around because I was fucking Nina's man.

With lust in his eyes, Rock spread my legs apart and ate my pussy like he'd never done before. Everywhere he touched on my body felt extra sensitive. The way he swirled his tongue inside of me while reaching up and firmly squeezing my nipples made me moan like a porn star. He licked on me so good that I almost stuck my fingers in my own pussy to taste it.

Rock looked deeply into my eyes and whispered, "I missed you so much, baby."

I wanted to believe him so badly, but the fact that he was engaged to Nina wouldn't allow me to. I had to protect my heart and look out for myself, because it was evident that every man in my life had failed me. So, rather than getting caught up in this emotional love triangle that Rock was trying to put me in, I blocked all of that shit and focused on busting off in his face.

Rock took his middle finger, pushed it deep into my soaked pussy, and made popping sounds with my natural juices, while sucking my clit. I nearly lost my fucking mind. He knew I loved to be freaked out and he did it so well. If that wasn't turning me on enough, the nigga flipped me over, propped me up on all fours, stuck his face between my ass check, and slurped the natural juices that seeped to the back like my ass was a sweet naval orange.

"Oh shit...ohhh...I'm cuming...I'm cuming," I screamed. The next thing I remembered was collapsing on my stomach and wanting to take a nap.

I fell asleep for about five minutes, but I quickly came to my senses. Rock was lying beside me, looking very comfortable, as if he was going to just eat my pussy and crawl back into my life. I had to show him it didn't work that easy. The head was the bomb, but he had to come correct to ever get back in my life.

"I'm about to get some rest and take care of a few errands later. I'll maybe call you tomorrow or whatever," I announced as I got out of bed, put my robe on, and hinted that it was time for his ass to leave.

Rock must of thought it was a game. He glanced at me and smiled, but I wasn't smiling. Slowly that smile disappeared, when he realized I was dead ass serious.

"You mean to tell me that you're still on the same bullshit. You haven't changed one fucking bit." Rock gathered his belongings and walked out the bedroom. He snatched his keys off the counter, damn near knocking down my antique vase that I paid a lot of money for. "Bitch, you're never going to change. You're going to die alone," he stated as he opened the front door.

"Who said anything about changing? You're the one with a whole fiancée at home. Do you think your tongue game is that good to make me turn into a side hoe for you?" I asked.

"Fuck you. That nigga, Deshawn messed your head up a long time ago. I was stupid to think I could save you."

"I don't need to be saved. I need to be loved. Goodbye."

Once again, Rock walked out of my life.

CHAPTER 19

Dead-End Heartbreak

A couple days went by and finally it was the day of no return. Today I set the ball in motion to rid Deshawn from my life permanently. It was around 8:30 pm, still a bit too early to head to Las Chicas, so I decided to watch a little television to waste some time.

I couldn't recall what show I ended up watching, but whatever it was it must have been boring as hell, or I was extremely tired because my ass fell asleep. All I knew was by the time I woke up and looked down at my phone, it was 10:00 pm. Damn! I had messed up… I messed up big time!

I jumped out of bed and made my way to the front door, not caring about what I was wearing, including the house slippers that I'd thrown on my feet. I looked at my phone as I ran out the door and saw that I had five missed calls from Myesha and a couple voicemail alerts. I tried to call her back, but her phone kept going to voicemail, so I checked my messages and she was on every single one.

"Please pick up, Jamaica. We're getting ready to leave out the house and head to the club to meet Deshawn."

"Jamaica, where are you?" Her last message was marked as urgent.

"Jamaica, I don't know where you are right now, but we just arrived in front of the club and Deshawn's car is parked in the rear where you said it would be, so he's definitely inside. I hope you're at the house by the time we leave here. Call me when you get this message."

I tried calling Myesha back one more time, hoping and praying that I didn't mess up my plans. The phone rang for what felt like eternity, but when I finally heard Myesha's voice, I felt a sense of relief.

"Girl, where have you been? I tried to call you about a million times," she answered.

"I overslept. I am so sorry. I just woke up about a minute ago, but I'm on my way to the house now. Where are you?" I asked.

"I'm parked outside of the club, waiting for ladies to come out with Deshawn. Lashel and I have been texting throughout the night. She just told me they've made their way up to VIP and are sitting with Deshawn. He's taking mad shots of Patron with them so it's just a matter of time before he leaves the club wasted."

"Are you serious?" I asked with a big ass smile on my face. "That was quick."

"I told you I would work everything out. Just be at the house so you can see how everything unfolds. I'm going to call you twice; once when we're on our way back to the house and once when we're actually outside."

"Okay, see you when you get here. Bye."

There was no turning back. If this plan went through without any hiccups, I could expect everything else would fall into place. I would finally be able to live my life without having to look over my shoulders.

I pulled up on the block, parked my car way around the corner, and power walked to the house. I wasted no time busting through the door, so I could get down to business. I walked from room to room, double-checking to make sure there were no traces of Jamaica Johnson anywhere. I knew I cleaned the house thoroughly a couple days ago, but I had to double check because even when he was drunk, Deshawn was observant.

After ensuring that everything was cool, I took a bottle of Cabernet Sauvignon upstairs to the office and prepared for Deshawn's arrival. I poured a nice glass of wine to calm my nerves and ease the tension in my body. As I scrolled down my Instagram newsfeed to see what everyone was up to on this fine Friday night, I received Myesha's first call.

"Hello," I eagerly answered.

"We got his ass. Lashel and Kelisa are driving in the car with him, and I'm following about four cars behind. Girl, he's pissy drunk, swerving in and out of lanes and shit."

"Okay, great. I'll be upstairs in the office. Hurry up and get here."

I sat patiently waiting for their arrival, which ultimately felt like the longest wait in world history. Finally, Myesha made her second call.

"Deshawn and the ladies just pulled into the driveway. I'm about to come through the back. I'll be upstairs shortly," she informed me.

Within minutes Myesha snuck through the back door and quietly made her way upstairs to the office. She was damn near out of breath from running up three flights of steps. Once she entered the room, I made sure all the locks were completely bolted. I turned on the monitors and saw that Deshawn and the ladies were already chilling in the lounge area.

Myesha and I both had our eyes and ears locked on the monitors. Through the speakers, I heard Deshawn's conversation, and for sure he was drunk as fuck.

"So who lives in this big ass house with the both of you?" he asked as he stumbled over the furniture.

"Just the two of us and our little sister. Our parents passed away years ago and we inherited this house," Kelisa lied.

Damn she was on point with that one. That was because these hoes lied on a regular basis. They could freestyle a bunch of lies without skipping a beat.

"Forget all this small talking. We didn't bring you back here to talk. We trying to get down and dirty with you," Lashel interrupted.

"Oh, we don't have to talk at all. Let's get right down to business," Deshawn stated, barely able to get his words out clearly. His words were slurred, making him sound like a complete drunken fool. "Let me see y'all do that freaky shit you were doing at the club. Do some lesbian shit for me," he requested.

Lashel and Kelisa began kissing and within seconds, they were naked, grinding all over each other. Deshawn took out a stack of hundreds and began making it rain on top of their bare bodies. Once they got him hot from the teaser, the ladies invited Deshawn to join in on their girl on girl action. He happily accepted their offer, and before you knew it, they were all getting it on.

I stopped watching once they started having sex because it was all business to me and I didn't care to see Deshawn's bare ass. For the remainder of the night, Myesha and I chilled and engaged in small talk, as Lashel and Kelisa put in work on Deshawn. She kept me entertained by filling me in on all the girls' love lives, including Nina's. With all the fucking and sucking they'd been doing, I was shocked to hear that they found time to have a love life. That shit was comical to me.

I kept glancing over at the monitors periodically as we talked to see what was going on. As much as I wanted to sit back, chop it up, and get the latest scoop on the girl, there was no way in hell I was going to kick my feet up and get comfortable with Deshawn's crazy ass under this roof.

After what felt like eternity, but was actually forty-five minutes later, Deshawn reached his peak and fell fast asleep with both ladies laying in his arms like he was the man. He woke up an hour later and got dressed. After putting his clothes on, he woke up Lashel and Kelisa.

"I'm about to be out," he announced.

"Damn, do you have to leave?" Kelisa asked. "You were the best we've ever had. My knees are still weak." She talked seductively as she stood before him bare naked, showing off her perky plumped breasts.

"Yes, he was girl," Lashel cosigned. "So when are we going to kick it with you again? I'm trying to fuck again real soon."

"Me too, but remember we're going out of town tomorrow and won't be back until Friday morning," Kelisa stated. "How about hooking up with us again on Friday night when we get back? Now that we're formally acquainted, I can be free to do all the freaky shit that I wanted to do to you."

"So, you're telling me that you held back on me tonight?" Deshawn replied with a stunned expression. "If you did all that and you were holding back, I can't imagine what else you got to offer."

Kelisa leaned over, planted a juicy kiss on him, and said, "Oh there's levels to this shit, daddy. I can always elevate and take you higher."

"Oh yeah? Well, meet me at the club on Friday and let's make it happen again," Deshawn ordered.

He left the house and Myesha went downstairs to meet the ladies shortly after to take them home. Once they pulled off the block, I also left the house and went home. I called Myesha the next morning and thanked her repeatedly, because I couldn't have pulled this off without her. We both decided that it would be wise for us to stay away from Las Chicas until Friday, just in case Deshawn decided to stake out the place. I called Shanks to let him know that he would be needed at the house all this week except Friday. Friday was off limits to everyone except Myesha, Lashel, Kelisa, and myself.

I called Rochelle and my mother and spent a lot of quality time with them during the week. We shopped until we dropped during the day, and went out to dinner almost every single night. Rochelle was happy because she was leaving for Atlanta soon and was excited about being on her own. Of course, my mother wasn't pleased, but she kept her feelings to herself.

One night while we were at dinner, my mother said, "Did I tell you girls that Pam called and left a message on my answering machine? She sounded really sad." My mother dialed her voicemail and played the message.

"*Mary, this is your sister. I know you hate me right now and I don't blame you because I don't know what I would do if the shoe was on the other foot. I'm not making money like I used to and can't afford to keep up with the expenses of the house anymore so I'm moving out. I would like to sign the deed over to you because it's only right. I guess karma is finally biting me in the ass. I have no money, no home, and no job. The worst part of all, is I don't have no family anymore. I called Cousin Ruth in Texas and she purchased a one-way plane ticket for me to come out there. She needs a nanny and says she could put me on her payroll as long as I take care of the children. I'm leaving in two weeks and would appreciate it if I could see you before I leave. I love you, sis. Goodbye.*"

I felt absolutely nothing after hearing that pathetic ass message. I could tell that Rochelle was on the same page with me. She rolled her eyes the entire time.

My mother, on the other hand, was a different story. Despite all the shady shit that went down, she still loved her sister so it was just a matter of time before she tried to justify her sleeping with her husband. My mother was going to forgive that trifling bitch sooner or later.

"I hope you're not falling for this crap? She's only sorry because she got caught. She could care less about you or this family. But I tell you one thing, she should be lucky it was Jamaica who caught her ass and not me because I would have bashed her skull in," Rochelle blurted. I was glad she said something because I was dying to.

"I'm not taking the blame off Pam because she's one hundred and ten percent wrong, but it takes two to tango. How could you forgive and still love your father, yet hate Pam when he's just as guilty as she is?" my mother asked.

"Because she's your sister and at the end of the day, Daddy's a man that you met. Blood should be always thicker than water. You're sitting here defending her like you really want her back in your life. I swear you're taking this too lightly."

"I agree," I added. "Mommy, you've always been gullible for Aunt Pam and it's about time you stop. If you forgive her, she's only going to hurt you again."

"I'm not forgiving Pam that easily, so you two certainly don't have to worry about that. I only saved her message because she talked about signing the deed of her house to me and I was thinking that Jamaica could possibly move in when she leaves."

Wait, what did my mother just say? "Wow, I never thought about it, but that's a great idea. I was sitting here renting my condo and paying thousands of dollars every month, when I could be living in a big ass house paying less. Plus, I'd be closer to home, and now that Rochelle was leaving for college and my father was out of the house, my mother was really going to need me.

"That sounds like an excellent idea. I was already thinking about purchasing a house and moving closer to home, so that would work out perfectly. I can move in as soon as Aunt Pam moves out," I stated.

"That's music to my ears. I will get the process started immediately. I'll call my lawyer and have him meet with Pam to handle the paperwork. Once she signs over the house, I'll give it to you and make sure that everything is legal and legit."

I was beyond happy after receiving that news. My mother was even more excited about me moving back to Harford County than I was. She began purchasing and putting down payments on all sorts of things for the house. We went from shopping for clothes and shoes, to furniture shopping for the remainder of the week. I became so consumed with the prospects of moving, that I didn't realize how fast the days were flying by.

When Thursday rolled around, I was more motivated to take Deshawn out than ever before. I had too much at stake, including my life, so there was definitely no turning back. Myesha and I spoke a lot on this particular day to cover all ends. Like a coach would do before a big game, I prepped and prepared her for any stumbling blocks the ladies could run into dealing with Deshawn. I explained his likes and dislikes repeatedly, until she felt she knew him just as well as I did. During our last conversation, I gave the specific orders that needed to be carried out precisely. The ladies didn't have room to freestyle. Everything they did tomorrow had to be exactly how I instructed or their lives could be on the chopping block right next to mine.

"I want Lashel and Kelisa to go back to the club and leave with Deshawn like they did the first time. Explain to them that when they get back to the house, get him comfortable by any means necessary, but most importantly, I need them to get him drunk as fuck again. I will provide the liquor this time. It's very important they take him to the middle room, the one with the Baltimore Raven's theme. Once he's completely drunk out of his fucking mind and passed out, I want them to leave the house and leave the rest up to me."

"What if they ask me why do they have to leave? What do you want me to tell them?"

"You don't have to tell those bitches shit. All they need to know is that once you say get the fuck out, they need to get the fuck out. Also, make sure that all the recording devices are working properly and all the batteries are charged up."

"Okay, I got that part, but what do you need me to do in particular? At least tell me what's going to take place after they leave so I can be on point," Myesha probed.

"You know that I'm a very private girl when it comes to certain things. The least you know about tomorrow's plans, the better off you are. Trust me, once I start working, everything is going to become obvious to you."

"Jamaica, this is not going to become deadly, is it? I have to ask you this because if it is I do not want to be involved."

"Calm your nerves. Nothing is going to turn deadly unless Deshawn finds out what's going down and flips out on Lashel and Kelisa."

Myesha laughed thinking I was joking, but I was dead ass serious. Them bitches were ghost if Deshawn suspected that they were setting him up.

"Well get some rest because we've got a long day ahead of us. Let's just keep our fingers crossed and pray that everything goes as planned so that you can finally walk away from this nigga for good," Myesha stated.

"Everything will be perfect if everyone follows my lead. No one goes on my hit list and comes off without being dealt with. No one!"

"I hear that. Well after tomorrow, that's one name that you can cross off," Myesha declared.

"Indeed," I replied, laughing on the inside because this bitch didn't know that her name was up next.

CHAPTER 20

Welcome to Jam Rock

I was already at the Las Chicas house by noon the next day setting everything up. I looked ridiculous, dressed in a blond wig, dark sunshades, and an old-woman-looking scarf covering my neck and lower face area. I thought this thing out completely. Deshawn was already familiar with the house so it was important for me to be low-key until my work was done. Not to mention, this absurd disguise came in handy when I went down the strip earlier to grab $200 worth of OxyContin and Ecstasy pills. I didn't want anyone recognizing me out there coping like a junky.

I walked from room to room, checking all the monitors and audio machines. After confirming that everything was good, I went into the kitchen and cooked all of Deshawn's favorite foods. I also whipped up a batch of my mother's famous Jamaican rum punch, added my own ingredients, and renamed it Citrus Hurricane. I needed Deshawn to feel relaxed and comfortable enough to let his guard down completely around the ladies so that I could work my magic, and for sure, my Citrus Hurricane would do the trick.

The house was clean just the way he liked it, with the sweet aroma of apple green scented candles soaring through the air. Beautiful rose petals were placed up the steps, and down the hallway leading into the bedroom where it would all go down. Strawberries and champagne would be on chill by the bedside waiting for him like the king that he thought he was. If Deshawn thought he was treated like royalty the last time he was here, he was going to be blown away with tonight's ambiance.

Myesha dropped by to check on me before linking up with Kelisa and Lashel. I was sipping on my drink feeling extra nice when she arrived. Typically, I would have been nervous as hell knowing that I had to face Deshawn soon, however, tonight was different. I felt empowered and in charge of my own destiny. It was time for me to boss up and show this nigga that I was just as crazy and powerful as he was.

"I'm on my way to pick the ladies up. Are there any last minute details you need to tell me so that I can pass it onto them?"

"Just remind the ladies to keep pouring the Citrus Hurricane for Deshawn and make sure that he drinks every drop of it. However, the ladies cannot take even a sip of that drink. That drink is for Deshawn only," I warned.

"Wait, why can't the ladies have a drink with him?" Myesha probed. "That's going to send up a big red flag. Deshawn's no dummy. If he notices the ladies pouring him drinks and they're not drinking, he's going to question that."

"Look, I made this drink extra strong and I need these girls sober all night. Taking just a sip of it will knock them off their feet. Deshawn drinks hard liquor every day so it won't have the same impact on him as it would on them. All Lashel and Kelisa have to do is pour themselves a glass of red wine. He won't know the difference because the colors are the same. Not to mention, Deshawn is going to be wasted by the time he gets here, and won't be able to think clearly," I stated.

"It almost time for me to meet the ladies so I'm heading back out. I'll call you once we reach the club so keep your cell phone near."

"It's right here in my pocket," I stated, as I pulled my cell phone out and waved it in the air. "Trust me, I'm not falling asleep and losing track of time tonight. I'm on high alert."

"You better be," Myesha stated as she snickered and walked away.

I sat in the office, sipping my drink, and thinking. I thought about my family. Wondering was this really the end of my parents' marriage and the impact it would have on our family. I thought about Rochelle going off to college, being on her own for the very first time, and questioned if she was prepared for the real world. The situation with Rock and me crossed my mind a few times. I truly didn't know how I was going to react if he actually married Nina.

Then there was Myesha, my ex-best-friend, who was smiling in my face and stabbing me in my back at the same time. I appreciated everything she was doing for me, but still couldn't put her levels of betrayal aside to forgive and forget.

And of course, Deshawn was heavily on my mind. Although I was being cool, I was very much aware of the monster that would be here soon. If I'd had the choice, I would have chosen to be anywhere but here, but the situation was out of my hands. Deshawn put my back against the wall, so I had to find a way out. Unfortunately, the measures that I had to take were extremely drastic.

I was lost in my thoughts when my cell phone rang, startling me. It was Myesha telling me they just pulled off from the club and were on their way to the house.

"This is it," I said, as I downed the last of the wine in my glass.

The first thing I did was run downstairs and reheat the food so that it would be warm when Deshawn arrived. I also put the champagne and strawberries on ice by the bedside, lit candies throughout the room, and dimmed the lights. I set the mood for this nigga so that he knew that tonight was all about him.

I received the second phone call from Myesha as I walked back into the office, nervously stating, "I'm on my way through the back door now. They should be pulling up in less than a minute or two."

Within seconds the back door slammed and I heard her stilettos rushing up the steps. Finally, *BOOOOM*, she burst into the office, barely able to catch her breath.

"I'm so glad this is the last time I have to do this shit. It is nerve-wracking trying to outdrive a nigga who's going one hundred ten miles per hour. I was in front of him and before I knew it, I caught a glimpse of his car speeding up on me, so I had to turn on the back road and put the pedal to the metal," she explained, still out of breath.

"I almost forgot how fast that fool drove after leaving the club. He doesn't linger around after handling business just in case someone is outside plotting on him, so he drives like a fucking maniac until he gets to his destination, and in his psychotic mind, that makes the situation safer for him. Trust me, he had his gun tucked under the seat the entire time his stupid ass was driving like that."

Myesha's neck nearly snapped off, as she abruptly turned around and looked at me like I was crazy. "Wait one damn minute. So, you mean to tell me that Deshawn's coming here with his gun?"

"Maybe. If he's the same Deshawn that I was engaged to years ago, hell yeah. He's bringing his gun tonight and more than likely had it on him the other night, which is why I stressed to get him drunk as hell. Don't be nervous; everything is going to be fine. I've thought this out and covered just about everything that can go wrong."

"I'm just going to sit here and say a silent prayer until this nigga leaves the house. If you say you have the situation under control, I can only trust and believe that you do," Myesha replied.

As we were talking, I looked over at the monitors and saw Deshawn and the ladies walking through the door. Just like the last time, he was already smashed.

Kelisa and Deshawn walked into the chill area as Lashel went into the kitchen to make his plate and pour him a tall cup of Citrus Hurricane. He smashed his food in less than five minutes and downed the cup of punch in one take, like he was starving.

I looked into his eyes and realized that he wasn't only drunk, the nigga was high as shit. This was perfect for me because that meant his ass would be out of commission sooner than expected.

"Baby, you look like you're tired. Why don't you make yourself comfortable," Kelisa suggested as she leaned over and began untying Deshawn's tennis shoes and loosening the buttons on his shirt.

"Yeah, we have the whole night ahead of us," Lashel added. "Let's sit back, relax, have some drinks, and enjoy the night."

"I don't have a problem with that," Deshawn replied, as he took out a blunt and sparked it up. "Y'all hitting this?"

"Hell, yeah," Lashel answered, as she poured him another drink. "We know you got that fire."

Deshawn took a few hits of the blunt and passed it to Lashel. She hit it and passed it to Kelisa. The three sat in the chill area, watching some random ass movie. Although the ladies were smoking, they were still on their game. As soon as Deshawn put his empty cup down, Lashel would fill it right back up. He continued drinking and drinking until his eyes started to roll back. He kept dozing off and jumping up, trying to hang, but that juice had his body on lock.

Sensing that he could pass out at any second and wouldn't make it to the bedroom, Kelisa suggested, "Let's go to the bedroom so you can lay down while my sister and I have our way with you, daddy." She took Deshawn's hand and led him up the steps.

He was so fucked up that he didn't even see the rose petals on the floor. He stumbled up the steps, walked into the bedroom, and fell out on his back.

The moment Deshawn's body touched the bed, his dick was already out his pants and in Kelisa's mouth. She sucked him off as Lashel licked and slurped on his balls.

"Y'all missed this big dick, huh? Yeah suck that shit and don't fucking move your face until it's covered with my kids," Deshawn demanded.

"Oh, we're going to swallow all of that," Lashel stated as she reached over and poured Deshawn another cup of Citrus Hurricane. "Sip on your drink and get real nice for us, because tonight we're going to turn your world inside out." Lashel went back on her knees and continued tag-teaming Deshawn's dick with Kelisa.

Just as he'd been doing all night, Deshawn knocked his drink back like it was water, and after a while he began to take notice that it was doing something to his body, but by then it was already too late. "What the hell is in this drink?" he inquired. "This shit creeped up on me."

"It's my aunt's signature drink called Citrus Hurricane because once it's in your system, everything erupts."

"Yeah, but what's in it? I feel funny," he replied, barely able to speak clearly. He tried to lift his head, but it fell back onto the pillow like dead weight. "Everything's going dark and my heart's racing. Tell me what the fuck is in this drink," he demanded.

Kelisa and Lashel ignored him, and continued having their way with him. I busted out laughing as I watched the terror in Deshawn's eyes. He was scared out of his mind, but didn't have the strength to walk away. It was funny how the tables turned because this was what he did to me in a sense. I was powerless and didn't have the strength to fight back. Until today. The irony of the situation amused the fuck out of me.

"Jamaica, what the hell did you put in that punch? Please tell me the truth. Did you poison him or something?" Myesha asked.

"You don't have anything to worry about. Deshawn is very drunk right now, but that's about it. We both know what he's capable of when he's sober, so I made his drink extra strong. That's all that's going on."

"I just want to be informed because we are in this together. If you go down, I go down and I would be pissed if I got locked up for some shit I didn't even know about."

"I'm not going down and you're not going down either," I stated. "The only person that's going down in this house is Deshawn."

After putting Myesha's mind at ease, I focused my attention back on Deshawn, who by now realized that something was seriously wrong. I didn't think I'd ever seen him this vulnerable.

He reached into his pocket, took out his cell phone, and began scrolling through his contact list.

"Who are you calling, baby?" Lashel asked as she passionately kissed his neck while taking the cell phone out of his hand.

"I'm fucked up, yo. I'm seeing about three of you standing in front of me. I don't feel like myself. I need to call my boy, Corey to come and pick me up."

"No, don't do that," Kelisa yelled out.

The dumb bitch panicked and reacted too quickly, and just as I thought, Deshawn picked up on it and looked at her strangely.

I got up and bolted all the locks in the office because I just knew that shit was about to go left. Fortunately, she was able to handle the situation before it escalated.

Kelisa gently took the phone out of Deshawn's hand and began sucking on his fingers. "We don't want you to leave. We waited all week to see you, daddy. Why don't you have another drink, calm your nerves, and let us take care of you tonight."

"No, I don't need another drink. It's fucking me up," Deshawn slurred as he tried to push the cup away. His eyes kept rolling to the back of his head, he was sweating bullets, and breathing hard. "Something is wrong," he stated, before falling back on the pillow and putting his hand over his forehead.

"You're just drunk and experiencing hangover symptoms. And you know what they say, the best way to cure a hangover is to continue drinking, so drink this last cup of punch and lay down," Lashel insisted.

Deshawn's good sense was already impaired, so he made the *smart* decision to take Lashel's advice. He had another drink and roughly ten minutes later, he fell out cold.

Lashel and Kelisa kept trying to wake Deshawn, but he wasn't budging. They shook his body so hard I thought his head was going to snap off his neck. After several unsuccessful attempts to revive him, the two buffoons frantically ran out of the room and left the house.

As soon as they were out of sight, I took out the masquerade mask that I had hidden in my bag, put it over my face, and said, "Showtime," in a very devious voice.

I looked over at Myesha sitting in the corner with the most nervous look on her face. "Now watch a pro in action. I want you to stay up here and keep the monitors rolling and recording. I'll be back in twenty to thirty minutes."

"What the fuck is going on?" Myesha asked. "Oh my God, I didn't sign up for this shit. What's wrong with Deshawn and why do you have this mask on?" She paced with a look of terror.

"I told you a long time ago the less you know the better off you are. Just sit back and enjoy the show." I walked out the door, made my way downstairs and entered the bedroom where Deshawn was still laid out cold. I walked to the bed and stood over top of the man who dismantled my life and scorned my heart for life. He had so much power over me in the past, but now he lay powerless. Something in me wanted to take out my knife and plunge it into his chest, but that would have been too easy. I was going to do what he did to me. I going to psychologically murder this bastard.

I went into the bathroom, wet a cold rag, and gently placed it over Deshawn's forehead. I then put some smelling salt under his nose and slapped his face as hard as possible until he awakened from the semi-coma. He kept attempting to open his weakened eyes but they were too heavy. Every time he managed to open them, they would shut, but I smacked his face again. I did this until he finally woke all the way up, but he was still very much immobilized.

"Wake up, honey," I softly whispered into his ears. "How are you feeling?"

Deshawn covered his entire forehead with both hands, as if he had a massive migraine, and mumbled, "My head hurts. I need to call my homeboy, Corey. Please call Corey for me."

"Who is Corey? Your boss?" I questioned.

"My boss? Hell no, I don't have no boss. I'm the fucking boss," Deshawn corrected. He tried to lift his head up again, but it fell back down.

"You know men with power turn me on so bad. Hearing stories about the way they take control makes me want to do anything just to be down." I began caressing Deshawn's dick. Despite being heavily intoxicated, he still managed to become fully erect. Yet, he laid helplessly on the bed unable to push me away even if he wanted to.

"What are you doing to me?" he asked.

Without answering, I inserted his dick deeply into my wet mouth and began sucking him off. I was actually enjoying this revenge a little more than I had anticipated. I almost forgot how big and juicy Deshawn's dick was. I got so caught up in my own sexual pleasures, that I almost forgot the real reason my lips were wrapped around his dick. It wasn't until I heard him moan in elation that I snapped back to reality.

"Daddy, please tell me more about your business," I probed. "Tell me how dangerous you are. I love dangerous men."

"What do you want to know," he asked provocatively as he licked his lips while rubbing his head. It was like, he was enjoying this bomb ass head that I was giving him, yet, he was still fucked up from the Citrus Hurricane. And that was exactly how I wanted him to be. I needed him too fucked up to be able to hurt me, but, alert enough to run his fucking mouth and give me all the information I needed to bring his ass down.

"What kind of drugs do you sell? Weed," I stated, knowing good and well weed was below his standards.

"Weed? Weed is for small timers. I'm in the big leagues, baby. I sling heroin all over East Baltimore." I began to moan as I sucked his hardened flesh with more force. "Oh, you like that, huh? You like to hear about the control and power that I have," Deshawn asked.

"Yes, daddy I love it. I just love a man with power and control. One who is above the law," I stated with his dick still snuggled in the back of my wet throat. "So how is it that you never get caught and where exactly do you sell that shit? I would love to come and see you in action one day."

"I got work from East Monument Street all the way to Park Heights Avenue. I just gave out some tester earlier today and the junkies were going crazy for the shit. As for why I've never been caught, that will never happen. I pay my workers really good and provide them with benefits. They know if they get caught, then they get caught. If they don't snitch, I'll continue to look out for them and their families until they get home. I even got a few police officers and State Attorneys on the books to ensure I never take a fall."

"Oh, when you say workers you mean Corey, right?" I explored deeper.

"Yes, his name is Corey but we call him Big C and there's also Michael known on the block as the Ice Man because he put a lot of dudes on ice for me, if you know what I mean."

"I think I know Corey and Michael from high school. What are their last names if you don't mind me asking?"

"Corey Stansbury and Michael Fullard," he involuntarily snitched. "Now, there's also Shawn Lewis, Timothy Watkins, Paul Johnson and our gangster bitch, Shelia Alexander AKA Shells. Those people will do anything for me and I mean anything I ask them to do. I own them. Those niggas can't eat without me," he explained with his eyes still completely closed. His words were still slurred, but comprehensive enough to turn over to the police.

"So when you say they'll do anything do you mean they would kill for you?" I opened my mouth as wide as I could and gave him powerful deep throat.

As I stated before, Deshawn's dick was big as shit, but I worked magic in that bedroom and sucked the shit out of his cock, only coming up to take a breath, and even then, I kept my juicy lips snuggled around the tip.

"Hell yeah they would kill for me. Do you know how many dudes those niggas have dropped for me? Man, this dude just owed me some money the other day and wouldn't pay up so we made his mother pay us back for him. Rather than give me the three hundred that he owed, his mother had to fork up five thousand for his funeral." Deshawn actually snickered as he recalled how he took the young man's life. "We murked his simple ass right in front of his son while he was picking him up from school, too. It wasn't even about the money. I spend that a night on strippers. It was about the principle of him owing me and not paying up."

I felt sick because I just heard about this murder on the news the other night. This nigga was truly heartless.

Needless to say from that point, Deshawn went on a confession spree, admitting to other murders he and his friends committed and even told me where three bodies were stashed this week. The idiot told me the name and location of his New York and California connects who shipped the drugs to him. The more I sucked and garbled his dick up, the more he incriminated himself.

When I concluded that I had enough information to bring Deshawn down to his knees, I decided that it was time to seal the deal. So, I took my mouth game to another level until he finally came down my throat and collapsed back into his semi-coma. I think the combination of alcohol, drugs, dopamine, and Jamaica's head game did the trick.

I was just about to pull the tapes from the recorders when suddenly I began to think about how he raped me and ejaculated on my face. I remembered how low he made me feel and at that very moment, I wanted him to feel even lower.

It took much strength but I was able to flip Deshawn over so that he was lying face down. Something inside of me wanted to hold his face deep into the pillow until he stopped breathing, but what I had in store for his ass would be much worse. Being that we were in a whore house, I knew all I had to do was simply open the top drawers and as expected, there were a bunch of props waiting. I pulled out a pretty red lace strap-on panty with a long tan dildo attached to it and greased it up with the bottle of Anal Ease that was sitting on the dresser. You already know what happened next.

Deshawn's ass was really tight when I first inserted the dildo inside of him, but I firmly plunged and worked my way inside. He woke up screaming out in agony.

"What the fuck are you doing?" he slurred. "Get the fuck off of me." He tried to lift himself from the bed but he had no strength because I just drained him. But it was mostly because his system was filled with "Ecstasy and OxyContin" fruit punch juice; AKA Citrus Hurricane. Yes, the drugs I purchased earlier were for my Citrus Hurricane punch.

Deshawn made several attempts to stop me from taking his manhood, but I was in total control.

"Shut the fuck up," I yelled. "Do you remember when you were talking to me like that? Bitch, be quiet and take this dick like a man." I kept slapping and spanking his ass as I inserted the dick into his virgin tunnel.

To my surprise, sodomizing Deshawn was therapeutic and it actually turned me on. Back and forth, I plunged deeper and deeper with my eyes tightly closed. The motion and friction from his ass cheeks slapping against my clitoris made me cum the hardest I had ever cum in my life.

"Yesses, yesss, yesssssssss bitch, I'm cumin; I'm cumin all up in this tight ass of yours," I moaned, as I felt an outpour of fluid rush from my body onto the shiny dildo that was covered with my natural juices.

I busted a good one and fell out on top of Deshawn's back like a nigga. After attempting to fight me off, Deshawn worked himself up, got overheated, and passed out once again, I kissed Deshawn on the side of his face and thanked him for giving me a great night of passion.

I used his t-shirt to wipe myself before walking around the room removing all the hidden recording devices that were planted earlier. I went back upstairs to the office to relieve Myesha from her post. The look she had on her face when I walked through the door was priceless. She stared at me like I was a cold-blooded killer.

"What the fuck did you just do, Jamaica? Why did you do all of that? More importantly, what the hell are you going to do with all that information he just told you? This is too much for me. I'm getting the fuck out of here because I do not want to be a part of this anymore. Do you understand the severity of what you just did?" Myesha scrammed around the room, gathering her belongings. "Oh my God, Jamaica, you fucked Deshawn. You fucked Deshawn in his ass. You fucking raped him and he's going to wake up and remember that shit. You had the mask on so he doesn't know it was you, but he will find out if he wakes up and finds you. We have to get out of here," Myesha demanded as she rushed to get out the door.

"Welcome to my world, girl. I'm going to start fucking up everybody who fucked me over, literally!" I handed her all the recordings of me Deshawn. "I want you to take these with you. I'm going to keep the copies that are up here in the office. I need you to go straight home and put these in a safe place."

"What? You're not coming with me? Do you plan on being here when that nigga wakes up?" Myesha asked, as the terror in her eyes heightened. "You must have a death wish or something. You need to get the hell out of here now."

"I have work to do and the night has just begun. All I need you to do is go home and put those tapes in a safe place until I pick them up from you."

"Are you crazy? I'm not leaving here without you," Myesha insisted.

"I'm not leaving and nothing you say is going to make me change my mind. I keep telling you that I've thought this out completely, but right now you're messing up my plans by still being here. You're putting both of our lives in danger. Please go while you still have the option. There's no telling what's going to happen to the both of us if Deshawn wakes up and sees you here."

"Okay, I'm leaving, but please keep me posted. Text me every chance you get."

"You got that," I lied.

After walking Myesha to the door, I went back into the bedroom, put my cell phone on silent, and cuddled next to Deshawn in the bed. When he woke up in the morning, I needed this face to be the first thing he saw.

Welcome to my crazy world. Welcome to Jamrock!

To Be Continued...

Jamaican Me Go Crazy
Part 2 Preview

Chapter 1
A Rude Awakening

I would be lying if I told you I slept a wink last night. How could anyone sleep comfortably while lying next to the devil himself? For most of the night, Deshawn tossed and turned, and talked in his sleep, although his words were extremely incoherent. I spent the majority of my time waiting for him to wake up. I swear, World War II seemed shorter than the wait I had to endure; however, around 6:30 a.m., Deshawn began to make slight movements in the bed. He turned to the left, then he turned to the right. He put his hands over his head and groaned in agony before finally opening his eyes, and just stared at the ceiling.

I watched as he laid in complete silence, with the most perplexed expression on his face.

Suddenly, Deshawn turned his face toward my direction and stared directly into my eyes. My heart nearly skipped a beat until I realized that he had no clue who I was because the room was still very dark, and for all he knew, Kelisa or Lashel was lying next to him.

After laying in silence in an attempt to gather his thoughts, Deshawn finally glanced at his watch, and to his surprise, he'd stayed a little longer than he had anticipated.

"I can't believe I stayed here all fucking night," he mumbled in disbelief. His body was still somewhat paralyzed from all the lethal substances that were still in his system.

He was utterly disorganized to the point that even I questioned if he was conscious of who he was or how he ended up at this house in the first place. "Wait, why do I feel so fucked up? What the hell was in that drink that y'all gave me last night," he asked as he looked over at me, desperately waiting for a response. Deshawn lifted his body midway off the bed and began deeply rubbing his lower back.

I suspected that the pain from my anal penetration began to sink into that ass; literally. Seeing the vulnerability in his eyes and hearing the fear in his voice made me feel ten feet tall. My plan wasn't 100% completed, yet I already felt accomplished.

"What the fuck happened here last night and where is your friend?" Deshawn asked as he became more and more furious by the fact that he was not in control of the situation. He was furious that his memory wasn't providing him with the answer to this questions, and most importantly, he was furious by my silence. My silence sent him into overdrive and his level of anger went from zero to a hundred real quick.

"Bitch, are you fucking dead? Do you think this is a fucking game? What was in that drink last night and what the fuck did you and your slut ass friend do to me?" Deshawn so desperately wanted an answer from me and I so desperately wasn't going to provide him with one.

To tell the truth, I was doing him a huge favor by not disclosing last night's festivities. I could imagine how he would react if I said, *"Oh last night I put a lethal amount of drugs and alcohol into your system and prayed that it was just enough to knock you out and not kill your evil ass. Luckily it worked, so once you became tremendously intoxicated, I tricked you into revealing your entire drug connections, which could land you and your affiliates in jail for a very long time. Oh yeah, I almost forgot, I fucked the dog shit out of you in your ass and busted the biggest nut on your back like you was my little bitch. That may be the reason why you're in pain right now."*

Deshawn was still weak from last night and his mind was extremely distorted, but I promise you, if I would have provided him with the answers to his questions, that psychotic nigga would have found the strength of one hundred men to get to me and he would have killed my ass before I could continue with my plan.

So yes, I kept my mouth shut and continued to lay in the dimmed room as I patiently waited for the right time to reveal myself.

Infuriated by my silence, Deshawn flew into rage, jumped out of the bed like the madman I'd known him to be, grabbed a handful of my hair, and forcefully hauled me out of the bed. "It's too fucking dark in here. Turn the lights on bitch," he demanded. "Where's the fucking light switch?"

Of course, I wasn't cooperating, so he griped my hair even tighter, damn near ripping strands from my scalp, as he walked around the room, feeling the walls up and down, looking for a light switch. After walking around, the darkened room while dragging my black ass behind him for a minute or so, he finally found what he was searching for.

Deshawn flicked on the light and at first, we were both slightly blinded by the sudden glare, however I knew it was important for me to keep my eyes open. Deshawn closed his eyes and squirmed, but still held onto me tightly. After blinking about fifteen times, he finally opened his eyes and stared at me like I had three heads attached to my neck. He closed his eyes once more and rubbed them, but when he opened them back up, I was still there, piercing through his evil eyes. The grip that he had on me intensified as he moved up closer to see if he was in fact seeing correctly, so I spared us both the time and energy by helping him understand that yes, Jamaica Johnson was in the motherfucking house.

"Your mind is not playing tricks on you, Deshawn. It's me, Jamaica in the flesh," I announced.

"What? Wait, how did you get in here?"

"How did I get in here?" I repeated. "Now are you talking about this house or your asshole because I got up in both last night." Just as I expected and already planned for, without any warning or even small talk, the brutal attack began. Deshawn punched me in my face repeatedly, before throwing me to the ground and proceeding to stomp the breath out of my body.

"Are you crazy or something? You must be fucking crazy being this close to me. Bitch, what are you up to and what did you do to me?" With every question he asked, a full forced kick came behind it like the question mark to his sentence. "You have to be out of your mind or have a death wish to even attempt to play these games with me, bitch."

"Yes, I am out of my mind; just like you are. You think you're the only monster in this world? Well thanks to you, there's another monster in town; another monster that you created," I yelled. Well, at least I attempted to yell before Deshawn's powerful kick landed smack dead in my chest, literally taking my breath away.

He kicked and stomped my tiny body in every direction imaginable like I was a ragdoll. When he became tired of kicking and stomping, he hovered over me and began strangling me senseless.

I tried to pull his hands away from my throat, but he was too strong. But then, Deshawn stopped as he felt, then saw the blood that streamed down the side of his leg. It was because he'd been moving around so vigorously that he started bleeding.

He looked down at me, and then back at his legs. He shoved me away from him. "Why am I bleeding? What did you do to me?

ANSWER ME, JAMAICA!" His loud baritone voice echoed through the house. "Why am I bleeding?"

"I told you exactly what I did to you already. Did you think I was lying? No baby, I was dead ass serious when I told you that I fucked the shit out of you and enjoyed every minute of that tight asshole of yours."

Deshawn lifted his fist above my face as I proceeded to stand up, and I knew that if I allowed that hit to connect I was as good as dead.

So, I hurried up and stood up and stated my case before he got the best of me. "Wait one minute. I have something important to tell you. Before you think about killing me, let me warn you that I have some very incriminating information on you that three other people have in their possessions, one of those people being my lawyer. I gave them word to hand deliver this information to the police in the case of my death, so I would think twice before doing something to me that you will surely regret for the rest of your life," I warned.

I had all of Deshawn's attention because he knew something very serious went down last night in this house. It was evident in the blood that was dripping out of his ass, so rather than beat my brains out of my skull as he truly wanted to do, he held his composure and allowed me to speak.

"Now if you remember anything about me, you know that I'm a planner and yes, I sat and planned this out for a while now just as you've been planning for me. The reason why your ass is bleeding and hurting is because I fucked you in it and before you go off on me and possibly kill me, let me show you one thing." I limped over to the camcorder, still feeling the pain from Deshawn's blows to my body, put the cassette tape in, and pressed play. I was hurt, but not to the extent that I was going to allow this sick monster to overpower me again. "Why don't you take a seat and listen to yourself? You should really try out for American Idol because I had no clue that you could sing so well," I teased.

Our images appeared on the television screen and Deshawn's whole demeanor changed. His facial expression shifted from furious to alarming as we both sat and listened as he confessed murders, named his connects, and revealed all sorts of incriminating secrets to me.

"You've been a bad boy, haven't you?" I taunted. "I just know the detectives would love to get a hold of this valuable information. Listen to you dropping a dime on your own friends, not to mention your connects. The Baltimore City Police would give me a reward for this buzz in their ears, don't you think? Could you imagine how heated it's going to get down in Internal Affairs when they find out that you have some of their top detectives and prosecutors on your payroll?"

I swear Deshawn became teary-eyed right before my own eyes. I had never seen this man so submissive and defenseless a day in my life. That's when I knew I had him exactly where I wanted him.

As if he wasn't already in distress, I actually saw homeboy's spirit stand up and rise from his body like it did in the movie Ghost, when our little love session started to play on the screen. His jaw dropped, meanwhile I was laughing my ass off, until I started to choke. Every time I stroked that ass, I yelled, "Bamm… Bamm" as I imitated my movements from last night, provoking the shit out of him.

"Bitch, you're dead," Deshawn said as he jumped from one side of the bed onto my body, and began strangling the life out of me. "I won't make the same mistake twice, bitch. You're not walking away alive this time around."

Coming soon to a bookstore near you!

ACKNOWLEDGMENTS

First and foremost, I would like to thank God, my source of power and strength. Father, you have given me opportunities that many people aren't fortunate to receive, and for your mercy, I will always be humbly grateful and thankful.

I would like to thank my wonderful parents, Dawn Lamb and Elon Wizzart for not only giving me life, but providing me with the best, and by the best, I mean something that's more valuable than anything money can buy. You two have shown me unconditional love, nurture, and protection, and have always made me feel like the world was in the grip of my hands.

To my joys, my two boys, Kaydin and Kyrin Michael Hill, thank you for choosing me to be your mommy. You've both given me a purpose to live and a reason to keep pushing, even when times are hard. Everything I do, I do for the two of you. I love you both beyond imagination.

To my grandparents, Olive and Aston Lamb, Lurline and Joseph Wizzart (RIP), and Panchita Mowatt, and my grandaunts Alma Mckie (RIP) and Lilith Martin, thank you for your wisdom, prayers, and encouragement. You all are the foundation that holds this family together.

Derron Bailey, Mylia Clarke, and Johnpaul Wizzart, I love you all and I'm extremely proud to be your big sister. Whether we're laughing at a funny joke, or crying on each other's shoulders, the bond we share is irreplaceable. To my second mother, Joan Evans aka Aunty Pinchie, we have a connection that's indescribable. You have always motivated me to be my own leader, and have been my biggest cheerleader. Thank you for being you!

Simone, Big Derrick, Von, and my entire family (there's a lot of you), I love you all from the bottom of my heart and soul. We've been through so much as a family, and although people could never understand the debts of the love that we share, there's no denying that we have something that's rare and priceless! JBR for LIFE!

Derrick Lamb aka Gary aka Father of the Family... You need no introduction. You need no explanation. You need no clarification because you are who you are, and I am who I am because of you. You stand alone, yet you stand a million men strong. I will always say this because it's true. Big cous, thank you for being a second father to me.

To my fiancé and best-friend, Tyran Hill, I owe my life to you. 1 Corinthian verse 3 states: "Love is patient, love is kind... Love never fails." My dear, love is you. Even if I thanked you a billion times for coming into my life and giving me everything that I gave up hopes of acquiring, I still couldn't thank you enough. You will be the last man that I love in this world and I look forward to being Mrs. Hill very soon.

Aunty Betty, Aunt Neda, Mr. Michael, and Mrs. Cynthia, thank you for your continuous love and support. Carmen Byrd and Shanee Cross, my besties for life. I thank you both for reading this book before anyone else, giving me constructive criticism, and challenging me to be great.

Last, but certainly not least, to my All-STARRS of friends and fans, I thank you all for rocking with me for all these years and supporting all my endeavors. None of this would be possible without you guys. Remember, no matter what you're going through in life, let your light shine through!

CPSIA information can be obtained
at www.ICGtesting.com
Printed in the USA
LVHW110156230520
656338LV00003B/221